BEYOND
THE
STARS

BEYOND
THE
STARS

Tales of Adventure
in Time and Space

This edition first published in
Great Britain in 1983 by

Octopus Books Limited
59 Grosvenor Street
London W1

Arrangement and illustrations © 1983 Hennerwood Publications Limited
Illustrated by Peter Dennis (Linda Rogers Associates)

Second impression, reprinted 1984

ISBN 0 86273 094 5

Printed and bound in Great Britain
by Collins Glasgow

CONTENTS

CONTENTS

ESCAPE FROM THE DEATH STAR

George Lucas

uke Skywalker, the old Jedi warrior Ben Kenobi, Han Solo and their companions are deep in the heart of the enemy battle station, the Death Star. Danger threatens on all sides as they struggle to free the young and beautiful Princess Leia from the clutches of the evil dark warlord, Darth Vader . . .

Lined with power cables and circuitry conduits that rose from the depths and vanished into the heavens, the service trench appeared to be hundreds of kilometers deep. The narrow catwalk running around one side looked like a starched thread glued on a glowing ocean. It was barely wide enough for one man to traverse.

One man edged his way along that treacherous walkway now, his gaze intent on something ahead of him instead of the awesome metal abyss below. The clacking sounds of enormous switching devices resounded like captive leviathans in the vast open space, tireless and never sleeping.

Two thick cables joined beneath an overlay panel. It was locked, but after careful inspection of sides, top and bottom, Ben Kenobi pressed the panel cover in a particular fashion causing it to spring aside. A blinking computer terminal was revealed beneath.

With equal care he performed several adjustments to the terminal. His actions were rewarded when several indicator lights on the board changed from red to blue.

Without warning, a secondary door close behind him opened. Hurriedly reclosing the panel cover, the old man slipped deeper into the shadows. A detachment of troopers had appeared in the portal, and the officer in charge moved to within a couple of meters of the motionless, hidden figure.

'Secure this area until the alert has been cancelled.'

As they began to disperse, Kenobi became one with the dark.

*

Chewbacca grunted and wheezed, and barely succeeded in forcing his thick torso through the hatchway opening with Luke's and Solo's help. That accomplished, Luke turned to take stock of their surroundings.

The hallway they had emerged into showed dust on the floor. It gave the impression of not having been used since the station had been built. Probably it was only a repair access corridor. He had no idea where they were.

Something hit the wall behind them with a massive *thunk*, and Luke yelled for everyone to watch out as a long, gelatinous limb worked its way through the hatch and flailed hopefully about in the open corridor. Solo aimed his pistol at it as Leia tried to slip past the half-paralyzed Chewbacca.

'Somebody get this big hairy walking carpet out of my way.' Suddenly she noticed what Solo was preparing to do. 'No, wait! It'll be heard!'

Solo ignored her and fired at the hatchway. The burst of energy was rewarded with a distant roar as an avalanche of weakened wall and beaming all but buried the creature in the chamber beyond.

Magnified by the narrow corridor, the sounds continued to roll and echo for long minutes afterward.

Luke shook his head in disgust, realizing that someone like Solo who spoke with the mouth of a gun
might not always act sensibly. Until now he had sort of
looked up to the Corellian. But the senseless gesture of
firing at the hatchway brought them, for the first time
in Luke's mind, to the same level.

The Princess's actions were more surprising than
Solo's, however. 'Listen,' she began, staring up at
him, 'I don't know where you came from, but I'm
grateful.' Almost as an afterthought she glanced back at
Luke, adding, 'To the both of you.' Her attention turned
back to Solo. 'But from now on you do as I tell you.'

Solo gaped at her. This time the smug smile
wouldn't come. 'Look, Your Holiness,' he was finally
able to stammer, 'let's get something straight. I take
orders only from one person—me.'

'It's a wonder you're still alive,' she shot back
smoothly. A quick look down the corridor and she had
started determinedly off in the other direction.

Solo looked at Luke, started to say something, then
hesitated and simply shook his head slowly. 'No
reward is worth this. I don't know if there's enough
credit in the universe to pay for putting up with *her* . . .
Hey, slow down!'

Leia had started around a bend in the corridor, and
they ran swiftly to catch up with her.

*

The half dozen troops milling around the entrance to
the power trench were more interested in discussing
the peculiar disturbance in the detention block than in
paying attention to their present boring duty. So
engrossed were they in speculation as to the cause of
the trouble that they failed to notice the fey wraith
behind them. It moved from shadow to shadow like a
night-stalking ferret, freezing when one of the troopers seemed to turn slightly in its direction, moving on
again as if walking on air.

Several minutes later one of the troopers frowned

inside his armor, turning to where he thought he had sensed a movement near the opening to the main passageway. There was nothing but an undefinable something which the ghost-like Kenobi had left behind. Acutely uncomfortable yet understandably unwilling to confess to hallucinations, the trooper turned back to the more prosaic conversation of his fellows.

*

Someone finally discovered the two unconscious guards tied in the service lockers on board the captured freighter. Both men remained comatose despite all efforts to revive them.

Under the direction of several bickering officers, troopers carried their two armorless comrades down the ramp and toward the nearest hospital bay. On the way they passed two forms hidden by a small opened service panel. Threepio and Artoo went unnoticed, despite their proximity to the hangar.

As soon as the troops had passed, Artoo finished removing a socket cover and hurriedly shoved his sensor arm into the opening. Lights commenced a wild flashing on his face and smoke started issuing from several seams in the small 'droid before a frantic Threepio could pull the arm free.

Immediately the smoke vanished, the undisciplined blinking faded to normalcy. Artoo emitted a few wilted beeps, successfully giving the impression of a human who had expected a glass of mild wine and instead unwittingly downed several gulps of something 180 proof.

'Well, next time watch where you stick your sensors,' Threepio chastised his companion. 'You could have fried your insides.' He eyed the socket. 'That's a power outlet, stupid, not an information terminal.'

Artoo whistled a mournful apology. Together they hunted for the proper outlet.

*

Luke, Solo, Chewbacca, and the Princess reached the end of an empty hallway. It dead-ended before a large window which overlooked a hangar, giving them a sweeping, tantalizing view of the freighter just below.

Pulling out his comlink and looking around them with increasing nervousness, Luke spoke into the pickup. 'See Threepio ... do you copy?'

There was a threatening pause, then, 'I read you, sir. We had to abandon the region around the office.'

'Are you both safe?'

'For the moment, though I'm not sanguine about my old age. We're in the main hangar, across from the ship.'

Luke looked towards the bay window in surprise. 'I can't see you across the bay—we must be right above you. Stand by. We'll join you as soon as we can.' He clicked off, smiling suddenly at Threepio's reference to his 'old age.' Sometimes the tall 'droid was more human than people.

'Wonder if the old man was able to knock out the tractor,' Solo was muttering as he surveyed the scene below. A dozen or so troopers were moving in and out of the freighter.

'Getting back to the ship's going to be like flying through the five Fire Rings of Fornax.'

Leia Organa turned long enough to glance in surprise from the ship to Solo. 'You came here in that wreck? You're braver than I thought.'

At once praised and insulted, Solo wasn't sure how to react. He settled for giving her a dirty look as they started back down the hallway, Chewbacca bringing up the rear.

Rounding a corner, the three humans came to an abrupt halt. So did the twenty Imperial troopers marching towards them. Reacting naturally—which is to say, without thinking—Solo drew his pistol and charged the platoon, yelling and howling in several languages at the top of his lungs.

Startled by the totally unexpected assault and wrongly assuming their attacker knew what he was doing, the troopers started to back away. Several wild shots from the Corellian's pistol initiated complete panic. Ranks and composure shattered, the troopers broke and fled down the passage.

Drunk with his own prowess, Solo continued the chase, turning to shout back at Luke, 'Get to the ship. I'll take care of these!'

'Are you out of your mind?' Luke yelled at him. 'Where do you think you're going?'

But Solo had already rounded a far bend in the corridor and didn't hear. Not that it would have made any difference.

Upset at his partner's disappearance, Chewbacca let out a thunderous if unsettled howl and rushed down the hallway after him. That left Luke and Leia standing alone in the empty corridor.

'Maybe I was too hard on your friend,' she confessed reluctantly. 'He certainly is courageous.'

'He certainly is an idiot!' a furious Luke countered tightly. 'I don't know what good it'll do us if he gets himself killed.' Muted alarms suddenly sounded from the bay below and behind them.

'That's done it,' Luke growled disgustedly. 'Let's go.' Together they started off in search of a way down to a hangar-deck level.

*

Solo continued his rout of all opposition, running at top speed down the long hallway, yelling and brandishing his pistol. Occasionally he got off a shot whose effect was more valuable psychologically than tactically.

Half the troops had already scattered down various subpassages and corridors. The ten troopers he continued to harry still raced headlong away from him, returning his fire only indifferently. Then they came up against a dead end, which forced them to turn and confront their opponents.

Seeing that the ten had halted, Solo likewise slowed. Gradually he came to a complete stop. Corellian and Imperials regarded one another silently. Several of the troopers were staring, not at Han but past him.

It suddenly occurred to Solo that he was very much alone, and the same thought was beginning to seep into the minds of the guards he was confronting. Embarrassment gave way rapidly to anger. Rifles and pistols started to come up. Solo took a step backward, fired one shot, then turned and ran like hell.

Chewbacca heard the whistle and crump of energy weapons firing as he lumbered lightly down the corridor. There was something odd about them, though: they sounded as if they were coming closer instead of moving away.

He was debating what to do when Solo came tearing around a corner and nearly ran him down. Seeing ten troopers in pursuit, the Wookie decided to reserve his questions for a less confused moment. He turned and followed Solo back up the hallway.

*

Luke grabbed the Princess and pulled her back into a recess. She was about to retort angrily at his brusqueness when the sound of marching feet caused her to shrink back into the darkness with him.

A squad of soldiers hurried past, responding to the alarms that continued to ring steadily. Luke looked out at the retreating backs and tried to catch his breath. 'Our only hope of reaching the ship is from the other side of the hangar. They already know someone's here.' He started back down the corridor, motioning for her to follow.

Two guards appeared at the far end of the passageway, paused, and pointed directly at them. Turning, Luke and Leia began running back the way they had come. A larger squad of troopers rounded the far bend and came racing towards them.

Blocked ahead and behind, they hunted frantically

for another way out. Then Leia spotted the cramped subhallway and gestured to it.

Luke fired at the nearest of their pursuers and joined her in running down the narrow passage. It looked like a minor service corridor. Behind them, pursuit sounded deafeningly loud in the confining space. But at least it minimized the amount of fire the troops could concentrate on them.

A thick hatchway appeared ahead. The lighting beyond turned dimmer, raising Luke's hopes. If they could lock the hatch even for a few moments and lose themselves somewhere beyond, they might have a chance of shaking their immediate tormentors.

But the hatch stayed open, showing no inclination to close automatically. Luke was about to let out a shout of triumph when the ground suddenly vanished ahead of him. His toes hanging over nothingness, he failed to regain his balance, succeeding just in time to nearly go over the edge of the retracted catwalk anyway as the Princess plowed into him from behind.

The catwalk had been reduced to a stub protruding into empty air. A cool draft caressed Luke's face as he studied walls that soared to unseen heights overhead and plunged to fathomless depths below. The service shaft was employed in circulating and recycling the atmosphere of the station.

At the moment Luke was too frightened and concerned to be angry with the Princess for nearly sending them over the edge. Besides, other dangers competed for his attention. A burst of energy exploded above their heads, sending metal slivers flying.

'I think we made a wrong turn,' he murmured, firing back at the advancing troops and illuminating the narrow corridor behind them with destruction.

An open hatchway showed on the other side of the chasm. It might as well have been a light-year away. Hunting along the rim of the doorway, Leia located a switch and hit it quickly. The hatch door behind them slid shut with a resounding boom. At least that cut off fire from the rapidly nearing soldiers. It also left the two fugitives balanced precariously on a small section of catwalk barely a meter square. If the remaining section were to unexpectedly withdraw into the wall, they would see more of the battle station's interior than either wished.

Gesturing for the Princess to move aside as much as possible, Luke shielded his eyes and aimed the pistol at the hatch controls. A brief burst of energy melted them flush with the wall, insuring that no one could open it easily from the other side. Then he turned his attention to the vast cavity blocking their path to the opposite portal. It beckoned invitingly—a small yellow rectangle of freedom.

Only the soft rush of air from below sounded until Luke commented, 'This is a shield-rated door, but it won't hold them back very long.'

'We've got to get across there somehow,' Leia

agreed, once more examining the metal bordering the sealed doorway. 'Find the controls for extending the bridge.'

Some desperate searching produced nothing, while an ominous pounding and hissing sounded from behind the frozen door. A small spot of white appeared in the center of the metal, then began to spread and smoke.

'They're coming through!' Luke groaned.

The Princess turned carefully to stare across the gap. 'This must be a single-unit bridge, with the controls only on the other side.'

Reaching up to the point at the panel holding the unreachable controls, Luke's hand caught on some-thing at his waist. A frustrated glance downward revealed the cause—and engendered a bit of practical insanity.

The cable coiled tightly in small loops was thin and fragile seeming, but it was general military-issue line and would have supported Chewbacca's weight eas-ily. It certainly ought to hold Leia and himself. Pulling the cable free of the waist catch, he gauged its length, matching it against the width of the abyss. This should span the distance with plenty to spare.

'What now?' the Princess inquired curiously.

Luke didn't reply. Instead, he removed a small but heavy power unit from the utility belt of his armor and tied one end of the cable around it. Making sure the wrapping was secure, he stepped as close to the edge of their uncertain perch as he dared.

Whirling the weighted end of the cord in increasing circles, he let it arc across the gorge. It struck an out-cropping of cylindrical conduits on the other side and fell downward. With forced patience he pulled the loose line back in, then recoiled it for another try.

Once again the weighted end orbited in ever greater circles, and again he flung it across the gap. He could feel the rising heat behind him as he let it go, heat from the melting metal doorway.

This time the heavy end looped around an outcropping of pipes above, wrapped itself several times around, and slipped, battery end down, into a crack between them. Leaning backward, he tugged and pulled on the cable, pulling on it at the same time as he tried to rest all his weight on it. The cable showed no sign of parting.

Wrapping the other end of the line several times around his waist and right arm, he reached out and pulled the Princess close to him with the other. The hatch door behind them was now a molten white, and liquid metal was running steadily from its borders.

Something warm and pleasant touched Luke's lips, alerting every nerve in his body. He looked down in shock at the Princess, his mouth still tingling from the kiss.

'Just for luck,' she murmured with a slight, almost embarrassed smile as she put her arms around him. 'We're going to need it.'

Gripping the thin cable as tightly as possible with his left hand, Luke put his right over it, took a deep breath, and jumped out into air. If he had miscalculated the degree of arc in their swing, they would miss the open hatch and slam into the metal wall to either side or below it. If that happened he doubted he could maintain his grip on the rope.

The heart-halting transit was accomplished in less time than that thought. In a moment Luke was on the other side, scrambling on his knees to make sure they didn't fall back into the pit. Leia released her hold on him with admirable timing. She rolled forward and into the open hatchway, climbing gracefully to her feet as Luke fought to untangle himself from the cable.

A distant whine became a loud hiss, then a groan as the hatch door on the other side gave way. It collapsed

inward and tumbled into the depths. If it touched bottom, Luke didn't hear it.

A few bolts struck the wall nearby. Luke turned his own weapon on the unsuccessful troopers and returned the fire even as Leia was pulling him into the passageway behind.

Once clear of the door he hit the activating switch. It shut tightly behind them. They would have several minutes, at least, without having to worry about being shot in the back. On the other hand, Luke didn't have the slightest idea where they were, and he found himself wondering what had happened to Han and Chewbacca.

*

Solo and his Wookie partner had succeeded in shaking a portion of their pursuers. But it seemed that whenever they slipped free of several soldiers, more appeared to take their place. No question about it: the word was out on them.

Ahead, a series of shield doors was beginning to close.

'Hurry, Chewie!' Solo urged.

Chewbacca grunted once, breathing like an over-used engine. Despite his immense strength, the Wookie was not built for long-distance sprinting. Only his enormous stride had enabled him to keep pace with the lithe Corellian. Chewbacca left a couple of hairs in one of the doors, but both slipped inside just before the five layers slammed shut.

'That ought to hold them for a while,' Solo crowed with delight. The Wookie growled something at him, but his partner fairly fluoresced with confidence.

'Of course I can find the ship from here—Corellians can't get lost.' There came another growl, slightly accusing this time. Solo shrugged. 'Tocneppil doesn't count; he wasn't a Corellian. Besides, I was drunk.'

*

Ben Kenobi ducked into the shadows of a narrow passageway, seeming to become part of the metal itself as a large cluster of troopers hurried past him. Pausing to make certain they had all passed, he checked the corridor ahead before starting down it. But he failed to see the dark silhouette which eclipsed the light far behind him.

*

Kenobi had avoided one patrol after another, slowly working his way back toward the docking bay holding the freighter. Just another two turns and he should be at the hangar. What he would do then would be determined by how inconspicuous his charges had been.

That young Luke, the adventurous Corellian and his partner, and the two robots had been involved in something other than quiet napping he already suspected from the amount of activity he had observed while making his way back from the power trench. Surely all those troops hadn't been out hunting just for him!

But something else was troubling them, judging from the references he had overheard concerning a certain important prisoner, now escaped. That discovery had puzzled him, until he considered the restless natures of both Luke and Han Solo. Undoubtedly they were involved in some fashion.

Ben sensed something directly ahead and slowed cautiously. It had a most familiar feel to it, a half-remembered mental odor he could not quite place.

Then the figure stepped out in front of him, blocking his entry to the hangar not five meters away. The outline and size of the figure completed the momentary puzzle. It was the maturity of the mind he had sensed that had temporarily confused him. His hand moved naturally to the hilt of his deactivated saber.

'I have been waiting a long time, Obi-wan Kenobi,' Darth Vader intoned solemnly. 'We meet again at last. The circle has been completed.' Kenobi sensed satisfaction beneath the hideous mask. 'The presence I sensed earlier could only have been you.'

Kenobi regarded the great form blocking his retreat and nodded slowly. He gave the impression of being more curious than impressed. 'You still have much to learn.'

'You were once my teacher,' Vader admitted, 'and I learned much from you. But the time of learning has long passed, and I am the master now.'

The logic that had constituted the missing link in his brilliant pupil remained as absent as before. There would be no reasoning here, Kenobi knew. Igniting his saber, he assumed the pose of warrior-ready, a movement accomplished with the ease and elegance of a dancer.

Rather roughly, Vader imitated the movement. Several minutes followed without motion as the two men remained staring at each other, as if waiting for some proper, as yet unspoken signal.

Kenobi blinked once, shook his head, and tried to clear his eyes, which had begun to water slightly. Sweat beaded up on his forehead, and his eyelids fluttered again.

'Your powers are weak,' Vader noted emotionlessly. 'Old man, you should never have come back. It will make your end less peaceful than you might have wished.'

'You sense only a part of the force, Darth,' Kenobi murmured with the assurance of one to whom death is merely another sensation, like sleeping or making love or touching a candle. 'As always, you perceive its reality as little as a utensil perceives the taste of food.'

Executing a move of incredible swiftness for one so old, Kenobi lunged at the massive shape. Vader blocked the stab with equal speed, riposting with a counterslash that Kenobi barely parried. Another parry and Kenobi countered again, using this opportunity to move around the towering Dark Lord.

They continued to trade blows, with the old man now backing towards the hangar. Once, his saber and Vader's locked, the interaction of the two energy fields producing a violent sparking and flashing. A low buzzing sound rose from the straining power units as each saber sought to override the other.

*

Threepio peeked around the entrance to the docking bay, worriedly counting the number of troopers milling around the deserted freighter.

'Where could they be? Oh, oh.'

He ducked back out of sight just as one of the guards glanced in his direction. A second, more cautious appraisal was more rewarding. It revealed Han Solo and Chewbacca hugging the wall of another tunnel on the far side of the bay.

Solo also was nonplussed at the number of guards. He muttered, 'Didn't we just leave this party?'

Chewbacca grunted, and both turned, only to relax and lower their weapons at the sight of Luke and the Princess.

'What kept you?' Solo quipped mirthlessly.

'We ran into,' Leia explained, panting heavily, 'some old friends.'

Luke was staring at the freighter. 'Is the ship all right?'

'Seems okay,' was Solo's analysis. 'It doesn't look like they've removed anything or disturbed her engines. The problem's going to be getting to it.'

Leia suddenly pointed to one of the opposite tunnels. 'Look!'

Illuminated by the flare from contacting energy fields, Ben Kenobi and Darth Vader were backing towards the bay. The fight attracted the attention of others beside the Senator. Every one of the guards moved in for a better view of the Olympian conflict.

'Now's our chance,' Solo observed, starting forward.

All seven of the troopers guarding the ship broke and rushed towards the combatants, going to the Dark Lord's aid. Threepio barely ducked aside as they ran past him. Turning back into the alcove, he yelled to his companion.

'Unplug yourself, Artoo. We're leaving.' As soon as the Artoo unit slipped his sensor arm free of the socket, the two 'droids began to slowly edge out into the open bay.

Kenobi heard the approaching commotion and spared a glance back into the hangar. The squad of troopers bearing down on him was enough to show that he was trapped.

Vader took immediate advantage of the momentary distraction to bring his saber over and down. Kenobi somehow managed to deflect the sweeping blow, at once parrying and turning a complete circle.

'You still have your skill, but your power fades. Prepare to meet the force, Obi-wan.'

Kenobi gauged the shrinking distance between the oncoming troops and himself, then turned a pitying gaze on Vader. 'This is a fight you cannot win, Darth. Your power has matured since I taught you, but I too have grown much since our parting. If my blade finds its mark, you will cease to exist. But if you cut me down, I will only become more powerful. Heed my words.'

'Your philosophies no longer confuse me, old man,' Vader growled contemptuously. 'I am the master now.'

Once again he lunged forward, feinting, and then slashing in a deadly downward arc with the saber. It struck home, cutting the old man cleanly in half. There was a brief flash as Kenobi's cloak fluttered to the deck in two neat sections.

But Ben Kenobi was not in it. Wary of some tricks, Vader poked at the empty cloak sections with the saber. There was no sign of the old man. He had vanished as though he had never existed.

The guards slowed their approach and joined Vader in examining the place where Kenobi had stood seconds before. Several of them muttered, and even the awesome presence of the Sith Lord couldn't keep a few of them from feeling a little afraid.

*

Once the guards had turned and dashed for the far tunnel, Solo and the others started for the starship—until Luke saw Kenobi cut in two. Instantly he shifted direction and was moving towards the guards.

'Ben!' he screamed, firing wildly towards the troops. Solo cursed, but turned to fire in support of Luke.

One of the energy bolts struck the safety release on the tunnel blast door. The emergency hold broken, the heavy door fairly exploded downward. Both the guards and Vader leaped clear—the guards into the bay and Vader backward, to the opposite side of the door.

Solo had turned and started for the entrance to the ship, but he paused as he saw Luke running towards the guards.

'It's too late!' Leia yelled at him. 'It's over.'

'No!' Luke half shouted, half sobbed.

A familiar, yet different voice rang in his ears —Ben's voice. 'Luke . . . listen!' was all it said.

Bewildered, Luke turned to hunt for the source of that admonition. He only saw Leia beckoning to him as she followed Artoo and Threepio up the ramp.

'Come on! There's no time.'

Hesitating, his mind still on that imagined voice (or was it imagined?), a confused Luke took aim and felled several soldiers before he, too, whirled and retreated into the freighter.

*

Dazed, Luke staggered towards the front of the ship. He barely noticed the sound of energy bolts, too weak to penetrate the ship's deflectors, exploding harmlessly outside. His own safety was currently of little concern to him. With misty eyes he stared as Chewbacca and Solo adjusted controls.

'I hope that old man managed to knock out that tractor beam,' the Corellian was saying, 'or this is going to be a very short ride.'

Ignoring him, Luke returned to the hold area and slumped into a seat, his head falling into his hands. Leia Organa regarded him quietly for a while, then removed her cloak. Moving to him, she placed it gently around his shoulders.

'There wasn't anything you could have done,' she whispered comfortingly. 'It was all over in an instant.'

'I can't believe he's gone,' came Luke's reply, his voice a ghost of a whisper. 'I can't.'

Solo shifted a lever, staring nervously ahead. But the massive bay door was constructed to respond to the approach of any vessel. The safety feature now served to facilitate their escape as the freighter slipped quickly past the still-opening door and out into free space.

'Nothing,' Solo sighed, studying several readouts with profound satisfaction. 'Not so much as an erg of come-hither. He did it, all right.'

Chewbacca rumbled something, and the pilot's attention shifted to another series of gauges. 'Right, Chewie. I forget, for a moment, that there are other ways of persuading us to return.' His teeth flashed in a grin of determination. 'But the only way they'll get us back in that traveling tomb is in pieces. Take over.'

Whirling, he ran out of the cockpit. 'Come with me, kid,' he shouted at Luke as he entered the hold. 'We're not out of this yet.'

Luke didn't respond, didn't move, and Leia turned an angry face to Solo. 'Leave him alone. Can't you see what the old man meant to him?'

An explosion jarred the ship, nearly tumbling Solo to the deck.

'So what? The old man gave himself to give us a chance to get away. You want to waste that, Luke? You want Kenobi to have wasted himself?'

Luke's head came up and he stared with vacant eyes at the Corellian. No, not quite vacant . . . There was something too old and unpleasant shining blindly in the back of them. Without a word, he threw off the cloak and joined Solo.

Giving him a reassuring smile, Solo gestured down a narrow accessway. Luke looked in the indicated direction, smiled grimly, and rushed down it as Solo started down the opposing passage.

Luke found himself in a large rotating bubble protruding from the side of the ship. A long, wicked-looking tube whose purpose was instantly apparent projected from the apex of the transparent hemisphere. Luke settled himself into the seat and commenced a rapid study of the controls. Activator here,

firing grip here ... He had fired such weapons a thousand times before—in his dreams.

Forward, Chewbacca and Leia were searching the speckled pit outside for the attacking fighters represented by firepricks on several screens. Chewbacca suddenly growled throatily and pulled back on several controls as Leia let out a yelp.

'Here they come.'

The starfield wheeled around Luke as an Imperial Tie fighter raced towards him and then swung overhead to vanish into the distance. Within the tiny cockpit its pilot frowned as the supposedly battered freighter darted out of range. Adjusting his own controls, he swung up and over in a high arc intended to take him on a fresh intercept course with the escaping ship.

Solo fired at another fighter, and its pilot nearly slammed his engine through its mountings as he fought to avoid the powerful energy bolts. As he did so, his hurried maneuver brought him under and around to the other side of the freighter. Even as he was lowering the glare reflector over his eyes, Luke opened up on the racing fighter.

Chewbacca was alternating his attention between the instruments and the tracking screens, while Leia strained to separate distant stars from near-by assassins.

Two fighters dove simultaneously on the twisting, spiraling freighter, trying to line their weapons on the unexpectedly flexible craft. Solo fired at the descending globes, and Luke followed with his own weapon a second later. Both fired on the starship and then shot past.

'They're coming in too fast,' Luke yelled into his comlink.

Another enemy bolt struck the freighter forward and was barely shunted aside by its deflectors. The cockpit shuddered violently, and gauges whined in protest at the quantity of energy they were being asked to monitor and compensate for.

Chewbacca muttered something to Leia, and she murmured a soft reply as if she almost understood.

Another fighter unloosed a barrage on the freighter, only this time the bolt pierced an overloaded screen and actually struck the side of the ship. Though partially deflected, it still carried enough power to blow out a large control panel in the main passageway, sending a rain of sparks and smoke in all directions. Artoo Detoo started stolidly towards the miniature inferno as the ship lurched crazily, throwing the less stable Threepio into a cabinet full of component chips.

A warning light began to wink for attention in the cockpit. Chewbacca muttered to Leia, who stared at him worriedly and wished for the gift of Wookie-gab.

Then a fighter floated down on the damaged freighter, right into Luke's sights. His mouth moving silently, Luke fired at it. The incredibly agile little vessel darted out of his range, but as it passed beneath them Solo picked it up instantly, and commenced a steady following fire. Without warning the fighter erupted in an incredible flash of multicolored light, throwing a billion bits of superheated metal to every section of the cosmos.

Solo whirled and gave Luke a victory wave, which the younger man gleefully returned. Then they turned back to their weapons as yet another fighter stormed over the freighter's hull, firing at its transmitter dish.

In the middle of the main passageway, angry flames raged around a stubby cylindrical shape. A fine white powdery spray issued from Artoo Detoo's head. Wherever it touched, the fire retreated sharply.

Luke tried to relax, to become a part of the weapon. Almost without being aware of it, he was firing at a retreating Imperial. When he blinked, it was to see the flaming fragments of the enemy craft forming a perfect

ball of light outside the turret. It was his turn to spin and flash the Corellian a grin of triumph.

In the cockpit, Leia paid close attention to scattered readouts as well as searching the sky for additional ships. She directed her voice towards an open mike.

'There are still two more of them out there. Looks like we've lost the lateral monitors and the starboard deflector shield.'

'Don't worry,' Solo told her, with as much hope as confidence, 'she'll hold together.' He gave the walls a pleading stare. 'You hear me, ship? Hold together! Chewie, try to keep them on our port side. If we—'

He was forced to break off as a Tie fighter seemed to materialize out of nowhere, energy bolts reaching out from it towards him. Its companion craft came up on the freighter's other side and Luke found himself firing steadily at it, ignoring the immensely powerful energy it threw at him. At the last possible instant before it passed out of range, he swung the weapon's nozzle minutely, his finger tightening convulsively on the fire control. The Imperial fighter turned into a rapidly expanding cloud of phosphorescing dust. The other fighter apparently considered the shrunken odds, turned, and retreated at top speed.

'We've made it!' Leia shouted, turning to give the startled Wookie an unexpected hug. He growled at her—very softly.

TRIAL BY COMBAT

Jay Williams

Kathryn came to herself suddenly, fully awake and conscious. There was none of the fuzziness of sleep, none of the lingering disorientation after an anaesthetic. She knew just where she was: on the bridge of a D-class cruiser, and from the blinking red light it was clear that the ship was at action stations. But she didn't know how she knew that, and worse yet, she didn't know how she had got there.

She glanced down at herself. She was still herself, at any rate there were the customary curves in the same places, but the blue coverall with the gold rings on the sleeves was that of a space officer. A faint prompting somewhere in her head added, *a Commander*. The thought made her stomach drop, as if she were in a fast lift.

She had no time for more. A blue-clad figure beside her said, 'Shall we open fire, sir?'

Part of her grinned at the survival of that antique word, 'sir', wherever a ship's command was concerned, regardless of sex; the more conscious part felt nothing but panic. Had she been transported somehow into another body? If so, there should be another part of her brain which would tell her automatically what to do, but there was nothing, no hint, only her own memories which somehow faded and became completely vague when she tried to recall anything beyond her graduation from Upper School—a holiday in Corsica, something about visiting an aunt, a dark-haired boy with an interest in biology, a return to Greater Brighton and her parents, and then an absolute blank.

She pulled herself together. She was, at least, quick-thinking and adaptable, and something had to be done at once. She looked around the bridge, and felt she could guess at some of what was happening. She was standing before a small console on which lights blinked and there was a small speaker and a microphone. The man beside her, with two rings on his sleeve to her three, was probably the First Officer. A curved panel some distance off, studded with dials, levers and knobs, must be the ship's controls, with half a dozen men and women before them in padded seats, waiting for her commands. The red light flashed on and off; somewhere an alarm buzzed. A large screen at the level of her eyes showed her the black field of space with two brilliant points on it.

'Sir—' the First Officer began.

'Yes, just a minute,' Kathryn said. 'I felt dizzy. Sorry. What's the position?'

The words came fluently, without thought, out of memories of her passionate study of history, of books about sea and space warfare. They seemed, at any rate, to be the right ones.

'Shall I call the doc?' the First Officer said, and when she shook her head, went on, 'Two small combat ships intercepting. They've ordered us off.'

A strange, high-pitched, snapping sort of voice broke in, coming from the disc of the speaker. ('There they are again, sir,' the First Officer interjected.)

'Here is commander of *Ardek*. You are to turn back,'

the voice said, or yapped. 'This is last warning.' There was, Kathryn thought, something faintly oriental about it.

'Very well, er, Number One.' She wished desperately she knew what his name was. 'Open fire.'

'Shoot!' said the First Officer.

His command was repeated by another voice. A woman's hand came down on a red button. The ship jarred faintly under Kathryn's feet. In the screen, she saw the abrupt tracery of criss-cross silver lines, and tiny sparkles appeared around the bright spots. Another officer, a very young man with pimples above his bushy beard, came languidly over to stand beside the First Officer.

'We'll get it in a minute, Mr Cawthorne,' he remarked.

As he spoke, there came a deep-toned crunch. A giant fist walloped the side of the control room and Kathryn all but fell. She was glad to see that the others had staggered, too. A light began flashing, at first red, then amber. She understood at once that the enemy ships had returned fire.

From her reading, she knew that there was little for her to do until a moment of decision came; she could safely leave routine to her First Officer. He was already saying calmly, 'Damage control. Report.'

Voices from the speaker muttered: 'Wing station, nil.' 'Bow station, nil.' 'Perimeter Able, two hits, all contained.' After a moment, the First Officer said, 'Nothing serious, sir. A few superficial holes in the outer hull.'

'Carry on, please, Mr Cawthorne,' Kathryn said.

Her mind was all on orientating herself. Cawthorne said to the bearded young man, 'Lock in and continue firing, Mr Hogg.' The other passed on the order. Kathryn gazed at the screen, where the two enemy ships were now darting about evasively, then at the busy people before the controls. Once again she tried to

remember, anything at all, anything that would give her a hint as to how she had come here. She must have passed through university, as she had hoped she would, and then have gone on to space, which was strange because she had always thought of herself as becoming a historian. It must have been a long time ago, in any case, for her to have climbed the ladder to the command of a cruiser. Could some wound received in action be plaguing her now, something that had given her a temporary amnesia? It might be so: the First Officer's words about calling the doctor and the calm with which he had accepted her excuse seemed to show he expected something of the sort. It was damnable, but once this action was over perhaps she would see the doctor after all. On the other hand, perhaps it would all pass off.

The ship shuddered underfoot again—another hit—and bringing her attention back to the screen she saw that one of the enemy was now glittering in a different way, dark red; it must have been badly hurt. Its companion was weaving about it, darting in and away, in an erratic manner. She frowned, watching it, and then said, before she thought, 'Mr Cawthorne.'

'Yes, sir.'

She went on, boldly, 'Look at that, on the screen. Doesn't it seem to you that that ship is trying to draw our fire away from the one that's been hit?'

He studied the screen for a moment, and then said, 'Yes, it looks that way. Gallant of him—'

She bit her lip, wondering what was the right thing to say, and then took the plunge. 'Have we communications open to them?'

He glanced at her sharply, but all he said was, 'Yes, sir.'

Well, from all she had read and studied, a commander's word was gospel, no matter how crazy it sounded. 'Ask them to surrender,' she said.

His face expressionless, he touched a switch and

said into the microphone, 'Stand by, enemy ship. This is ISC *Ganymede*. We call upon you to surrender. Cease firing and show a signal.'

The loudspeaker hummed quietly for a moment or two, and then the alien voice, this time with a snarl in it, said, 'Never! Our orders are no one to land on this planet. Even if we die, we fight you.'

It cut off abruptly, and Kathryn saw the dark red dot suddenly disintegrate into a cloud of spangles.

'Direct hit,' said the Gunnery Officer, the bearded young man.

At the same instant, one of the men at the controls said, 'Three more enemy ships in sight, bearing two-oh-three-nine slash four-four.'

Both Kathryn and the First Officer stared at the screen. An arrow-shaped pattern appeared in one corner and then split apart. Over the speaker, they could hear the faint, growling voices of the aliens, talking their own language.

A thought flashed across Kathryn's mind, but before she could give it words, the enemy spoke once more. '*Ardek* here. Turn back, I warn you.'

The pattern had broken; the bright dots of the fighters spread wide. The Gunnery Officer was giving calm orders, and the tracery of the return fire filled the screen like a web of silver. Twice more the cruiser jarred to enemy hits.

We should take evasive action, Kathryn told herself, out of some memory of a sea battle in the twentieth century, and didn't realize she had said the words aloud until the First Officer replied 'Right, sir,' and began barking commands.

The screen showed only blackness now. The cruiser had darted aside, turned sharply, and sped away, momentarily out of range. Then, into the blackness, swam two, three, four points of light.

'They won't give up so easily,' said Cawthorne, half to himself.

'No, they won't,' Kathryn said. 'But meanwhile, we have a minute or two to breathe.'

If only I could remember! she thought. It was almost too much for her. Perhaps she ought to give up, confess to her amnesia, and let the First Officer take over? But there was a stubborn streak in her, and a sense of passionate curiosity which kept her determined to go on, to try to find out what was happening and how to cope with it.

Meanwhile, the First Officer was handing her a sheet of paper, torn from a machine. 'The position print-out, sir,' he said.

She stared, at first blankly, then with slowly-growing comprehension at the rows of figures and letters. She was able to interpret what seemed like gibberish: Gnmd 4 dir hts Per A—that was *Ganymede*, of course, her own ship, four direct hits, and she remembered Perimeter Able from the earlier report. Then, various figures; her mind raced, and she guessed that they must be the positions of the enemy ships in relation to her own, their speeds, their courses. Several rows of equations, which she skipped, and then a neat, computer-drawn chart, a large circle, a smaller irregular one, four crosses in various places, and a large red arrowhead. The latter must be *Ganymede*, then her attackers; the large circle must be the planet they were trying to reach, and the smaller one perhaps a satellite, or a space station—perhaps the base from which the fighters had come.

'Our orders, as you know, sir, are to land on that planet,' the First Officer was saying.

'Yes, I know.' Kathryn had already guessed as much.

'We'll have to close with them again. So far, as you can see from the damage control report, we're in good shape. Able has had to evacuate one compartment. Two dead.'

She had already noted that on the print-out:

caslts–2, which she had guessed to mean two casualties. She closed her eyes for an instant, trying to concentrate, trying to bring together the details of all she
had learned so far.

'Are you all right, sir?' The First Officer sounded
concerned.

'Yes, I'm fine. Just trying to think. You may attack
again, Mr Cawthorne.'

She felt sure it was the right thing to say; at any rate,
the First Officer seemed satisfied. She could visualize
her own ship, now, a barbed red shape, with the
smaller crosses diving at it so that the image arose in
her mind of a bull worried by dogs.

One of the fighters flared and vanished from the
screen. Another suddenly dropped away, clearly
damaged beyond manoeuvring. And still the leader, a
brighter speck than the others, dived in upon the
cruiser, firing bravely, followed by his single companion.

'They've got guts, all right,' Cawthorne muttered.
'We'll finish 'em off, though.'

'No!' Kathryn said, sharply. Then, as he stared, she
added. 'I don't see the necessity for more killing. I
have an idea.'

It had come from a recollection, vague but persist-
ent, of famous fights against odds, of medieval battles
settled by hand-to-hand encounters, of those stirring
words in the mouth of King Henry V:

Ride thou unto the horsemen on yon hill:
If they will fight with us, bid them come down,
Or void the field.

But mostly, it came from all those things she had so far
observed which began to click together in her mind
and form a pattern. She depressed the switch on the
console as she had seen Cawthorne do, and spoke into
the microphone.

'*Ardek!* This is the commanding officer of ISC *Ganymede*. Do you hear me?'

'Here is *Ardek*,' came the answer. 'I hear you.'

'It is my intention to avoid further loss of life on either side. You must see that we are stronger than you.'

'We will not surrender. More of us will come.'

'Very well. Then I challenge you, personally, to a duel.' Her throat closed on the word, and she was conscious of Cawthorne, beside her, turning to gaze at her in astonishment. 'If you win, we will withdraw. If I win, you must let us pass. Do you agree?'

The amplifier hummed for a moment; then the high-pitched voice replied, 'I agree. Where we fight?'

'There is a satellite of your planet nearby. I have seen it on my report. I will have myself put down there on any spot you choose. As for weapons, let us each use a single hand-weapon, nothing more.'

'Very well.'

As Kathryn snapped up the switch, Cawthorne said, 'Sir, I must protest. This is irregular, against all regulations, and it's dangerous as well—'

She raised a hand. 'I know all that, Mr Cawthorne. But I am certain I can defeat him. I suspected he'd agree to a duel. If you've been watching him in action you can see that he is impetuous and gallant, not the kind of officer who can resist such a challenge. But there's something else. He never fired the first shot. Hadn't you noticed? He only fights on the defensive.'

'But—'

'No buts. I'm going. That's an order.' She found that it gave her an unexpected pleasure to say the words. There were some satisfactions in being in command, even if she couldn't remember how she had got there.

They set a course for the satellite which had appeared on her print-out, and raised it in minutes, a vast, uneven globe of rock and dust pitted by craters. Co-ordinates for a landing were arranged with *Ardek*'s commander, and Kathryn was ferried down by a small scout ship. As she had surmised, the satellite was used as a base, and the enemy commander had informed her that it had an atmosphere provided by great machines which released oxygen from the soil, thin but breathable, so that space-suits were unnecessary.

She found herself on the floor of a crater, and she could see at once why the enemy had chosen it, for it was a wide space, sloping gently upwards to high rocky walls all around and strewn sparsely with immense boulders behind which someone who thought of defence rather than attack could take cover and watch to see what his opponent would do. But, Kathryn thought grimly, I am not going to be lured into fighting *his* way. Examples sprang to her mind from a dozen points in history in which the guerrilla tactics of surprise, of suddenness, of speed had all counted for more than weight and firepower. She could see the enemy's small fighter—it carried no scout-ship—coming down out of the royal blue of the sky, and at once, with the great bounds the lesser gravity made possible, she made off at high speed for the rim of the crater, carrying under her arm the bundle she had brought with her.

She had guessed at the low gravity because of the smallness of the satellite, and her recollection of many telecasts of the research and mining parties on the moon of her own world came to help her. Her first couple of jumps were awkward, but she quickly mastered the kangaroo leaps and as *Ardek* settled in a cloud of silvery dust, she vanished into the sharp-edged shadows. She had been on the point of asking Cawthorne's advice about weapons, but a touch at her belt had revealed that she was wearing some sort of side-arm, and she had decided that that would be enough for her. She wanted nothing that would encumber her. She unholstered it now and studied it.

She had never in her life handled a pistol, but it was simple enough to work out. The handle adapted itself snugly to her fist; this stud beneath the forefinger must be a trigger, and a closer look showed another flat lever which was marked with an arrow. When she pushed it in the direction of the arrow, a red mark showed. This, then, either prepared it for firing or kept it from doing so. She would simply have to try both ways. She assumed the thing was loaded; the captain of a war-ship would hardly carry an empty pistol. She had no idea how it fired, or how many times, but she hadn't wanted to expose her ignorance since, if she had done so, Cawthorne might well have prevented her from going.

She could see the enemy commander in the distance. He stepped out of his ship, gazed about, and sprang for the cover of a rock some distance off. A minute or two later, *Ardek* shot upwards. Kathryn marked that rock well, although it was obscured momentarily by the flame and dust of the ship's take-off. Before the ship was well off the ground, she had begun working her way around the edge of the crater, keeping in the shadow where her dark uniform made her invisible, and moving swiftly.

She had to assume that her opponent had seen her running for cover as he came down. If so, he would have his eye on the spot where she had vanished. If he was the kind of fighter she thought he was, he would wait for her to make a short rush out, working towards him and keeping behind rocks. But now she had followed a considerable arc of the crater's circle and was some distance from where she had started. There were plenty of upright, jagged rocks along the wall's foot and she paused behind one of them and unwrapped her bundle.

She had asked for a pillow and any light-coloured garment. They had given her a pair of pale khaki fatigues, into which she now stuffed the pillow. She set it down at the edge of the rock so that it projected a little way like the bulge of a head and shoulder. She sighted along it with her pistol, making sure there was no obstruction between it and the great boulder where the other commander lay hidden. Then she pressed the stud. Nothing happened.

'Now I know,' she thought, with a grimace. She moved the lever so that the red mark no longer showed, and tried again.

This time, there was a sharp crack. A small bright flame appeared and vanished; from the boulder chips flew. A pause, and then *Ardek*'s commander fired. His weapon made a loud roar, and the ground near Kathryn's hiding place was ploughed by a long scorch-mark from which black smoke rose.

But Kathryn herself was no longer there. She had guessed that her shot from a wholly unexpected direction would surprise him and make him duck, and in that split-second she had leaped, a long flat jump

which took her five metres away and into the shelter of another rock.

There, she waited. He must be straining his eyes, and with luck he would eventually make out the pale bulge at the edge of the rock she had left. Again, he fired. Once again she moved, and gained another four or five metres.

His third shot grazed the edge of the pillow-stuffed overalls. There was a brief spurt of flame and the dummy was knocked to one side. From the enemy's viewpoint it must have looked, as it moved with flapping sleeves, very much like a body. It now lay a trifle more exposed, still smouldering.

And then the waiting began. Kathryn's last jump had carried her to the shelter of an upthrust needle of stone which did not altogether conceal her. She made herself as flat as she could and lay frozen, gripping the butt of her pistol so hard that her hand hurt. The minutes dragged. He was being very cautious. She could imagine him behind his rock, straining his eyes —or whatever aliens like him used for eyes—watching the faint light-coloured shape for the slightest movement. He *must* think he had hit her. She willed it with all her might.

At last, he appeared. Two bounds, and he had streaked from his position to another, a boulder some ten metres nearer the dummy. Again, he waited. So did Kathryn. Another advance by him, and this one brought him at an angle so that he could now see more of the dummy. It also brought him closer to Kathryn.

She dared not lift her head yet, but she could see him clearly, his body tense in a green uniform, his pistol ready. She could not see his face, but his shape was certainly manlike. *Come on*, she cried inside her head. *Just one more jump*.

He might have heard her unspoken command. He seemed to relax, to make up his mind. Lifting his pistol, he stepped into the open and made that last jump which brought him within a dozen paces of her position. She held him in the sights of her weapon.

She didn't shoot. Instead, she called, 'Don't move!'

She saw him start at the voice coming from the wrong direction. His gun wavered; he stood uncertainly.

'I have you covered,' she shouted. 'Drop your weapon.'

He did so. She scrambled to her feet and stepped into view, pointing her pistol firmly at him. He caught the movement from the corner of his eye and turned to face her. They stood looking at each other for half a dozen heartbeats, and then she dropped her arm.

There was no hostility in her at the sight of him close to, but amusement and gladness. It was all so winningly familiar: that blunt muzzle, those drooping ears, the mournful but affectionate brown eyes, and even the hands covered with fine, silky hair, could be seen to have once been paws. The ancient canine bond drew her, and drew him as well for he leaped up awkwardly towards her, fawning about her, touching her with hard-nailed fingers.

And then everything was clear to her, the defensive fighting, the gallantry, the barking, growling speech, and even that question which had come to her earlier: where had these aliens learned English?

'But then—' she said, bemused, 'then this is our own moon, and that planet Earth itself!'

'Yes, yes,' he cried. 'We have guarded it all these centuries, as we promised you. Welcome home, mistress!'

'Very good,' said a voice, seeming to come from the depths of space.

Slowly, Kathryn's vision blurred and cleared; the lunar landscape thinned away reluctantly and through it she could see a room which took shape, solidified, and became real. A white-haired man was smiling at

her and nodding reassuringly, and at that her memory flooded back.

'Ah!' she exclaimed. 'The test! Was that it? You didn't explain that it would be—'

'I know,' said the Examiner. 'You see, there must be no way for you to prepare yourself for it. But let us see how you scored.'

She could feel the cone above her head, the metal attachments to her temples and the back of her skull. Her hands rested in metal cups and there was a spongy material under her fingers. A steel case stood upright at her side, and the Examiner inspected a sheet which protruded from a slot in it.

'Yes,' he said. 'Adjustment and orientation to new surroundings, excellent. Ability to decode and general linguistics, very good. Imagination, superior. Deductive ability, inquisitiveness ... hm, hm ... reaction times—all very satisfactory. Considerable tenacity of purpose, use of your own educational background—not at all bad, considering the circumstances.'

'Does that mean—?' she began, anxiously.

'As I told you, Kathryn, the examination is not at all in conventional subjects. After all, this university has thousands of applicants, and we cannot accept mere rote learning from the few hundred we choose. We are looking for other qualities in our candidates, even in one who intends to specialize in history. But to answer your question—'

He chuckled, and his old eyes crinkled in amusement.

'I think we can say, "Welcome to the university, mistress,"' he finished.

THE LIGHTS OF THE CITY

Garry Kilworth

Serpers were probably not the ugliest aliens in the galaxy, but their hostility towards humans made them seem so. They walked upright, like people, but their four limbs were very thin and sinewy. I think this was because they had no bones in their arms, just rings of muscle. Their heads were flat and fanned out like a cobra's, and they had a way of looking at you through narrow, yellow eyes. That's why I sometimes called them snakeheads.

The dark hours were long on their world. The days were short with very weak sunshine. Serpers used their flat, hood-like necks to catch the warmth of the sunlight.

Scarlet was a favourite colour amongst them. They wore loose clothing with many folds and wrinkles. The colour of the material was often reflected on their hairless oily skin, but sometimes they covered every inch of their flesh and only allowed a slit to see through. They were fairly primitive, of course. Like most aliens in that part of the galaxy, when they fought, which seemed to be most of the time, they did so with spears and swords. It is true I once saw one with a crossbow but I believe he must have been killed shortly afterwards because I only saw the weapon that one time.

We humans, on the other hand, gave our word before we left Earth, that we would do no harm to any intelligent life—such a promise made it difficult for us to defend ourselves. By the way, my name is Todd Arith. The Serpers laughed at me because my blue eyes and black hair reminded them of the mounts they rode—dark, woolly creatures, with wicked-looking horns that were used to steer them.

I was born on Serpers' World but my parents came from old Earth, which was many light years away. Ever since the Serpers attacked our city, I had lived in the mountains. Most of my people escaped in a space-ship but in all the panic I lost my parents and the ship took off without me. Now, I was the only human left on the planet. I was twelve Earth years of age when I first ran to hide in the mountains. That was three Earth years ago. The Serpers had attacked us in the dead of night. There had been much confusion: people run-ning this way and that, and Serpers chasing them with their ugly weapons. The night had swallowed our screams with gusto and there had been many horrible incidents which, when I think of them, make me trem-ble even now.

*

The Serpers were coming for me. This time, though, I knew they weren't intending to kill me. I had seen what was happening to their fields. They had tried to make use of the technology the humans had left behind. But it had got out of control and they didn't know what to do. They needed me. There was no one else for them to turn to. So they ignored their pride and began to climb the mountain where I lived.

'Come on, you barbarians,' I shouted into the wind, standing on a tall rock above them. Then I began to climb, making it the second time in my life that I had seriously been pursued by them. Only this time they wanted my help, not my life. Still, I wasn't going to make it easy for them.

The herders could have caught me quickly, of course. Some of the young, athletic warriors, nimble as rock creatures, could have sprung from ledge to ledge as fast as I. But those that were coming were the old chiefs and since they wanted my help they could not take me by force. There were no sinewy, muscled Serpers in strips of bright, jangling armour climbing up the crags. Instead, it was a slow procession of fumbling elders, followed by their servants and sons. Elders of the tribes of Farmers, Herdsmen and, perhaps stronger and more stately than the rest, Elders of the Tribe of Warriors.

I sat crosslegged on a flat rock outside my cave and waited for them to arrive. Three Earth years I had lived in these merciless mountains and I knew their dark, rugged corners as well as the corners of my own mind. They arrived.

Calef of the Herdsmen was to be the first to speak. I knew this because his face, fringed by the hood, trembled. Also he was the weakest of the three leaders.

'You mock us, young one,' he began breathlessly.

'No more than you deserve,' I snorted. I was being brave now that I was needed but I could not carry it too far if I wished to escape from the world that had me trapped. My vague plans allowed for some anger on my part. They would expect a certain amount of spirit, otherwise they would have been suspicious.

'We need your help, human,' the Herdsman continued. 'Great cracks have appeared in our fields—cracks wide enough to swallow farms. The land is swelling as if it is about to burst and we are afraid it will destroy us all.'

I stared hard at them. I wanted them to humble themselves before me. To beg my forgiveness with their eyes, if not their mouths. The only one that did not turn away was Kang of the Warriors, and even he twisted uncomfortably, making his leather breastplate creak in the silence. His tongue ran over the metal band in his mouth that had replaced his battle-broken teeth.

'You snakehead,' I cried. 'You dare to ask me for help?'

They accepted this insult in silence. They were desperate. Kang gripped his weapon until his fingers showed white.

'Speak,' he said but quietly enough. His wide nose with the jewel embedded in the bridge twitched as he spoke. It was the only sign that I had managed to anger him.

'Tell me why you attacked our city,' I ordered, 'before I help you.'

It was the third member of the group, Pougerchan of the Farmers, that answered my request. He was a thin, grizzled man in a huge coat.

'We hated you. We could see you walking with silver skins on strips of curving copper from tower to tower, laughing and calling to one another ... and your lights never went out. We were jealous of the newcomers to our world. The humans.'

He was speaking about my parents and my people, when we lived in the city at the foot of the mountains. We had always had light in this place of darkness. An invisible forcefield around our city had protected us. Then, one night, the power had run out and the Ser-

pers had got through the forcefield and attacked us in the dark. My mother and father and the rest of the humans escaped in a spaceship but I had run the wrong way. Now I supposed my parents thought I was dead. The lights of the city had not been on since that time.

I looked up. I could see the fuzzy shape of the moon. That was where I believed my parents were. They had escaped to the moon and built another city. On really dark nights I thought I could see their lights shining. Of course, they had probably returned to look for me, but by that time I had climbed the mountain and was hiding, shivering in fright, at the back of the cave I eventually made my home.

Once the Serpers had finished talking, I told them my terms. I would help them—if they let me go back into the old city just for one night. They agreed.

With the chiefs there was a young Serper about my age. I asked who he was.

'He is Jagan, the wizard's son,' one of the elders answered. 'He knows as many things as yourself.' These defiant words were an attempt at saving face.

'If he knows so much he can stop your fields expanding,' I answered sarcastically. Jagan laughed out loud and shook his head. It was difficult not to like him, even though he was a snakehead.

The next day I gathered my rags around me and walked down the mountainside. They had left a bundle of what they considered fine clothes in my path. I

took the hint and put them on—pulling the hood over my head. They hated the sight of my skin. Anyway, I needed something to protect me against the cold winds of the valleys.

The plains below me were cracked like giant crazy paving and I raised my eyes to where the great volcano the natives called Skerg-pall stood like a gigantic rotten tooth that jutted from the centre of our great island. The volcano's roots stretched their claw-like points far out into the fertile fields. The volcano dominated the whole island.

I could not see the crater top. For many years now it had been encircled by the forcefield. The Serpers had used the city forcefield to plug their volcano and stop it from erupting. It was the wrong thing to do, of course. The steam and boiling mud had to find a way out somewhere and the pressure was building up underneath the fields. Soon there would be an almighty explosion and the whole island would disappear from the face of the world. It had happened once on Earth, to a place called Krakatoa.

The elders met me in the foothills. A stinking, clamorous mob followed us over the fields to inspect one of the largest cracks, a wide abyss that separated buildings of the same farm.

'How deep is it?' I asked, kicking a stone into the chasm. We did not hear it hit the bottom. It seemed to fall forever.

Kang said, 'Shall I lower someone down? When the screaming stops we will know they have reached the middle of the world.'

The idea obviously pleased him. He looked like a man who had just discovered his own genius.

'Certainly not,' I cried, appalled at the thought. Some of the nearest Serper females were taking no chances; they backed rapidly out of sight behind the men.

However, Kang merely gave one of his characteristic

shrugs and wiped some surplus saliva from his lips with his beard.

We then had a look at several more of the huge cracks in the fields—the whole countryside was criss-crossed with them—but wherever we walked the crowd followed and hampered our movements.

They treated the whole episode as an excuse for a holiday. Mounted Serper youths with clubs and glinting shields were dashing at each other. They weaved in and out of greasy females and youngsters trying to knock one another out of the saddle. The elders had brought jugs of ale and were getting drunker by the moment, arguing politics and starting fist fights. I asked if Jagan could show me what I wanted to see, alone.

Kang secured us a couple of mounts, a quiet one for me as I had never ridden one of the beasts in my life. Jagan and I set out to tour the fields and visit Skerg-pall, the source of their troubles.

It took three nights of hard riding to reach the edge of the volcano and my mount had a lather seeping through its coat which had soaked through my clothes and down into my new boots. My wet slippery legs rubbing backwards and forwards along the animal's back made my skin extremely sore. I suggested to Jagan that we dismount and walk for a while.

'You do much magic?' I asked him.

'I am first to see the raincloud that ends a drought. This is their magic.'

'That is very shrewd of you. Is all your magic so easily explained?'

He had a long red hood that flapped in the wind. He turned his yellow eyes on me and replied, 'Most of it.'

I wanted to question him on the forcefield: that invisible dome-shaped shield we had invented to keep aliens out of our cities.

'And who suggested putting the forcefield on top of the volcano to prevent it erupting?' I asked. It was this

that held the giant bubble of red lava high above us, on the volcano lip. It seemed as if any moment it would burst and flood the land in fire.

'My father. The wizard. His intentions were good.'

'Well, it's too late for placing the blame now, but we can't switch off the forcefield. The lava would pour over the farms in the valley, destroying them.'

Jagan's face was full of concern and I wondered how such an intelligent youth survived amongst the callous, brutish oafs whom he called his brothers. Probably there were more like him, but I was prejudiced against the many because of the few that had slaughtered my people.

He said, 'We must consult with the elders. You must tell us what we can do.'

'I am grateful for your confidence in me. I just hope it's not misplaced,' I said, climbing on to my tame beast.

*

When we got back, I asked the elders to let me make a quick visit to my old city.

Inside the buildings the walls were green with mould and the rooms stank. All of our beautiful possessions were gone, stolen by the Serpers.

The streetlamps were still there though, high and out of reach of everything, even time. They were embedded like rock crystals in the giant arches that spanned the city. Those smooth, curving forms crisscrossed over the city; untouched by earthquakes because of the city's floating foundations; so high that the clouds passed beneath them.

I spent the rest of the four-hour day searching what was left of the city. Just as the blood-red light began draining away from the sky, I found what I wanted. The metal was rustless and it had been covered with protective sheeting. It was a machine my uncle used to drive, a vehicle with a corkscrew-pointed nose that would drill through rock. All I had to do was find some

fuel and I was sure the machine would burst into life at the first touch of the button. I had seen my uncle do it many times and our machines are built to last.

'Well what is this?' growled Kang suspiciously, kicking the rock borer on the flank as I showed the machine to the elders.

'It is the god of unicorns,' said Pougerchan, touching the huge shiny nose and smiling to show the only four teeth he had left in his head.

'It's a rock-borer,' I answered. 'We used it to cut tunnels through mountain passes and bore down below the surface when we found it necessary. For mines. The nose drill is made from one of the hardest minerals known.'

Calef was walking around it and looking upwards at its massive proportions. Jagan followed him.

Jagan shuddered. 'And with this machine we cut a hole down through the rock to the lava bed below and allow the steam and mud to escape? Somewhere where it will do no harm to us and where the sides of the tunnel will be strong enough to stop the world from cracking in two? And what magic will guide this wondrous metal beast?'

'Someone has to drive it,' I said.

'I thought it was this way,' nodded Jagan.

The chiefs conferred and came up with a few names of criminals and generally despised local inhabitants that they were willing to get rid of, but Jagan spoke.

'I will drive the beast,' he said quietly, stroking its side. 'This was all my father's fault and he is too old and sick to wipe away his sins.'

'The youth has intelligence,' said Calef craftily.

'He has reliability,' added Pougerchan.

'And he *wants* to do it,' finished Kang.

'Jagan,' I said to him afterwards. 'I will wait with my mount. You can jump clear once the machine has been set on its course and we can both escape the eruption afterwards.'

'It'll be dangerous,' he said.

'I don't care. *You* don't deserve to die for *them*.'

*

The machine's fuel came from an underground ware-house. We put the small solar battery out into the sun to charge. Finally, I gave the courageous Jagan some lessons in handling the machine and we set off, Jagan in the machine which filled him with so much terror. The elders and I followed him, mounted on our beasts.

He handled the rock-borer well as it rumbled like a metal dragon over the uneven ground towards the place where he was to pierce the crust of the world. We had chosen a spot well away from any village or farm.

We stopped our mounts some distance from the point where Jagan was to begin drilling. Jagan did not pause. The machine moved on until it reached its destination. Then it halted, gleaming in the sunlight. At first I thought that something had gone wrong but soon it began to move into position.

The cat-tracks went up inside the shell at a touch of a button and the pistoned legs pushed out at the back to drive the already screwing nose into the earth. It was faster at digging than travelling overland and in a moment it was gone, the sand piling up around the edge of the giant worm hole. The others began riding away immediately, but I spurred my mount towards the hole and saw that Jagan had managed to jump free before the machine began its descent. He ran to me and climbed up on the back of my beast.

'Ride!' he shouted.

At first it was a hiss, then a scream, and finally a full-throated roar came from the vent. It was obvious then that the distance we had ridden was not going to be far enough. We had not covered very much more ground when the first ash blasted from the mouth of the hole and up into the atmosphere. The reverbera-tions were tremendous, shaking the ground like a piece of rag.

My mount danced to keep its footing, and twice my mouth struck the hard muscles of its neck causing me much pain. A moment later it was raining chunks of steaming rock the size of barrels and the noise was deafening. My mount followed that of Kang's, who was a magnificent rider for all his other faults. He weaved in and out of the boulders with the ease of an expert.

The four of us made it out of the danger area before the lava stream shot upwards like water from a high-powered hose. Bits of burning ash had landed on my clothes and hair but apart from a few blisters I was unscathed. Pougerchan, moaning softly, had an ugly burn running from his waist to his right knee and Kang had a small wound in his shoulder. Calef was unhurt but his mount was limping. We all looked towards the volcano and saw that the lava had begun to subside.

While the other two wrapped some rags around Pougerchan's thigh, I watched the fiery stream spurting heavenward. I had saved their world and my reward was a night in the city. The Serpers would keep their promise, I knew, but at dawn they would come for me. They would kill me then.

'The city is mine, though,' I said, still staring at the stream of lava, 'for tonight.'

When the drums stopped, the Serpers would come for me.

They had been feasting and dancing all night and filling the air with insane screams and laughter. Soon the dawn would arrive and they would remember my presence in the city. They would come, red-eyed with blood-lust, to perform one of their ritual murders.

When I was in the mountains I had not mattered to them. It was too much trouble to kill me. Now, they owed me their lives. It would be an intolerable burden to let me live.

It was night and I could not see the new volcano cone Jagan had created on the western shores

—though the glow from its fire was plainly visible. In fact I could not see very much at all beyond the city boundary, except one or two fires on the plain, a star or two, and of course the moon. That arid-looking place where I hoped my people now lived.

*

The drums muttered on. But I had got what I wanted. I was alone in my old city, racing through the streets. The solar batteries had had three years to charge themselves and there was plenty of power. I knew what I had to do.

During the night I had been running the streets of the vast city, throwing the switches and turning on the lights. The lamps on the arches were coming on, one by one. I needed as much light as I could get for I knew that this night would be my last chance. I had to call for help in the loudest voice I had—the lights of my old city.

Feverishly, I ran from lamp to lamp. Lights. Lights were coming on one after the other, to form bright bows across the roof of the city. Towers became tall columns of dazzling brilliance.

Someone would be watching.

Someone on the moon would have his eyes on this world and would see the city swathed in light after three years. Someone had to be watching. They would know. They would see the glow and they would know that one of their own was alive in the old city. Surely they would guess that?

Or would they?

Another tower, and another light. Perhaps they were not on the moon after all, but on some distant planet, too far away to take the trouble to investigate the reappearance of the lights after all this time? Perhaps my eyes had tricked me into seeing a glow from the moon. Maybe they would come, a long way, and it would be too late to save me.

But if my people were on the moon . . .

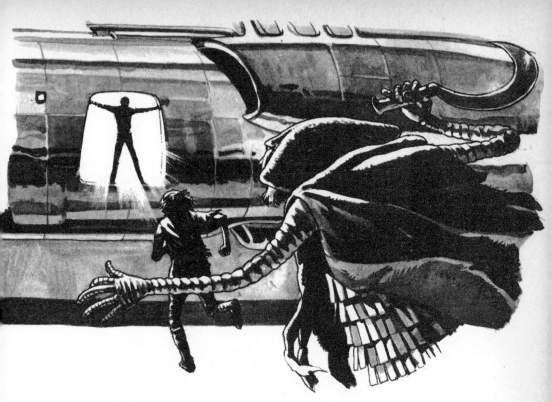

Another light.

And my parents insisted they investigate ...

And yet another.

Then it would take but a few hours to come and rescue me.

On and on I stumbled breathlessly through the night, through the thousands of doorways and along the flying pathways arching between each tower, until it was time for the dawn to unmask.

Had my people been watching?

I looked up into the fading darkness. It was difficult to see beyond the lights. If they had seen them they would be here very soon.

I searched the dawn skies outside—and was rewarded with a moving teardrop of silver, which might have been a shooting star, falling down the face of the sky. A shooting star ... or a spaceship.

While I watched the small dot moving downwards, I realized that something had happened, something had changed. I became aware that the drums had ceased throbbing, and all the world was still. The Serpers would soon be inside the city, they would enter again with their sickle-shaped swords.

I waited—but before the Serpers came there was a ship, the ship of my people, humming like a giant metal insect above the towers. Kang and his men must have seen it coming. I could imagine the Serpers moving more stealthily now—eyes glinting with anticipation. I stood in the centre of the main square shouting and waving my arms skyward—a perfect target for Kang's longbow archers.

'*Here I am. Here I am,*' I called to the ship.

I could hear the Serpers clanking and shuffling in the streets not far from the square.

'Quick, quick!' I shouted, as the ship moved over my head searching the city for the unlikely sight of human survivors. After all, the attack had taken place three Earthyears ago.

Then I remembered. My clothes. I looked like a native. They would see me and leave, thinking a foolish Serper youth had learned the trick of the lights and was playing bright games with the darkness.

I tore off the cloak and flung it to the ground—and at last the ship paused, and after a moment, descended.

Kang's chilling battle cry rang loud through the night and arrows began clanging against the far side of the ship. I walked swiftly towards it and as I did so a panel slid open. There, in the hatchway, was an almost-forgotten figure in a silver sheath. A hand beckoned, the light, shining behind it. Then, suddenly Kang rushed at me from out of the darkness. His huge, flat head was fanned out in rage, and he swung his mighty sword about him. I could hear it whistling in the dawn air; could see the flashing blade whirling. I ran and grasped the edge of the hatch.

The ship began to rise and I felt the sword nick my elbow. I was almost out of reach but with a roar Kang gripped my ankle and together we left the ground, dangling from the hatch.

My father reached down and began to pull me aboard but two bodies were too heavy for him. Already we were high above the city. Kang held on grimly to my foot but swung dangerously from side to side. His heavy sword was weighing both of us down but he would not let go of it. Then I felt suddenly lighter. Kang's hand had slipped. He went crashing down through the glass screens of one of the towers, his sword spinning through space beside him. The tower lights began to go out one by one as his body smashed through each brilliant panel.

My father pulled me aboard.

'Welcome home, son,' he said.

THROUGH THE MOONS
OF MOWL

Brian Earnshaw

The veteran starship *Dragonfall 5* is on her way to the planet Mowl with her crew, Tim, Sanchez, Old Elias and Big Mother, and their flying dog hound, Jerk. Also on board are Nigel Pony and the scientist, Professor Horgankriss. Together they are on a mission—to discover the secret of Mr Mowl and his Instant Ship . . .

Dragonfall 5 woke from her three days of orbiting sleep to the soft hum of her anti-gravs. With Old Elias alert at the rocket switches Tim eased the old ship gently round until she was pointing straight for the centre of Mowl.

Now the whole glory of silver light reflecting from the four hundred odd moons poured straight into the control cabin. A sphere composed of many other spheres, some large, some small, all brilliant, the moons of Mowl filled half the heavens ahead of them. Old Elias flipped down his eyeshade, the rest of the family crew reached for their goggles. Tim was at anti-grav controls, Sanchez was navigator at the laser radio, Big Mother was on standby as usual, with the rug she was making on her knee. Nigel Pony stood firmly on his four legs with his nose resting on Sanchez's shoulder. Jerk had gone to sleep.

'On target zero,' Tim called as the three long vanes

of their Galactic Integrator in the nose cone centred on to their course.

'Rockets five,' Old Elias called back, as he pulled down the firing rods for port and starboard wing pods.

Dragonfall quivered slightly from end to end and reared up a little upon itself. Her blue and silver livery flashed back light at the great white sun behind them almost as brilliantly as did the moons ahead of them. Down her sides was blazoned GHA in green letters, crossed with a black hypodermic needle, the badge of the Galactic Health Authority, their charter company.

Four . . .

Three . . .

Two . . .

One . . .

On two pillars of fire *Dragonfall* lunged forward at five, ten, twenty thousand miles an hour, straight for the barrier of moons that swung in stately order and grew ever larger ahead of them.

'She's riding rough, isn't she?' Old Elias spoke what they had all noticed; that their starship was shaking, quivering and almost kicking as her speed gathered.

'This far out she should be smooth as silk at twenty thousand.' Old Elias checked anxiously at his dials.

'Nothing wrong on my side,' called Tim.

Dragonfall lurched again, so violently that Big Mother had to snatch sharply at her rug.

'Land's sakes!' she said. 'It's a mercy I've got nothing on the stove!'

'I can't make it out,' Old Elias said in a worried tone.

'If an amateur could put a word in,' Nigel Pony drawled.

'What?' Old Elias snapped.

'A starship of this reverent vintage is likely to buck like a young colt when it drives at twenty thousand miles an hour through a dense oxygen atmosphere,' Nigel said softly.

'Dense oxygen atmosphere!' Old Elias shouted.

'What do you mean? Dense oxygen ends at the tropopause mark, sixteen miles up from planetary surface. There might be a bit of oxygen up to the stratopause at fifty miles out, but we're more than forty thousand miles out even from the moons. Must be one hundred and fifty thousand miles out from planetary surface. We're in almost pure vacuum.'

'Pardon me, folks,' Nigel continued, 'you're thinking in terms of ordinary planets and Mowl's no ordinary planet. Not on your life! Might I suggest you take an air sample and check the contents?'

Old Elias nodded, holding on tightly to the shivering control wheel. Tim reached forward and pressed three switches one after the other. A green panel lit up, set with figures.

'Wow!' Tim called in surprise. 'Nigel's right. The air's breathable already, oxygen's ninety per cent normal.'

'On Mowl's surface you'll find the oxygen is fifty per cent above normal,' said Nigel, 'that's why we're all so frisky! But if I were you folks I'd slow down some if you don't want sore seats all round.'

Old Elias fired the braking rockets, their speed dropped and the ride became easier.

'How do you get oxygen this far out?' Tim asked.

'Mowl's an old planet,' said Nigel casually. 'Old age and the stone grass working together have given us a ripe harvest of air.'

'What's stone grass?' asked Sanchez.

'If I recall my botany,' replied Nigel, 'it looks like long deep grass but technically it's a fungus. It can grow on soil, stone, just about anything. Most of those moons ahead of us are covered in it and, of course, it just about drips with oxygen. Me, I can't wait to get my teeth into a good mouthful of deep, dark, stone grass!'

'Does it taste nice?' asked Sanchez.

'There isn't a flavour to touch it in the whole wide universe,' Nigel smacked his lips noisily. 'Though I fear you folk will want to boil it or fry it or seethe it or something sad like that.'

'How about fresh with oil and vinegar, like lettuce?' suggested Big Mother.

'Pleasant for a change,' Nigel agreed.

'If this stone grass grows on the moons of Mowl,' Tim had been working things out, 'you could live on them if you could get to them. There must be plenty of oxygen to breathe and there's the grass to eat.'

'If we could get to them!' Nigel Pony snorted softly. 'Honey child! The history of Mowl goes back for many thousands of years, but it just does not record a time when my race was not living on the moons and travelling freely to them.'

Tim felt a little crushed.

'But you haven't developed space craft,' he protested, 'not until this Mr Mowl came up with the Instant Ship.'

'Instant Ship,' Nigel repeated thoughtfully. 'An uneasy name to my ears. It suggests an easy-to-prepare pudding. Add milk and then stir! You know what I mean?'

'But you didn't develop space flight, did you?' Tim persisted.

'When you live on the finest planet in the galaxy you don't spend much effort trying to fly away from it,' Nigel explained airily. 'But you are right. Until this remarkable creation of Mr Mowl we had developed no space drive. Our volcanoes pump up an inexhaustible supply of hydrohelioid gas. This is much lighter than air. By collecting it in oval balloons we construct cloud clippers which travel comfortably and reasonably swiftly between our planet and our moons.'

'What do you mean by "reasonably swiftly",' Tim pressed him.

'Brother,' said Nigel, 'I've got my hoofs above my head! I surrender! I'll come quietly! You've got me cornered. By reasonably swiftly, I mean it takes about a week. And what's a week when you've got fresh air and good company? No one hurries on Mowl.'

'Can I take it that you know these moons reasonably well?' asked Old Elias, moving restlessly in his seat.

'I was born on that one,' Nigel waved a hoof vaguely at the barrier of bright opal globes looming large ahead of them.

'Then I'd take it kindly,' said Old Elias, 'if you'd find us an easy road through them, 'cos I'm bothered if I can figure one out. According to my charts all galaxy-side ships land on one of the big moons.'

'That one there! The one we call Gate to the Dark,' Nigel pointed to the left. 'Then passengers travel on down to Mowl by cloud clipper.'

'What we want, though, is to do it under our own steam. To get down before the return entry of the Instant Ship,' Old Elias explained.

'The usual way through is between Gate to the Dark and Eye of the Sun, over there,' Nigel pointed. 'But that way might be too crowded for what we want. May I suggest the narrow but clear passage over to our right, thirty-five degrees, between Sighs of the Air and a minor moon called Wind Whipper.'

'Whatever you say,' Old Elias grunted.

'And might I . . .' Nigel Pony hesitated.

'You want to take over, I suppose,' Old Elias sounded cross.

'Folks, I'll be so careful you'd think a feather pillow was at the controls.'

Grudgingly Old Elias slid sideways and Nigel wriggled carefully into his seat. His two front hooves closed precisely upon the wheel.

'And could I trouble you for an eyeshade?'

Old Elias sighed and fitted his own on to Nigel's forelock.

'What a trial,' Nigel mused contentedly, 'that one's very own planet should be the most brilliant object in the known universe!'

Confidently *Dragonfall 5* closed in upon the moon wall. Their cabin flooded with almost intolerable light as the great spheres bulked about them. Mountains, plains and valleys were marked on their curves as they drew closer, but they still reflected silver light. Only as *Dragonfall* swung in a fiery arc and plunged into the gap between vast Sighs of the Air and small, broken Wind Whipper did the colours change.

'They're going dark green, now we're going past them. Dark green and shadowy,' called Sanchez.

'That's their real colour,' explained Nigel. 'The silver is only sun reflection. Think of all that stone grass. No! Stop tempting me. I've got to wait.'

Now *Dragonfall* blazed like a two-winged flame bird through the dark passage between the two moons. Though their way looked narrow it was at least thirty or forty miles wide.

'How is it that they don't bump into each other?' Sanchez asked as he gazed at the dark green slopes to left and right. 'With four hundred and eighty of them you'd think they'd crash sometimes.'

'Astronomers say they have quite often,' Nigel answered, 'but it was all millions of years ago and they've been going steady now for ages. They all hold each other in position.'

'It's gravity,' said Tim.

'Yes, isn't science wonderful?' Nigel snickered again, then peered forward into the darkness. 'Look, there's Mowl at last.'

Everyone stared into the gloom, which was such a contrast after the blaze of light they had been used to for the last three days. Far ahead of them, looking at this distance no larger than some of the moons they had just passed, was the dim green sphere of a planet mottled with faint silver patterns reflected down from the moons and the barely seen sun above it.

'Is that Mowl?' Sanchez was disappointed. 'Isn't it rather depressing living there?'

'Depressing!' Nigel exclaimed. 'To live in a perpetual green twilight as if surrounded by unripe cooking apples or lost in a forest of moss! How can you call that depressing? Mowl is the finest planet that ever was, and here's me coming back to it! I'm so happy I could sing. But I won't because your father will think I'm not concentrating on my flying and that wouldn't do at all. Just you wait and I'll show you. Mowl is free! It's the only planet where earth, air, fire and water all do more or less as they please.'

'Fire?' Sanchez questioned.

'Volcanoes and rivers of flame spout here there and everywhere,' Nigel replied. 'Look carefully and you can see some of the biggest craters from right up here.'

It was true. When they looked they could make out tiny crackled patterns of yellow and red in some areas.

'Water?' Tim asked.

Nigel threw back his head for a long, high, neighing laugh.

'Water,' he repeated. 'You know what happens to your seas on Earth where you've just got one medium-sized moon tugging at them?'

'Tides,' said Sanchez.

'Sometimes rising sixty feet,' added Tim.

'Right, folks,' said Nigel. 'Well, imagine what happens to our seas, which are much smaller than yours, with four hundred and eighty moons all heaving away with their gravities!'

'Golly,' said Tim, working it out.

'The sea must go mad!' said Sanchez.

'You've said it, folks,' crowed Nigel. 'Now you understand what I said about earth, air, fire and water doing what they please.'

'We must get our camera out,' said Big Mother. 'We're going to get some very good colour slides.'

'Reckon I'll take over the controls again,' Old Elias had been fretting as they'd come between the moons.

'I've got to fly while I can. We'll soon be grounded on some hick planet again, wasting away.'

He and Nigel Pony changed places. Nigel stood again behind Sanchez, handily near to the laser radio. Big Mother got up to prepare supper, a vegetable risotto with an enormous green salad for Nigel. Cooking smells filled the air and slowly, very slowly, the changing green disk of Mowl grew closer. Behind them the sky was monstrous with the black shapes of the moons. Only thin slivers of light reflected from the sun to Mowl, and then back up again to the moons to pattern them with rare silver.

'Large flying object twenty-eight miles distant,' Sanchez called from his 3D-radar screen, 'thirteen degrees right, forty-six degrees down.'

'We'll give that a wide berth,' Old Elias commented as he swung the starship to the left.

'Can you bring it up on your visi-screens?' Nigel asked.

'It should be well within range for a minute or two.' Tim adjusted the focus of the visi-screen and abruptly the picture of a strange ship sprang into view. A large cluster of oval balloons gathered like a pyramid to carry a broad flat deck with a shallow curved hull. Towers and turrets sprang from the deck in fantastic outline. They were painted black and gold, while the balloon cluster was in five shades of blue.

'Going up fast,' Tim remarked.

'Like a city in the sky,' said Sanchez.

Nigel leaned forward and sighed.

'That's a school cruise ship,' he said, 'going up to sample the various pastures of the moons. Ah me! That takes me back awhile.'

'Aren't all the pastures stone grass?' Sanchez asked.

'It never tastes the same in two different places,' Nigel explained. 'And it's the travel that really matters, not the object of travel. I can remember my

cruise school days now as if it were yesterday: dancing, singing, fighting.'

'Our school isn't like that,' Sanchez looked crossly
at Big Mother. 'They put us under mechanical in-fillers
all night and ask us questions all day! We hate it!'

'All life should be pleasure,' said Nigel. 'That's the
only true way to learn anything.'

Big Mother stirred uneasily. She had a hard time
persuading the boys to go to school just for a week
here and there, and she didn't want Nigel Pony putting them off even more.

'All very well,' she began . . .

Abruptly a shrill loud neighing, broken and changing from high to low notes, filled the cabin.

'It's the radio,' said Sanchez. 'Someone is trying to
get through to us. It's the horses at last!'

*

For a moment they hesitated, wondering how to cope
with this first contact from the horse world. While they
waited Nigel stepped briskly forward.

'I'd better answer it, folks,' he said. 'I talk the
language and you don't.'

'No!' said Old Elias quickly, 'let them speak English.
It's Intergalactic standard language for radio contact.'

Nigel Pony looked huffed. Sanchez spoke into the
microphone.

'*Dragonfall 5* speaking,' he said, 'inbound from the
galaxy. We are receiving you. Over, please.'

There was a brief pause, then the quiet drawl of a

horse speaking careful English came from the speaker.

'Mowl Base to *Dragonfall 5*. All ships inbound from the galaxy land at our Moon Base on Gate to the Dark. You are now within the moon circle and headed for Mowl. What is your purpose, please?'

Sanchez turned off his broadcast switch so that Mowl Base would not hear them talking and then turned to the crew. The door to the hold flew open at the same moment and Professor Horgankriss came in, partly to look for his supper, partly to find out what the neighing sound had been about.

'What do we tell them?' asked Sanchez. 'Are we still supposed to be a secret?'

'I don't think there's anything to be gained by hiding facts, is there, folks?' Nigel asked, looking around.

'Well,' Old Elias began, 'we might want to hang around a few thousand feet up until this Instant Ship...'

Smoothly Nigel interrupted him.

'What do you say, Professor? Haven't you decided to meet this Mr Mowl as he calls himself and have it out with him? You want to find out just what he's up to with his Proton Drive; pollution and all that!'

'Pollution,' the Professor caught the word as Big Mother handed him a steaming plate of savoury-smelling risotto. 'Oh yes, we've got to deal with that! Bring it out into the open! The only way!'

'And you don't want to wait first and run your own checks when the Instant Ship comes back from Earth?' Tim asked sensibly.

The Professor hesitated for a moment, then plunged his fork into a big mushroom, cupped full of brown rice.

'Negative!' he said fiercely.

'He means no,' the first three Minims whispered loudly overhead.

'Give me the microphone,' ordered the Professor with his mouth full of food. Sanchez passed it to him after a glance at his father.

'*Dragonfall* to Mowl. Do you hear me?' the Professor demanded.

'Not very well,' the radio voice replied.

The Professor swallowed once to empty his mouth and went on speaking. 'This is Professor Horgankriss of the Galactic Polytechnic speaking. I represent the Galactic Health Authority and I am arriving to monitor radiation hazards on Mowl following the flights of the new Instant Ship. I may have to forbid any further use of this Proton Drive so it is urgent, repeat urgent, that I should have a conference with Mr Mowl, its inventor, at the earliest opportunity. Over to you.'

The laser radio was silent. Nigel Pony lay back and looked satisfied. Tim looked at Sanchez and raised one eyebrow.

'He means . . .' whispered the first Minim very clearly in the silence. 'He is coming . . .' hissed the second.

'To stir up a lot of trouble,' ended the third.

The Minims rocked on their perch and hugged each other nervously.

'When I chartered this ship . . .' began the Professor angrily.

'Mowl Base to *Dragonfall 5*,' the voice from the radio broke in. 'You will land one mile due south of the volcano known as The White Mane of Fire. This is shown on standard star charts. You will wait there for an anti-gravity transport which will take you to inter-view Mr Mowl. Is this satisfactory?'

Professor Horgankriss smiled broadly.

'Most satisfactory,' he replied. 'Over and out.'

'Our pleasure,' said the radio voice. 'Over and out.'

'See,' the Professor turned to them. 'I've got it all settled. I'll show them! I'll get the real facts.'

Everyone settled down to their risotto before it got cold.

After supper, with Mowl a great green shadow growing through their front window ports, the boys started on the washing up, and Nigel, without being asked, got up to help them. The Professor had gone to sleep on the sofa, Big Mother was getting on with her rug and Old Elias was happy to be left alone at the controls.

'Come on,' said Sanchez, giving Nigel Pony a friendly nudge, 'tell us the truth.'

'Don't I always do that, folks?' Nigel grinned.

'Well, some of it,' said Tim tactfully. 'You don't actually tell lies.'

'Did you really work as a counting horse at Chipperfield's Circus?' Sanchez asked him.

'Really,' Nigel nodded, drying a plate carefully. 'But not for long. It gets boring pretending to be stupid, and my worst enemies never tell me I'm that.'

'But why did you do it?'

'You are a scientist, aren't you?' pressed Tim.

'Let's say I'm an expert on Mowl,' said Nigel cautiously. 'That's why I'm working with the Professor for the Health Authority.'

'But the circus?' Sanchez reminded him.

'That was a while ago and part of another job,' said Nigel vaguely. 'Let's say I wanted to find out what it was like to be a pony in a world where humans rule.'

'And what was it like?'

'Dry hay which gave me sneezing fits, sugar, carrots and a lot of small girls wanting to sit on me!' Nigel snorted as he remembered. 'It was the saddles and girths I really hated. You won't find saddles on Mowl, some horses might let you sit on them as a special favour because you've only got two legs, but you won't be allowed to ride them.'

'Oh!' Sanchez could not hide his disappointment. He had been looking forward to a whole planet full of horses, hoping that they wouldn't all be as clever as Nigel Pony.

Nigel looked sideways at him.

'You won't think much of me,' he said sadly, 'when you see the real horses on Mowl. They're big and beautiful and very fast.'

'You're all right,' Sanchez told him. 'You've got a super coat.'

'Small head, perfect shoulders, true action,' said Nigel gloomily, 'but only ten hands high. Ah well, it's the price of being intelligent!'

'And you really believe that this new Proton Drive could be dangerous?' Tim could see Nigel was getting depressed. 'You think it could tear the atmosphere apart and make radiation?'

'Ah, we don't know, do we?' Nigel hung up his tea-cloth neatly. 'That's the interesting thing about the Instant Ship and the Proton Drive, we just don't know anything about it. One minute no one has heard of it, the next minute it's big news all over the galaxy and all the big space-ship lines are queuing up to try and buy it.'

'They're down there now,' he jerked his head in the direction of the green planet. 'If our Professor wants a chat with the great Mr Mowl he's going to find that there are a lot of other people with the same idea. Yet we don't know a thing, that's what interests me about the Proton Drive—masses of money but no hard facts. Of course it could be dangerous. It may use a huge laser of gas to project a radiation beam that could blot out a planet with a twitch of its tail. Still nothing's blotted out dear old Mowl yet, has it? And if anyone can get to the bottom of the mystery it's the Professor. Don't you agree?'

They looked over to where the Professor was having a nap with his silk handkerchief over his face. Sanchez did not think that the Professor was very likely to get to the bottom of any mystery and he did not believe that Nigel Pony thought he would do so either. Sanchez looked sideways at Nigel and found that Nigel was looking sideways at him. They all burst out laughing.

'Of course,' said Tim when they'd quietened down a little, 'the strangest thing of all is that Pan Galactic and Trans Galaxy Airways are ready to spend millions of credits and risk tearing up the atmosphere just to get people across the galaxy in three seconds instead of three hours.'

'That's not their fault, it's people's faults for not having three hours to spare,' said Sanchez. 'If people would refuse to pay more to go faster, then the space ships would go slower, like these horses do when they take a whole week to get from Mowl to its moons.'

'You can't expect everyone to be as intelligent as a horse,' said Nigel kindly. 'It's all a matter of the confidence you get from having four efficient legs. Now, though I don't expect he'll be very pleased, I'm going to offer your father some help with our landing.'

Dragonfall swooped down on Mowl in a great arc from the North Pole to the South Pole. From sixty thousand feet up the planet still looked dark and shadowy but speckled by hundreds of fire pits and lakes of flame from the many volcanoes. Once around the South Pole they streaked up the other side of the planet, crossing a small dark sea.

'Nearly there now, folks!' Nigel pointed to a line of plume-topped volcanoes along the curve of the horizon, 'The one we call The White Mane of Fire is that tall slim one, the second on the left.'

'Rocket in retro-brakes to force three!' ordered Old Elias.

'Force three retros away,' Tim called back.

Dragonfall's rocket pods swung into reverse on her

short curved back wings, and coughed flame that fell behind them in roman-candle balls of red fire.

'Force five retros!' ordered Old Elias as the slender volcano with its white feather of drooping incandescent gas drew nearer.

'Force five away,' replied Tim.

'Project anti-gravs at quarter strength and free wheel,' said Old Elias and turned on the anti-gravs himself. A hum of partial weightlessness ran through the old ship.

'You'll pardon an amateur . . .' began Nigel.

'Eh! What's that?' Old Elias growled.

'But I wouldn't fly directly over the crater of White Mane of Fire if I were captain,' Nigel continued.

'Well you're not!' snapped Old Elias, and at eight thousand feet he drove directly across the volcano's fire pit.

With a great whoosh *Dragonfall 5* shot upwards four thousand feet in a few seconds, carried headlong by a gush of lighter-than-air hydrohelioid gas from the volcano. Jerk, the Minims, Big Mother and Big Mother's rug all ended up in a heap by the cooking stove. From down below in the cargo-hold came a crash of breaking glass and a shout of 'All my precious instruments!' from the Professor.

'That'll larn 'em to fasten their safety belts,' said Old Elias as he fought back into control.

'There's usually a thermal up-draught over the top,' remarked Nigel, whose four legs had kept him firm. 'That's where we should land.' He pointed down.

Old Elias glared in the direction Nigel had pointed.

'There's a ditch of fiery lava right around the area,' he snorted.

'One mile due south was what we were told,' Nigel reminded him.

Her rockets silent, buoyed partly by her anti-gravs, *Dragonfall* swung like a blue and silver gull, down,

down over the weird green land, threaded with its ribbons of fire.

'Anti-gravs full strength!'

In a soft whirr of gentle power they landed, a careful three pointer, on a rolling meadow of long dark grass.

'Perfect!' Nigel commented, stepping over into the corner to help Big Mother to her feet, and letting the Minims use him as a ladder back up to their perch. 'Three cheers for our captain!'

THE STAR

H. G. Wells

It was on the first day of the new year that the announcement was made, almost simultaneously from three observatories, that the motion of the planet Neptune, the outermost of all the plants that wheel about the sun, had become very erratic. Ogilvy had already called attention to a suspected retardation in its velocity in December. Such a piece of news was scarcely calculated to interest a world the greater portion of whose inhabitants were unaware of the existence of the planet Neptune, nor outside the astronomical profession did the subsequent discovery of a faint remote speck of light in the region of the perturbed planet cause any very great excitement.

Scientific people, however, found the intelligence remarkable enough, even before it became known that the new body was rapidly growing larger and brighter, that its motion was quite different from the orderly progress of the planets, and that the deflection of Neptune and its satellite was becoming now of an unprecedented kind.

Few people without a training in science can realize the huge isolation of the solar system. The sun with its specs of planets, its dust of planetoids, and its impalpable comets, swims in a vacant immensity that almost defeats the imagination. Beyond the orbit of Neptune there is space, vacant so far as human observation has penetrated, without warmth or light or sound, blank emptiness, for twenty million times a million miles. That is the smallest estimate of the distance to be traversed before the very nearest of the stars is attained. And, saving a few comets more unsubstantial than the thinnest flame, no matter had ever to human knowledge crossed this gulf of space, until early in the twentieth century this strange wanderer appeared. A vast mass of matter it was, bulky, heavy, rushing without warning out of the black mystery of the sky into the radiance of the sun. By the second day it was clearly visible to any decent instrument, as a speck with a barely sensible diameter, in the constellation Leo near Regulus. In a little while an opera glass could attain it.

On the third day of the new year the newspaper readers of two hemispheres were made aware for the first time of the real importance of this unusual apparition in the heavens. 'A Planetary Collision,' one London paper headed the news, and proclaimed Duchaine's opinion that this strange new planet would probably collide with Neptune. The leader writers enlarged upon the topic. So that in most of the capitals of the world, on January 3rd, there was an expectation, however vague, of some imminent phenomenon in the sky; and as the night followed the sunset round the globe, thousands of men turned their eyes skyward to see—the old familiar stars just as they had always been.

Until it was dawn in London and Pollux setting and the stars overhead grown pale. The winter's dawn it was, a sickly filtering accumulation of daylight, and the light of gas and candle shone yellow in the windows to show where people were astir. But the yawning policeman saw the thing, the busy crowds in the markets stopped agape, workmen going to their work betimes, milkmen, the drivers of news-carts, dissipation going home jaded and pale, homeless wanderers, sentinels on their beats, and in the country, labourers trudging afield, poachers slinking home, all over the dusky quickening country it could be seen—and out at sea by seamen watching for the day—a great white star, come suddenly into the westward sky!

Brighter it was than any star in our skies; brighter than the evening star at its brightest. It still glowed out white and large, no mere twinkling spot of light, but a small round clear shining disc, an hour after the day had come. And where science has not reached, men stared and feared, telling one another of the wars and pestilences that are foreshadowed by these fiery signs in the Heavens. Sturdy Boers, dusky Hottentots, Gold Coast negroes, Frenchmen, Spaniards, Portuguese, stood in the warmth of the sunrise watching the setting of this strange new star.

And in a hundred observatories there had been suppressed excitement, rising almost to shouting pitch, as the two remote bodies had rushed together, and a hurrying to and fro to gather photographic apparatus and spectroscope, and this appliance and that, to record this novel astonishing sight, the destruction of a world. For it was a world, a sister planet of our earth, far greater than our earth indeed, that had so suddenly flashed into flaming death. Neptune it was, had been struck, fairly and squarely, by the strange planet from outer space and the heat of the concussion had incontinently turned two solid globes into one vast mass of incandescence. Round the world that day, two hours before the dawn, went the pallid great white star, fading only as it sank westward and the sun mounted above it. Everywhere men marvelled at it, but of all those who saw it none could have marvelled more than those sailors, habitual watchers of the stars, who far away at sea had heard nothing of its advent and saw it now rise like a pigmy moon and climb zenithward and hang overhead and sink west-ward with the passing of the night.

And when next it rose over Europe everywhere were crowds of watchers on hilly slopes, on house-roofs, in open spaces, staring eastward for the rising of the great new star. It rose with a white glow in front of it, like the glare of a white fire, and those who had seen it come into existence the night before cried out at the sight of it. 'It is larger,' they cried. 'It is brighter!' And, indeed the moon a quarter full and sinking in the west was in its apparent size beyond comparison, but scarcely in all its breadth had it as much brightness now as the little circle of the strange new star.

'It is brighter!' cried the people clustering in the streets. But in the dim observatories the watchers held their breath and peered at one another. *'It is nearer,'* they said. *'Nearer!'*

And voice after voice repeated, 'It is nearer,' and the clicking telegraph took that up, and it trembled along telephone wires, and in a thousand cities grimy com-positors fingered the type. 'It is nearer.' Men writing in offices, struck with a strange realization, flung down their pens; men talking in a thousand places suddenly came upon a grotesque possibility in those words, 'It is nearer.' It hurried along awakening streets, it was shouted down the frost-stilled ways of quiet villages, men who had read these things from the throbbing tape stood in yellow-lit doorways shouting the news to the passers-by. 'It is nearer.' Pretty women, flushed and glittering, heard the news told jestingly between the dances, and feigned an intelligent interest they did not feel. 'Nearer! Indeed. How curious! How very, very clever people must be to find out things like that!'

Lonely tramps faring through the wintry night murmured those words to comfort themselves—looking skyward. 'It has need to be nearer, for the night's as cold as charity. Don't seem much warmth from it if it *is* nearer, all the same.'

'What is a new star to me?' cried the weeping woman kneeling beside her dead.

The schoolboy, rising early for his examination work, puzzled it out for himself—with the great white star, shining broad and bright through the frost flowers of his window. 'Centrifugal, centripetal,' he said, with his chin on his fist. 'Stop a planet in its flight, rob it of its centrifugal force, what then? Centripetal has it, and down it falls into the sun! And this—!'

'Do *we* come in the way? I wonder—'

The light of that day went the way of its brethren, and with the later watches of the frosty darkness rose the strange star again. And it was now so bright that the waxing moon seemed but a pale yellow ghost of itself, hanging huge in the sunset. In a South African city a great man had married, and the streets were alight to welcome his return with his bride. 'Even the skies have illuminated,' said the flatterer. Under Capricorn, two negro lovers, daring the wild beasts and evil spirits, for love of one another, crouched together in a cane brake where the fireflies hovered. 'That is our star,' they whispered, and felt strangely comforted by the sweet brilliance of its light.

The master mathematician sat in his private room and pushed the papers from him. His calculations were already finished. In a small white phial there still remained a little of the drug that had kept him awake and active for four long nights. Each day, serene, explicit, patient as ever, he had given his lecture to his students, and then had come back at once to this momentous calculation. His face was grave, a little drawn and hectic from his drugged activity. For some time he seemed lost in thought. Then he went to the window, and the blind went up with a click. Halfway up the sky, over the clustering roofs, chimneys and steeples of the city, hung the star.

He looked at it as one might look into the eyes of a brave enemy. 'You may kill me,' he said after a silence. 'But I can hold you—and all the universe for that matter—in the grip of this little brain. I would not change. Even now.'

He looked at the little phial. 'There will be no need of sleep again,' he said. The next day at noon, punctual to the minute, he entered his lecture theatre, put his hat on the end of the table as his habit was, and carefully selected a large piece of chalk. It was a joke among his students that he could not lecture without that piece of chalk to fumble in his fingers, and once he had been stricken to impotence by their hiding his supply. He came and looked under his grey eyebrows at the rising tiers of young fresh faces, and spoke with his accustomed studied commonness of phrasing. 'Circumstances have arisen—circumstances beyond my

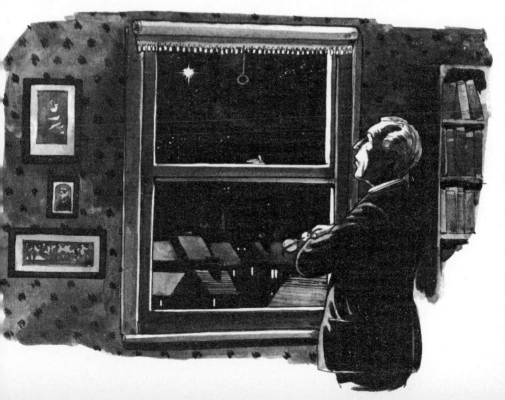

control,' he said and paused, 'which will debar me
from completing the course I had designed. It would
seem, gentlemen, if I may put the thing clearly and
briefly, that—Man has lived in vain.'

The students glanced at one another. Had they
heard aright? Mad? Raised eyebrows and grinning lips
there were, but one or two faces remained intent upon
his calm grey-fringed face. 'It will be interesting,' he
was saying, 'to devote this morning to an exposition,
so far as I can make it clear to you, of the calculations
that have led me to this conclusion. Let us assume—'

He turned towards the blackboard, meditating a
diagram in the way that was usual to him. 'What was
that about "lived in vain"?' whispered one student to
another. 'Listen,' said the other, nodding towards the
lecturer.

And presently they began to understand.

That night the star rose later, for its proper eastward
motion had carried it some way across Leo towards
Virgo, and its brightness was so great that the sky
became a luminous blue as it rose, and every star was
hidden in its turn, save only Jupiter near the zenith,
Capella, Aldebaran, Sirius and the pointers of the
Bear. It was very white and beautiful. In many parts of
the world that night a pallid halo encircled it about. It
was perceptibly larger; in the clear refractive sky of the
tropics it seemed as if it were nearly a quarter the size of
the moon. The frost was still on the ground in
England, but the world was as brightly lit as if it were
midsummer moonlight. One could see to read quite
ordinary print by that cold clear light, and in the cities
the lamps burnt yellow and wan.

And everywhere the world was awake that night,
and throughout Christendom a sombre murmur hung
in the keen air over the country side like the belling of
bees in the heather, and this murmurous tumult grew
to a clangour in the cities. It was the tolling of the bells
in a million belfry towers and steeples, summoning

the people to sleep no more, to sin no more, but to gather in their churches and pray. And overhead, growing larger and brighter as the earth rolled on its way and the night passed, rose the dazzling star.

And the streets and houses were alight in all the cities, the shipyards glared, and whatever roads led to high country were lit and crowded all night long. And in all the seas about the civilized lands, ships with throbbing engines, and ships with bellying sails, crowded with men and living creatures, were standing out to ocean and the north. For already the warning of the master mathematician had been telegraphed all over the world, and translated into a hundred tongues. The new planet and Neptune, locked in a fiery embrace, were whirling headlong, ever faster and faster towards the sun. Already every second this blazing mass flew a hundred miles, and every second its terrific velocity increased. As it flew now, indeed, it must pass a hundred million of miles wide of the earth and scarcely affect it. But near its destined path, as yet only slightly perturbed, spun the mighty planet Jupiter and his moons sweeping splendid round the sun. Every moment now the attraction between the fiery star and the greatest of the planets grew stronger. And the result of that attraction? Inevitably Jupiter would be deflected from his orbit into an elliptical path, and the burning star, swung by his attraction wide of its sunward rush, would 'describe a curved path' and perhaps collide with, and certainly pass very close to, our earth. 'Earthquakes, volcanic outbreaks, cyclones, sea waves, floods, and a steady rise in temperature to I know not what limit'—so prophesied the master mathematician.

And overhead, to carry out his words, lonely and cold and livid, blazed the star of the coming doom.

To many who stared at it that night until their eyes ached, it seemed that it was visibly approaching. And that night, too, the weather changed, and the frost that

had gripped all Central Europe and France and England softened towards a thaw.

But you must not imagine because I have spoken of people praying through the night and people going aboard ships and people fleeing towards mountainous country that the whole world was already in a terror because of the star. As a matter of fact, use and wont still ruled the world, and save for the talk of idle moments and the splendour of the night, nine human beings out of ten were still busy at their common occupations. In all the cities the shops, save one here and there, opened and closed at their proper hours, the doctor and the undertaker plied their trades, the workers gathered in the factories, soldiers drilled, scholars studied, lovers sought one another, thieves lurked and fled, politicians planned their schemes. The presses of the newspapers roared through the nights, and many a priest of this church and that would not open his holy building to further what he considered a foolish panic. The newspapers insisted on the lesson of the year 1000—for then, too, people had anticipated the end. The star was no star—mere gas—a comet; and were it a star it could not possibly strike the earth. There was no precedent for such a thing. Common sense was sturdy everywhere, scornful, jesting, a little inclined to persecute the obdurate fearful. That night, at seven-fifteen by Greenwich time, the star would be at its nearest to Jupiter. Then the world would see the turn things would take. The master mathematician's grim warnings were treated by many as so much mere elaborate self-advertisement. Common sense at last, a little heated by argument, signified its unalterable convictions by going to bed. So, too, barbarism and savagery, already tired of the novelty, went about their mighty business, and save for a howling dog here and there, the beast world left the star unheeded.

And yet, when at last the watchers in the European

States saw the star rise, an hour later it is true, but no larger than it had been the night before, there were still plenty awake to laugh at the master mathematician—to take the danger as if it had passed.

But hereafter the laughter ceased. The star grew—it grew with a terrible steadiness hour after hour, a little larger each hour, a little nearer the midnight zenith, and brighter and brighter, until it had turned night into a second day. Had it come straight to the earth instead of in a curved path, had it lost no velocity to Jupiter, it must have leapt the intervening gulf in a day, but as it was it took five days altogether to come by our planet. The next night it had become a third the size of the moon before it set to English eyes, and the thaw was assured. It rose over America near the size of the moon, but blinding white to look at, and *hot*; and a breath of hot wind blew now with its rising and gathering strength, and in Virginia, and Brazil, and down the St Lawrence valley, it shone intermittently through a driving reek of thunder-clouds, flickering violet lightning, and hail unprecedented. In Manitoba was a thaw and devastating floods. And upon all the mountains of the earth the snow and ice began to melt that night, and all the rivers coming out of high country flowed thick and turbid, and soon—in their upper reaches—with swirling trees and the bodies of beasts and men. They rose steadily, steadily in the ghostly brilliance, and came trickling over their banks at last, behind the flying population of their valleys.

And along the coast of Argentina and up the South Atlantic the tides were higher than had ever been in the memory of man, and the storms drove the waters in many cases scores of miles inland, drowning whole cities. And so great grew the heat during the night that the rising of the sun was like the coming of a shadow. The earthquakes began and grew until all down America from the Arctic Circle to Cape Horn, hillsides were sliding, fissures were opening, and houses and

walls crumbling to destruction. The whole side of Cotopaxi slipped out in one vast convulsion, and a tumult of lava poured out so high and broad and swift and liquid that in one day it reached the sea.

So the star, with the wan moon in its wake, marched across the Pacific, trailed the thunderstorms like the hem of a robe, and the growing tidal wave that toiled behind it, frothing and eager, poured over island and island and swept them clear of men. Until that wave came at last—in a blinding light and with the breath of a furnace, swift and terrible it came—a wall of water, fifty feet high, roaring hungrily, upon the long coasts of Asia, and swept inland across the plains of China. For a space the star, hotter now and larger and brighter than the sun in its strength, showed with pitiless brilliance the wide and populous country; towns and villages with their pagodas and trees, roads, wide cultivated fields, millions of sleepless people staring in helpless terror at the incandescent sky, and then, low and growing, came the murmur of the flood. And thus it was with millions of men that night—a flight nowhither, with limbs heavy with heat and breath fierce and scant, and the flood like a wall swift and white behind. And then death.

China was lit glowing white, but over Japan and Java and all the islands of Eastern Asia the great star was a ball of dull red fire because of the steam and smoke and ashes the volcanoes were spouting forth to salute its coming. Above was the lava, hot gases and ash, and below the seething floods, and the whole earth swayed and rumbled with the earthquake shocks. Soon the immemorial snows of Thibet and the Himalaya were melting and pouring down by ten million deepening converging channels upon the plains of Burmah and Hindostan. The tangled summits of the Indian jungles were aflame in a thousand places, and below the hurrying waters around the stems were dark objects that still struggled feebly and reflected the blood-red tongues of fire. And in a rudderless confusion a multitude of men and women fled down the broad river-ways to that one last hope of men—the open sea.

Larger grew the star, and larger, hotter, and brighter with a terrible swiftness now. The tropical ocean had lost its phosphorescence, and the whirling stream rose in ghostly wreaths from the black waves that plunged incessantly, speckled with storm-tossed ships.

And then came a wonder. It seemed to those who in Europe watched for the rising of the star that the world must have ceased its rotation. In a thousand open spaces of down and upland the people who had fled thither from the floods and the falling houses and sliding slopes of hill watched for that rising in vain. Hour followed hour through a terrible suspense, and the star rose not. Once again men set their eyes upon the old constellations they had counted lost to them forever. In England it was hot and clear overhead, though the ground quivered perpetually, but in the tropics, Sirius and Capella and Aldebaran showed through a veil of steam. And when at last the great star rose near ten hours late, the sun rose close upon it, and in the centre of its white heart was a disc of black.

Over Asia it was the star had begun to fall behind the movement of the sky, and then suddenly, as it hung over India, its light had been veiled. All the plain of India from the mouth of the Indus to the mouths of the Ganges was a shallow waste of shining water that night, out of which rose temples and palaces, mounds and hills, black with people. Every minaret was a clustering mass of people, who fell one by one into the turbid waters, as heat and terror overcame them. The whole land seemed a-wailing, and suddenly there swept a shadow across that furnace of despair, and a breath of cold wind, and a gathering of clouds, out of the cooling air. Men looking up, near blinded, at the star, saw that a black disc was creeping across the

light. It was the moon, coming between the star and
the earth. And even as men cried to God at this respite,
out of the East with a strange inexplicable swiftness
sprang the sun. And then star, sun and moon rushed
together across the heavens.

So it was that presently, to the European watchers,
star and sun rose close upon each other, drove headlong for a space and then slower, and at last came to
rest, star and sun merged into one glare of flame at the
zenith of the sky. The moon no longer eclipsed the star
but was lost to sight in the brilliance of the sky. And
though those who were still alive regarded it for the
most part with that dull stupidity that hunger, fatigue,
heat and despair engender, there were still men who
could perceive the meaning of these signs. Star and
earth had been at their nearest, had swung about one
another, and the star had passed. Already it was receding, swifter and swifter, in the last stage of its headlong journey downward into the sun.

And then the clouds gathered, blotting out the
vision of the sky, the thunder and lightning wove a
garment round the world; all over the earth was such a
downpour of rain as men had never before seen, and
where the volcanoes flared red against the cloud
canopy there descended torrents of mud. Everywhere
the waters were pouring off the land, leaving mud-
silted ruins, and the earth littered like a storm-worn
beach with all that had floated, and the dead bodies of
the men and brutes, its children. For days the water

streamed off the land, sweeping away soil and trees
and houses in the way, and piling huge dykes and
scooping out Titanic gullies over the country side.
Those were the days of darkness that followed the star
and the heat. All through them, and for many weeks
and months, the earthquakes continued.

But the star had passed, and men, hunger-driven
and gathering courage only slowly, might creep back
to their ruined cities, buried granaries, and sodden
fields. Such few ships as had escaped the storms of
that time came stunned and shattered and sounding
their way cautiously through the new marks and
shoals of once familiar ports. And as the storms subsided men perceived that everywhere the days were
hotter than of yore, and the sun larger, and the moon,
shrunk to a third of its former size, took now fourscore
days between its new and new.

But of the new brotherhood that grew presently
among men, of the saving of laws and books and
machines, of the strange change that had come over
Iceland and Greenland and the shores of Baffin's Bay,
so that the sailors coming there presently found them
green and gracious, and could scarce believe their
eyes, this story does not tell. Nor of the movement of
mankind now that the earth was hotter, northward
and southward towards the poles of the earth. It con-
cerns itself only with the coming and the passing of the
Star.

The Martian astronomers—for there are astronomers on Mars, although they are very different beings from men—were naturally profoundly interested in these things. They saw them from their own standpoint of course. 'Considering the mass and temperature of the missile that was flung through our solar system into the sun,' one wrote, 'it is astonishing what a little damage the earth, which it missed so narrowly, has sustained. All the familiar continental markings and the masses of the seas remain intact, and indeed the only difference seems to be a shrinkage of the white discoloration (supposed to be frozen water) round either pole.' Which only shows how small the vastest of human catastrophes may seem, at a distance of a few million miles.

JOHNSON

Guy Weiner

It took a whole year to programme the tutor robot for young Hal.

It was a very fine and up-to-date robot, humanoid and highly sophisticated, atomic powered and with additional infra-red vision. Registration number 10.HN.50.N.

When it arrived, the number roughly stencilled on the packing case, 10HN50N, gave it its name at once. Johnson it became, and the name fitted the character perfectly.

Johnson had been specially programmed to complete Hal's education on his Grand Galactic Tour, the final stage of the training of a child from a wealthy family before he took up the responsibilities of adulthood.

It brought him into contact with many different races of people, and it broadened his outlook in meeting with the minds of those other than humans.

And it induced self-reliance, as he travelled with only his tutor. Through the vast empty regions of space, touching at most of the inhabited planets of the Solcen Federation.

There he would study the cultures and history of alien peoples, and build up an understanding of the basic requirements of individual lifestyles.

But Hal and Johnson had to get to know each other first, and for six months after Johnson was first activated they travelled the different lands of Earth together, learning each others' habits and ways of thought, and Johnson's locating coils became tuned to the brainwave pattern of his pupil.

'The Safety, Health and Well-being' of his pupil were the overriding tenets that had been built into Johnson's brain circuitry, as they were into all tutor robots, and parents felt no misgivings at putting the care of their children into the hands of these robots.

Came the time for blast-off on the Grand Tour, and, with no special farewells, Johnson took the little ship out from holding dock and into orbit under low-drive, his single passenger watching his skilled movement at the control panel, steel fingers flipping switches, and unwinking glassy eyes checking instruments as he waited for the exact moment to change to hyper-drive.

For the first two years of the five-year tour, Hal entered into the lives of many strange and differing civilizations.

The great caverns, ever growing bigger, of Six Alpha Centauri IV, where generations of four-armed people lived and died without ever coming to the surface of their planet, or seeing the heavens and the beauty of their twin suns.

The glass people of Clist, whose silicon-based metabolism made them brittle and cold, but whose keen intelligence and sense of organization had brought the Federation into being.

And the great pyramid cities of the giant outer moon of Krinar, the middle planet, whence early space pioneers had brought civilization to the first peoples of Central America, the Middle East and the Indus valley on Earth.

Then came the month-long haul to the little-known worlds of Sirius, remote and seldom visited. Little was known of the ways and habits of their peoples.

'We could both learn much, Hal,' said Johnson. 'We could gather material for the thesis for your doctorate.'

'Oh, you're always harping on education and the future when all I want to do just now is enjoy myself and have fun.'

'But are you not enjoying yourself, Hal? With all this travelling to new places? And we also meet Earth people, even in these far-flung worlds.'

'Yes,' Hal replied, 'but I have the constant feeling at the back of my mind that it's all for a reason, my education. Not just plain fun for no reason at all.'

'I'm sorry, but I'm not programmed for just plain fun for no reason at all. Everything must have its purpose; that's the way I'm made.'

'Oh, it's not your fault.' Hal felt a twinge of conscience. 'I'm in that sort of mood. I just don't want to be me, the son of a high senator and the grandson of a president.'

The click of the distant signal of the Proximity Scanner drew their attention, and they turned to study the screen, dotted with minute points of light where the feeler beams reached out to several light-minutes around them.

'There,' said Johnson, pointing to a glowing speck in the centre of the screen. 'It looks like a planet, and we're heading straight for it.'

Hal brightened; this was better.

Weeks of empty space, with the scanner finding only dust clouds, chunks of rock and the occasional planetoid, had started to become boring.

As they drew closer to the planet the analysers sent their search beams down to the surface, and by the time the view had grown to a green- and blue-dappled disc filling two-thirds of the screen, the condition cards were slapping out from the dispenser.

'Earth-type planet. Gravity point ninety-four. Atmosphere breathable. Humidity low. Vegetable and animal life.' And a host of other pieces of information that Johnson carefully studied to make sure of there being no forces inimical to his young charge.

But everything seemed safe and in order, oddly so for so remote a planet, though Johnson felt a strange uncertainty that his analysers couldn't pin-point.

However, he put the ship in orbit and prepared to make contact with any intelligences that might exist down there.

The directory gave little information beyond its size and position with regard to Sirius, that blazed far distant in the blackness of space, its tiny companion star only a dot in the myriads of other stars that crowded the sky.

Soon the telescope showed that there were signs of intelligence on the planet below.

Cultivated fields, monorail tracks, well-ordered cities spread over miles of land, and on the broad oceans of the Northern Hemisphere, shipping of all sizes sailed between distant ports.

The space ship secured in orbit, the dinghy was swung out, and Hal and Johnson prepared to land on the alien planet.

Down through wispy cloud banks the little vessel dived, to level off and sink down towards a large, smooth, park-like area outside the entrance of the largest city that had appeared in the scanners.

Hovering high over the park, they watched as a line of human-looking figures, marching in procession, filed out from the city gate and formed a large circle on the grass-like surface.

Four of the figures, waving coloured pennants, marched around the circle, and ended by planting the wind-blown pennants in a large square.

Hal turned to Johnson.

'It looks as though that's a welcoming party,' he

said to the robot. 'Shall we land and meet them?'

'I see no objection,' was the reply. 'They don't appear to be hostile.'

The reaction beams were gradually turned down, lowering the gleaming hemisphere towards the waiting figures.

As the landing legs sprawled outwards, and the dinghy rocked slightly on contact, the power died away and they could see from the view-ports the circle of figures closing in towards them.

There was no sign of fear as the man-like people came forward, and Hal was surprised how really human they seemed. They were tall and carried themselves with great dignity. Heads, arms, legs like men of Earth. Even their features were similar.

They were dressed in many-coloured gowns, with thick-soled sandals on their feet, and they seemed to be wearing some sort of dark head-dress, from the centre of which a projection rose, bending over at the top and bulging into an egg-shaped knob that bobbed up and down as they walked.

'Like a group of actors from an old Japanese play,' was Hal's comment.

After a final test of the atmosphere, the access port was opened, the ramp lowered and the two visitors strode down to meet the people of the alien planet.

The ring of people had stopped, and one of their number, taller and fatter than his companions, came forward to greet the two space travellers.

He came to within a few feet of Hal and Johnson and bowed low, the knob on the bobbing projection weaving from one to the other as though it was examining them.

And it was.

A thick eyelid on the knob lifted and a big glassy eye stared at them, taking in all the details of the two.

*

And even as the fat man straightened up and looked

at them with the ordinary eyes of his face, and extended both hands in greeting, the cranial eye still stared.

Hal held out his own hands and grasped those of the alien, while Johnson activated the electronic communicator that he'd brought along.

The brightly clad alien was speaking to them, and the communicator hissed and bubbled for a moment or two as it analysed the sounds and translated the words into English.

'—been some years since space ships of the Federation have called at Griml, but we have records of such visits.' The communicator picked him up in mid-sentence. 'You are welcome, and His Majesty has ordered that you be brought into his presence as honoured guests.'

Hal bowed back and thanked him for his courtesy, but his eyes kept turning to the single swaying eye above the alien's head.

The ring of people then began a low chant that was strangely soothing, formed up into two files and started a slow march back towards the city, with their visitors walking apart between the two lines.

As the marching men fed in through the open gate and Johnson came level with the portal, a bell began ringing loudly and two guards sprang forward to bar his way.

'No robots are permitted within the city,' the communicator crackled. 'They can be programmed for assassination.'

'Hal,' Johnson shouted forward to his pupil. 'You can't go in there without me. It's my duty . . .'

Hal came back to him, laughing.

'Oh, it's all right, Johnson. They're quite friendly. And don't forget we're honoured guests; at least I am. I'll take the communicator. Wait for me, I won't be long, and I'll sing out if I need help.'

He laughed again and carried on with his conductor,

leaving Johnson fretting and hunting through his electronic brain for an answer to this one.

Then he hurried back to the dinghy for another
communicator, and at the same time he slipped a
wicked little stun-gun into his pocket.

Inside the great State Hall of the palace in the city,
Hal was led forward into the presence of the high king
of the powerful country of Tarn.

The king must have been very ancient, for he was a
little wizened figure, sitting cross-legged on a plain
black stone slab in the midst of the splendour and
colour of the State Hall.

The king's cranial eye watched closely as Hal
advanced towards him and bowed low.

They exchanged greetings, Hal allowing the king to
assume that he was an accredited ambassador from
the Solcen Federation. He was steadily learning to be a
diplomat.

Then food was brought and Hal sat with the king
and his courtiers, carefully trying each of the fruits and
meats before eating them. He felt the need of Johnson
and his comestible probe, but he was now left to make
his own decisions.

Carefully he sipped a pale blue, wine-like liquid and
found it very agreeable. He drank more.

'There is much I would learn about your world,' he
said to the king. 'We have but little information at
Solcen Centre on Earth about this planet.'

'Alas, we are far behind your peoples in many
ways,' replied His Majesty. 'But I will show you all I
can.'

He signed to the fat courtier who had conducted Hal
into the city, who rose and stepped up on to the royal
slab, bowing low to the king and to Hal.

'This is my chief minister, Lai,' said the king. 'A
person of great learning.'

His cranial eye bobbed in the minister's direction.

'Bring maps and distance scanners,' he ordered, 'so

that we can show Ambassador Hal as much of our world as we can.'

When Lai had departed on his errand, the king's eye turned again to Hal.

'Here on this planet of Griml,' he began, 'we lack many of the advantages that the Federation worlds have. Most of all, the peace that world-wide government brings. We still have the quarrels, yes, and wars, brought about by separate, power-hungry nations. Our great cities have high walls for defence, and we still have to maintain battle forces and armaments against those who pretend to be our friends.'

Hal began to think that he had fallen among a very primitive people.

'You are wise, indeed,' the king went on. 'Wise to have made your landfall here, at Tarn, and not at one of the smaller nations. Tarn is the most powerful country on Griml—and the most civilized.'

His voice dropped to a deep whisper, and he half pointed to two sombrely dressed figures who sat talking close together.

'I speak low,' he went on, 'for their envoys feast among my courtiers here. But if you had landed at Barron or Zano, they would as likely have killed you, and taken your ship to use against Tarn.'

Hal began to wonder if Johnson knew more than he had told him.

The return of Lai with several attendants changed the conversation.

They unrolled maps and spread them on the royal black slab.

A large black box with a glass-like front panel was set up at the edge.

And there, amid the babble of talk in the great hall, lit by the long sloping beams of sunlight through the tall window openings, Hal learned much of the strange primitive world of Griml.

Chief Minister Lai, with a long pointer, showed on the maps how the great country of Tarn, with its royal city and hundreds of walled satellite cities, controlled the vast fertile lands of the south temperate zone: while beyond the scorching deserts to the north, a hundred small countries clustered, divided by broad seas and towering crags.

The screen of the distance scanner lit up, to show in quick succession armies of men marching and training in mock warfare, and fleets of oval aircraft, each underslung with rows of pointed death-bombs.

Hal was astonished that such antiquated behaviour should be surviving on any world that had the knowledge of the past history of Earth.

He sat back in his cushions, slowly sipping more of the pale wine, and pondering the stupidity of peoples who do not learn from the mistakes of the past.

The king seemed to be aware of his thoughts. His heavy-lidded cranial eye looked away from the screen and studied Hal's face, trying to look into his mind.

'I am very old, Hal,' came his deep voice. 'And I think I can read men well. Your arrival here is fortunate. If, when you report back to the Solcen Federation on your mission, you can persuade them of the justice of the position of Tarn, then perhaps the Federation will provide us with the weapons to show these enemies of ours, who call themselves our friends, the error of their ways.'

He paused and his voice took on a ringing tohe of pride.

'Then we could apply to take our equal place in the Federation, as a united planet.'

Hal listened to the king's extraordinary request.

It was like a school history lesson. Political motives, muddled, dishonest and incongruous, coming from the lips of a king who claimed to be civilized.

He tried to follow the reasoning, but the pale wine that he had been swallowing was having its effect. He began to feel drowsy. The kaleidoscope of coloured marbles and gilded columns began to swing around, and he slept, stretched out on the softness of a crimson carpet.

'A very nice young man,' the king muttered to Minister Lai. 'A great pity that he goes through life half blind. We must do all we can to help him. Let him report to the Federation on our kindness.'

*

The warm yellow Sirian sunrise slanted through the arched windows of the bedroom to which he had been taken, and Hal woke into a new life.

He was amused at himself. Yes, he'd got drunk last night. Better not tell Johnson.

Poor old Johnson. He was probably still waiting at the city gate for him. Perhaps he could get a message through.

He sat up to try and call someone, and he felt a strange soreness on the top of his head.

Reaching up he touched a muscular projection that felt like part of himself.

As he thought about it he sensed the eyelid opening, and his vision sharpened.

Tiny details of the walls and columns of the room came to add to his ordinary vision, and he closed his cranial eye in stupefaction.

With realization he began to panic, and he called out in fear. The people of Tarn had grafted a cranial eye on to his head.

He didn't want it. He would be a monster back on Earth. He had no use for it.

He called out in panic again.

A door panel slid aside and two of the aliens hurried in to his side where he sat wide-eyed and shouting.

He stared at them blankly for a few moments, then sprang from the bed and switched on the communicator that had been set on a near-by table.

'Take it away—take it away,' he shouted.

The eye flicked open and weaved about frantically as he stared with it at the two blank faces.

'Hush, hush,' they soothed him. 'We know it must be a shock to a half blind man suddenly to be able to see properly. But try it first. Get used to it. It can then be removed if you so wish it.'

Under the influence of their quiet voices he began to calm down.

And he began to re-think his position, and even to experiment with his new eye, which he had tried to keep tightly closed.

Lifting the eyelid slowly and gingerly, he closed his other eyes.

Everything stood out sharp and clear. He found that he had a number of different lenses in the cranial eye that he could use separately or combine at will.

He stood at a window looking out at distant things telescopically. The nearer buildings and the hills beyond the city wall.

He brought the far gate into focus, looking for Johnson, but he was nowhere to be seen. That didn't worry
him, as he knew that his tutor could tune in to his
brainwave pattern, and find him anywhere within ten
miles or so.

Then he looked up into the sky and watched as his
orbiting space ship swam into view, so close that he
could see even the rivets of the shell.

Changing lenses, he studied with delight the
minute grains of the stone window sill, the structure of
the skin of his hand.

His guides led him to a completely dark laboratory,
where, to his surprise, everything was visible to his
new eye. Clearly he could make out the shapes of the
instruments, and the figures and features of his companions. He had now an ability that he had envied in
Johnson—infra-red vision.

He found that he could swing the eye almost
through a complete circle and see what was behind
him, but that he had to close his ordinary eyes when he
did that, as he became confused and dizzy at the
combined views.

What would Johnson say to it all? He might even ask
the aliens to fit a cranial eye to his own head. But
would it work with a robot's circuitry?

Still, Hal thought, he must let his tutor see the
wonder of it. A special eye, telescopic, microscopic,
sensitive to infra-red light, among a host of other
abilities. Yes, this was something new for Johnson to
learn.

He asked to go to his robot at the city gate, and, with
the greatest of politeness, his companions said that
they would return soon to escort him there.

While they were away Hal continued to experiment
with the eye on top of his head, where he found that
the soreness he had felt on first awakening had disappeared.

The hair had re-grown to the base of the eye-stalk,

and he wondered at the great skill of the Grimlian surgeons.

Soon his guides returned, accompanied by four more gorgeously clad courtiers, who bowed low as they entered.

With the greatest of politeness they escorted Hal to the palace entrance and along the marble paved road to the gate in the city wall.

Using his new eye he watched Johnson standing and waiting for him as he approached, a severe look of disapproval on his human-like face. A look that changed to puzzlement and then realization as Hal got closer.

'Hal,' shouted the robot as his charge passed through the gate with his companions. 'What have they done to you? Why did you let them do it? Oh, I should have been there with you.'

Hal grinned broadly.

'They did it out of kindness, Johnson. And it's wonderful, really wonderful.' And he began to relate the wonders of his new vision, and to tell of the feast that he'd had with the great king, and how much he'd learned of events on Griml.

Johnson took it all in and fed it into his computer circuitry. He checked the decisions against his programme and free-will systems, balanced against the Primary Tenets of the Safety, Health and Well-being, and accepted the resultant course of action.

'Kindness nothing. They've made a monster of you,' the robot snorted. 'You're not going back into that city, Hal. Certainly not without me. Goodness knows what else they'd do to you. We must return to the ship at once.'

And he turned away towards the dinghy squatting between the fluttering flags.

But Hal didn't follow him. He drew back to where the group of courtiers waited for him to return.

'Johnson,' he called, a determined expression

replacing the smile on his face, 'I am an honoured guest here. I am accepted as the accredited representative of the Federation. I am in no danger, and this new eye is a fine thing, a gift from these people.'

The Grimlians stood in a silent group by the gate. No communicator had been switched on and they apparently understood nothing of the exchanges between Hal and the robot.

'They want to use you, Hal,' insisted Johnson as he came back to his charge. 'To use you to influence the Federation to supply them with sophisticated weapons with which to carry on their wars of conquest.'

'I know that well enough, Johnson, but I think that I am quite capable of resisting their requests at the Solcen Council.'

The robot stood silent. The coldness in Hal's voice struck hard at his receptor circuitry. The rapport between them seemed to be dissolving away, but he could sense the danger to the lad of leaving him alone in the hands of the Grimlians.

'They will pervert your mind, Hal,' he burst out. 'Brainwash you and mislead you as to their motives. Let us go now, before they have a chance.'

But Hal was already moving away in the midst of the group of courtiers. His new eye seemed to Johnson as it bobbed up and down, to have a life of its own and to be surveying him with a sort of sinister mockery.

'I shall be back in a day or two,' Hal called back to him. 'Wait here for me.'

It was an order, a command, and it conflicted with the overriding tenets built into the robot.

That damned eye was already exerting its influence. With its stalk rooted deep in Hal's brain, it was distorting his mental processes.

Something must be done to rescue him from the clutches of the Grimlians.

He stood staring disconsolately after the receding group beyond the city gate, where two guards stood regarding him with suspicion.

Then he turned and began to follow a narrow path that ran along the line of the thirty-foot city wall.

For many hours he trudged beside the meandering wall. It was blank and featureless, with no windows or projections, and he could see the helmets of patrolling guards as they passed between the battlements.

He completed the circuit of the long wall. There was only the one gate, and it was hopeless to try and pass there. There was, of course, the dinghy, but to cross the wall unobserved with it was quite out of the question.

He began a second circuit of the wall. It was illogical that there should be no other outlet from the city. An escape route, perhaps more than one, in the event of an enemy taking the gate by assault.

He ranged further out, across the parklands that surrounded the city, searching among the clumps of trees for some secret entrance.

Johnson was unhappy. Or rather, his brain circuits were registering discordant pulse-patterns where there should be smooth harmony. Which meant that Johnson was unhappy.

Hal drawing away from him like that left an odd gulf in the relationship between them that had been so good.

He wandered among the trees puzzling over it, as he continued to hunt for an entrance to the city.

Then it struck him as odd that there should be those clumps of trees. They would be perfect cover for any enemy forces attacking the city, and surely the Grimlians would realize that. There must be some other reason for leaving the trees there, and he began to search carefully among the undergrowth.

And he found what he was looking for: a square

pivoted stone, almost invisible in its age-old green moss. Below it was a long flight of steps, and at the foot of the steps a dank low tunnel heading straight towards the city wall.

Using his infra-red vision Johnson moved slowly forward into the darkness, along the debris-strewn passageway, in places almost blocked with fallen earth and stones. Past broken and crumbled wooden door-ways leading to side passages that must have formed a bewildering labyrinth in the distant past.

But he kept on his careful way towards the city wall, until, pushing aside long trailing creepers, he emerged into a small enclosed garden, long-neglected and overgrown.

A splashing fountain overflowed its blue marble basin, sending a little stream bubbling through the thick undergrowth, the only sound in the gathering darkness of late evening.

The robot stood in the concealing shrubbery, slowly turning as his locator coils, attuned to Hal's brainwave patterns, sought the direction in which to find his charge.

From the neglected grotto the signal led him along a twisting path and out on to a wide sward, beyond which the great king's palace loomed against the night sky, windows sparkling with brilliant lights.

As he made his watchful way between the beds of flowers, Johnson's mind was still disturbed by Hal's rejection of him and his advice and warnings, but he

kept on until he was close to the palace wall below a broad window.

He felt the near presence of Hal and, after peering around into the darkness to see that he was unobserved, he began his climb to the room above.

Steel fingers gripping into the heavy carvings that covered the stonework of the wall, he raised himself until he could peer into the room.

Two figures were there.

Hal reclined on a low couch, seemingly asleep. His facial eyes were closed and he appeared quite relaxed, but his heavy cranial eye stared unwinkingly at a large screen set in the wall.

By the side of the couch Minister Lai sat talking in a low voice into the communicator, from which wires led to earphones set on Hal's head.

Steadily the cranial eye watched the colour patterns sweeping across the screen. Patterns intermixed with scenes of Griml, with its inhabitants occupied in peaceful and civilized living.

Soft, soothing music pulsated from the screen to accompany the pictures.

The music changed to deep sinister tones as the screen showed other countries. Scenes of Barron and Zano arming against Griml. Brutalizing education of the young people, and scenes of evil witchcraft.

The eye was brainwashing Hal, deep and direct into his mind.

Johnson stared horrified at the scene in the room,

then slowly he drew the stun-gun from his pocket.

Setting the lever at high-power, he pointed the gun at the brightly-clad Minister and fired.

There was no sound, but the fat figure of Lai slumped sideways and rolled off his chair to the floor. Johnson hoped that the powerful shock had killed him.

Slowly the great eye springing from Hal's head turned towards the robot and stared with such malevolence that, had Johnson been human, he would have fled from the horror of it.

But the robot was being driven by the ultimate urge for Hal's safety.

With the lever of the gun at low-power, he fired at the recumbent form of his charge, holding the pressure until he saw the cranial eye slowly close and slump down on its stalk.

Climbing across the sill of the window into the room, the robot gathered the limp form of Hal in his arms and carried him across to the window, where he tore down a long cord from the curtains, tied it around the lad's body and lowered him to the ground outside.

As Johnson crossed the grounds again with the unconscious Hal across his shoulder, the limp cranial eye banging against his back gave the robot a sickening feeling of disgust.

Through the long tunnel under the wall and out into the dark parklands, where the ship's dinghy sprawled waiting.

Hal came to his senses slowly. He could hear the hum of the ship on hyper-drive. He opened his eyes. He was in the sick bay, lying staring up at the white-painted deckhead, and the horror of what had been happening to him flooded into his mind.

The way the Grimlians had tried to manipulate him, to use him for their own ends, and the way the strange eye had soured his relationship with Johnson.

His head felt a little sore on top, and reaching up he

felt an adhesive bandage, and he remembered the delights and the power of that sinister cranial eye—but Johnson the robot had done his duty. He had made him into a normal young man again, fit to be the next president of the Solcen Federation.

THE SMALLEST DRAGONBOY

Anne McCaffrey

 lthough Keevan lengthened his walking stride as far as his legs would stretch, he couldn't quite keep up with the other candidates. He knew he would be teased again.

Just as he knew many other things that his foster mother told him he ought not to know, Keevan knew that Beterli, the most senior of the boys, set that spanking pace just to embarrass him, the smallest dragonboy. Keevan would arrive, tail fork-end of the group, breathless, chest heaving, and maybe rated a stern look from the instructing wingsecond.

Dragonriders, even if they were still only hopeful candidates for the glowing eggs which were hardening on the hot sands of the Hatching Ground cavern, were expected to be punctual and prepared. Sloth was not tolerated by the Weyrleader of Benden Weyr. A good record was especially important now. It was very near hatching time, when the baby dragons would crack their mottled shells and stagger forth to choose their lifetime companions. The very thought of that glorious moment made Keevan's breath catch in his throat. To be chosen—to be a dragonrider! To sit astride the neck of the winged beast with the jewelled eyes; to be his friend in telepathic communion with him for life; to be his companion in good times and fighting extremes; to fly effortlessly over the lands of Pern! Or, thrillingly, *between* to any point anywhere on the world! Flying *between* was done on dragonback or not at all, and it was dangerous.

Keevan glanced upward, past the black mouths of the weyr caves in which grown dragons and their chosen riders lived, towards the Star Stones that crowned the ridge of the old volcano that was Benden Weyr. On the height, the blue watch-dragon, his rider mounted on his neck, stretched the great transparent pinions that carried him on the winds of Pern to fight the evil Thread that fell at certain times from the sky. The many-faceted rainbow jewels of his eyes glistened momentarily in the greeny sun. He folded his great wings to his back, and the watchpair resumed their statuesque pose of alertness.

Then the enticing view was obscured as Keevan passed into the Hatching Ground cavern. The sands underfoot were hot, even through the heavy wher-hide boots. How the bootmaker had protested having to sew so small! Keevan was forced to wonder again why being small was reprehensible. People were always calling him 'babe' and shooing him away as being 'too small' or 'too young' for this or that.

Keevan was constantly working, twice as hard as any other boy his age, to prove himself capable. What if his muscles weren't as big as Beterli's? They were just as hard. And if he couldn't overpower anyone in a wrestling match, he could outdistance everyone in a foot race.

'Maybe if you run fast enough,' Beterli had jeered on the occasion when Keevan had been goaded to boast of his swiftness, 'you could catch a dragon. That's the only way you'll make a dragonrider.'

'You just wait and see, Beterli, you just wait,' Keevan had replied. He would have liked to wipe the contemptuous expression from Beterli's face, but the guy didn't fight fair even when the wingsecond was watching. 'No one knows what Impresses a dragon!'

'They've got to be able to *find* you first, babe!'

Yes, being the smallest candidate was not an enviable position. It was therefore imperative that Keevan Impress a dragon in his first hatching. That would wipe the smile off every face in the cavern, and accord him the respect due any dragonrider, even the smallest one.

Besides, no one knew exactly what Impressed the baby dragons as they struggled from their shells in search of their lifetime partners.

'I like to believe that dragons see into a man's heart,' Keevan's foster mother, Mende, told him. 'If they find goodness, honesty, a flexible mind, patience, courage—and you've that in quantity, dear Keevan—that's what dragons look for. I've seen many a well-grown lad left standing on the sands on Hatching Day, in favour of someone not so strong or tall or handsome. And if my memory serves me'—which it usually did—Mende knew every word of every Harper's tale worth telling, although Keevan did not interrupt her to say so—'I don't believe that F'lar, our Weyrleader, was all that tall when bronze Mnementh chose him. And Mnementh was the only bronze dragon of that hatching.'

Dreams of Impressing a bronze were beyond Keevan's boldest reflections, although that goal dominated the thoughts of every other hopeful candidate. Green dragons were small and fast and more numerous. There was more prestige to Impressing a blue or a brown than a green. Being practical, Keevan seldom dreamed as high as a big fighting brown, like Canth, F'nor's fine fellow, the biggest brown on all Pern. But to fly a bronze? Bronzes were almost as big as the queen, and only they took the air when a queen flew at mating time. A bronze rider could aspire to become a Weyrleader! Well, Keevan would console himself, brown riders could aspire to become wingseconds, and that wasn't bad. He'd even settle for a green dragon: they were small, but so was he. No matter! He simply had to Impress a dragon his first time in the Hatching Ground. Then no one in the Weyr would taunt him any more for being so small.

Shells, thought Keevan now, but the sands are hot!

'Impression is imminent, candidates,' the wing-second was saying as everyone crowded respectfully close to him. 'See the extent of the striations on this promising egg.' The stretch marks *were* larger than yesterday.

Everyone leaned forward and nodded thoughtfully. That particular egg was the one Beterli had marked as his own, and no other candidate dared, on pain of being beaten by Beterli on the first opportunity, to approach it. The egg was marked by a large yellowish splotch in the shape of a dragon backwinging to land, talons outstretched to grasp rock. Everyone knew that bronze eggs bore distinctive markings. And naturally, Beterli, who'd been presented at eight Impressions already and was the biggest of the candidates, had chosen it.

'I'd say that the great opening day is almost upon us,' the wingsecond went on, and then his face assumed a grave expression. 'As we well know, there are only forty eggs and there are seventy-two candidates. Some of you may be disappointed on the great day. That doesn't necessarily mean that you aren't dragonrider material, just that *the* dragon for you hasn't been shelled. You'll have other hatchings, and it's no disgrace to be left behind an Impression or two. Or more.'

Keevan was positive that the wingsecond's eyes rested on Beterli, who'd been stood off at so many Impressions already. Keevan tried to squinch down so the wingsecond wouldn't notice him. Keevan had been reminded too often that he was eligible to be a candidate by one day only. He, of all the hopefuls, was most likely to be left standing on the great day. One

more reason why he simply had to Impress at his first hatching.

'Now move about among the eggs,' the wingsecond said. 'Touch them. We don't know that it does any good, but it certainly doesn't do any harm.'

Some of the boys laughed nervously, but everyone immediately began to circulate among the eggs. Beterli stepped up officiously to 'his' egg, daring anyone to come near it. Keevan smiled, because he had already touched it ... every inspection day ... as the others were leaving the Hatching Ground, when no one could see him crouch and stroke it.

Keevan had an egg he concentrated on, too, one drawn slightly to the far side of the others. The shell bore a soft greenish blue tinge with a faint creamy swirl design. The consensus was that this egg contained a mere green, so Keevan was rarely bothered by rivals. He was somewhat perturbed then to see Beterli wandering over to him.

'I don't know why you're allowed in this Impression, Keevan. There are enough of us without a babe,' Beterli said, shaking his head.

'I'm of age,' Keevan kept his voice level, telling himself not to be bothered by mere words.

'Yah!' Beterli made a show of standing on his toe tips. 'You can't even see over an egg: Hatching Day, you better get in front or the dragons won't see you at all. 'Course you could get run down that way in the mad scramble. Oh, I forget, you can run fast, can't you?'

'You'd better make sure a dragon sees *you*, this time, Beterli,' Keevan replied. 'You're almost overage, aren't you?'

Beterli flushed and took a step forward, hand half raised. Keevan stood his ground, but if Beterli advanced one more step, he would call the wingsecond. No one fought on the Hatching Ground. Surely Beterli knew that much.

Fortunately, at that moment, the wingsecond called the boys together and led them from the Hatching Ground to start on evening chores.

There were 'glows' to be replenished in the main kitchen caverns and sleeping cubicles, the major hallways, and the queen's apartment. Firestone sacks to be filled against Thread attack, and black rock brought to the kitchen hearths. The boys fell to their chores, tantalized by the odours of roasting meat. The population of the Weyr began to assemble for the evening meal, and the dragonriders came in from the Feeding Ground or their sweep checks.

It was the time of day Keevan liked best: once the chores were done, before dinner was served, a fellow could often get close to the dragonriders and listen to their talk. Tonight Keevan's father, K'last, was at the main dragonrider table. It puzzled Keevan how his father, a brown rider and a tall man, could *be* his father—because he, Keevan, was so small. It obviously never puzzled K'last when he deigned to notice his small son; 'In a few more turns, you'll be as tall as I am—or taller!'

K'last was pouring Benden wine for all around the table. The dragonriders were relaxing. There'd be no Thread attack for three more days, and they'd be in the mood to tell tall tales, better than Harper yarns, about impossible manoeuvres they'd. done a-dragonback. When Thread attack was closer, their talk would change to a discussion of tactics of evasion, of going *between*, how long to suspend there until the burning but fragile Thread would freeze and crack and fall harmlessly off dragon and man. They would dispute the exact moment to feed firestone to the dragon so he'd have the best flame ready to sear Thread midair and render it harmless to ground—and man—below. There was such a lot to know and understand about being a dragonrider that sometimes Keevan was overwhelmed. How would he ever be able to remember everything he ought to know at the right moment? He couldn't dare ask such a question; this would only have given additional weight to the notion that he was too young to be a dragonrider.

'Having older candidates makes good sense,' L'vel was saying, as Keevan settled down near the table. 'Why waste four to five years of a dragon's fighting prime until a rider grows up enough to stand the rigours?' L'vel had Impressed a blue of Ramoth's first clutch. Most of the candidates thought L'vel was marvellous because he spoke up in front of the older riders, who awed them. 'That was well enough in the Interval when you didn't need to mount the full Weyr complement to fight Thread. But not now. Not with more eligible candidates than ever. Let the babes wait.'

'Any boy who is over twelve Turns has the right to stand in the Hatching Ground,' K'last replied, a slight smile on his face. He never argued or got angry. Keevan wished he were more like his father. And oh, how he wished he were a brown rider! 'Only a dragon . . . each particular dragon . . . knows what he wants in a rider. We certainly can't tell. Time and again the theorists,' and K'last's smile deepened as his eyes swept round the table, 'are surprised by dragon choice. *They* never seem to make mistakes, however.'

'Now, K'last, just look at the roster this Impression. Seventy-two boys and only forty eggs. Drop off the twelve youngest, and there's still a good field for the hatchlings to choose from. Shells! There are a couple of weyrlings unable to see over a wher egg much less a dragon's. And years before they can ride Thread!'

'True enough, but the Weyr is scarcely under fighting strength, and if the youngest Impress, they'll be old enough to fight when the oldest of our current dragons go *between* from senility.'

'Half the Weyrbred lads have already been through several Impressions,' one of the bronze riders said then. 'I'd say drop some of *them* off this time. Give the untried a chance.'

'There's nothing wrong in presenting a clutch with as wide a choice as possible,' said the Weyrleader, who had joined the table with Lessa, the Weyrwoman.

'Has there ever been a case,' she said, smiling in her odd way at the riders, 'where a hatchling didn't choose?'

Her suggestion was almost heretical and drew astonished gasps from everyone, including the boys.

F'lar laughed. 'You say the most outrageous things, Lessa.'

'Well, *has* there ever been a case where a dragon didn't choose?'

'Can't say as I recall one,' K'last replied.

'Then we continue in this tradition,' Lessa said firmly, as if that ended the matter.

But it didn't. The argument ranged from one table to the other all through the dinner, with some favouring a weeding out of the candidates to the most likely, lopping off those who were very young or who had had multiple opportunities to Impress. All the candidates were in a swivet, though such a departure from tradition would be to the advantage of many. As the evening progressed, more riders favoured eliminating the youngest and those who'd passed four or more Impressions unchosen. Keevan felt that he could bear such a dictum if only Beterli was eliminated. But this seemed less likely than that Keevan would be turfed out, since the Weyr's need was for fighting dragons and older riders.

By the time the evening meal was over, no decision had been reached, although the Weyrleader had promised to give the matter due consideration.

He might have slept on the problem, but few of the candidates did. Tempers were uncertain in the sleeping caverns next morning as the boys were routed out of their beds to carry water and black rock and cover the 'glows'. Mende had to call Keevan to order twice for clumsiness.

'Whatever is the matter with you, boy?' she demanded in exasperation when he tipped black rock short of the bin and sooted up the hearth.

'They're going to keep me from this Impression.'

'What?' Mende stared at him. 'Who?'

'You heard them talking at dinner last night. They're going to turf the babes from the hatching.'

Mende regarded him a moment longer before touching his arm gently. 'There's lots of talk around a supper table, Keevan. And it cools as soon as the supper. I've heard the same nonsense before every hatching, but nothing is ever changed.'

'There's always a first time,' Keevan answered, copying one of her own phrases.

'That'll be enough of that, Keevan. Finish your job. If the clutch does hatch today, we'll need full rock bins for the feast, and you won't be around to do the filling. All my fosterlings make dragonriders.'

'The first time?' Keevan was bold enough to ask as he scooted off with the rockbarrow.

Perhaps, Keevan thought later, if he hadn't been on that chore just when Beterli was also fetching black rock, things might have turned out differently. But he dutifully trundled the barrow to the outdoor bunker for another load just as Beterli arrived on a similar errand.

'Heard the news, babe?' asked Beterli. He was grinning from ear to ear, and he put an unnecessary emphasis on the final insulting word.

'The eggs are cracking?' Keevan all but dropped the loaded shovel. Several anxieties flicked through his mind then: he was black with rock dust—would he have time to wash before donning the white tunic of candidacy? And if the eggs were hatching, why hadn't

the candidates been recalled by the wingsecond?

'Naw! Guess again!' Beterli was much too pleased with himself.

With a sinking heart, Keevan knew what the news must be, and he could only stare with intense desolation at the older boy.

'C'mon! Guess, babe!'

'I've no time for guessing games,' Keevan managed to say with indifference. He began to shovel black rock into his barrow as fast as he could.

'I said, "guess".' Beterli grabbed the shovel.

'And I said I'd no time for guessing games.'

Beterli wrenched the shovel from Keevan's hands. 'Guess!'

'I'll have the shovel back, Beterli.' Keevan straightened up, but he didn't come to Beterli's bulky shoulder. From somewhere other boys appeared, some with barrows, some mysteriously alerted to the prospect of a confrontation among their numbers.

'Babes don't give orders to candidates around here, babe!'

Someone sniggered and Keevan knew, incredibly, that he must have been dropped from the candidacy.

He yanked the shovel from Beterli's loosened grasp. Snarling, the older boy tried to regain possession, but Keevan clung with all his strength to the handle and was dragged back and forth as the stronger boy jerked the shovel about.

With a sudden unexpected movement, Beterli rammed the handle into Keevan's chest, knocking him over the barrow handles. Keevan felt a sharp, painful jab behind his left ear, an unbearable pain in his right shin and then a painless nothingness.

Mende's angry voice roused him and, startled, he tried to throw back the covers, thinking he'd overslept. But he couldn't move, so firmly was he tucked into his bed. And then the constriction of a bandage on his head and the dull sickishness in his leg brought back recent occurrences.

'Hatching?' he cried.

'No, lovey,' said Mende, and her voice was suddenly very kind, her hand cool and gentle on his forehead. 'Though there's some as won't be at any hatching again.' Her voice took on a stern edge.

Keevan looked beyond her to see the Weyrwoman, who was frowning with irritation.

'Keevan, will you tell me what occurred at the black-rock bunker?' Lessa asked, but her voice wasn't angry.

He remembered Beterli now, and the quarrel over the shovel and . . . what had Mende said about some not being at any hatching? Much as he hated Beterli, he couldn't bring himself to tattle on Beterli and force him out of candidacy.

'Come, lad,' and a note of impatience crept into the Weyrwoman's voice. 'I merely want to know what happened from you, too. Mende said she sent you for black rock. Beterli—and every weyrling in the cavern—seems to have been on the same errand. What happened?'

'Beterli took the shovel. I hadn't finished with it.'

'There's more than one shovel. What did he *say* to you?'

'He'd heard the news.'

'What news?' The Weyrwoman was suddenly amused.

'That . . . that . . . there'd been changes.'

'Is that what he said?'

'Not exactly.'

'What did he say? C'mon, lad. I've heard from everyone else, you know.'

'He said for me to guess the news.'

'And you fell for that old gag?' The Weyrwoman's irritation returned.

'Consider all the talk last night at supper, Lessa,' said Mende. 'Of course the boy would think he'd been eliminated.'

'In fact, he is, with a broken skull and leg.' She touched his arm, a rare gesture of sympathy for her. 'Be that as it may, Keevan, you'll have other Impressions. Beterli will not. There are certain rules that must be observed by all candidates, and his conduct proves him unacceptable to the Weyr.'

She smiled at Mende and then left.

'I'm still a candidate?' Keevan asked urgently.

'Well, you are and you aren't, lovey,' his foster mother said. 'Is the numb weed working?' she asked, and when he nodded, she said, 'You just rest. I'll bring you some nice broth.'

At any other time in his life, Keevan would have relished such cosseting, but he lay there worrying. Beterli had been dismissed. Would the others think it was his fault? But everyone had been there! Beterli provoked the fight. His worry increased, because although he heard excited comings and goings in the

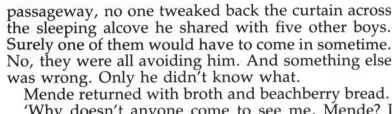

passageway, no one tweaked back the curtain across the sleeping alcove he shared with five other boys. Surely one of them would have to come in sometime. No, they were all avoiding him. And something else was wrong. Only he didn't know what.

Mende returned with broth and beachberry bread.

'Why doesn't anyone come to see me, Mende? I haven't done anything wrong, have I? I didn't ask to have Beterli turfed out.'

Mende soothed him, saying everyone was busy with noontime chores and no one was angry with him. They were giving him a chance to rest in quiet. The numb weed made him drowsy, and her words were fair enough. He permitted his fears to dissipate. Until he heard the humming. It started low, too low to be heard. Rather he felt it in the broken shin bone and his sore head. And thought, at first, it was an effect of the numb weed. Then the hum grew, augmented by additional sources. Two things registered suddenly in Keevan's groggy mind: the only white candidate's robe still on the pegs in the chamber was his; and dragons hummed when a clutch was being laid or being hatched. Impression! And he was flat abed.

Bitter, bitter disappointment turned the warm broth sour in his belly. Even the small voice telling him that he'd have other opportunities failed to alleviate his crushing depression. *This* was the Impression that mattered! This was his chance to show *everyone* from Mende to K'last to L'vel and even the Weyrleaders that he, Keevan, was worthy of being a dragonrider.

He twisted in bed, fighting against the tears that threatened to choke him. Dragonmen don't cry! Dragonmen learn to live with pain. . . .

Pain? The leg didn't actually pain him as he rolled about on his bedding. His head felt sort of stiff from the tightness of the bandage. He sat up, an effort in itself since the numb weed made exertion difficult. He touched the splintered leg, but the knee was unhampered. He had no feeling in his bone, really. He swung himself carefully to the side of his bed and slowly stood. The room wanted to swim about him. He closed his eyes, which made the dizziness worse, and he had to clutch the wall.

Gingerly he took a step. The broken leg dragged. It hurt in spite of the numb weed, but what was pain to a dragonman?

No one had said he couldn't go to the Impression. 'You are and you aren't,' were Mende's exact words.

Clinging to the wall, he jerked off his bedshirt. Stretching his arm to the utmost, he flipped his white candidate's tunic from the peg. Jamming first one arm and then the other into the holes, he pulled it over his head. Too bad about the belt. He couldn't wait. He hobbled to the door, hung on to the curtain to steady himself. The weight on his leg was unwieldy. He'd not get very far without something to lean on. Down by the bathing pool was one of the long crook-necked poles used to retrieve clothes from the hot washing troughs. But it was down there, and he was on the level above. And there was no one nearby to come to his aid: everyone would be in the Hatching Ground right now, eagerly waiting for the first egg to crack.

The humming increased in volume and tempo, an urgency to which Keevan responded, knowing that his time was all too limited if he was to join the ranks of the hopeful boys standing about the cracking eggs. But if he hurried down the ramp, he'd fall flat on his face.

He could, of course, go flat on his rear end, the way crawling children did. He sat down, the jar sending a stab of pain through his leg and up to the wound on the back of his head. Gritting his teeth and blinking away the tears, Keevan scrabbled down the ramp. He

had to wait a moment at the bottom to catch his breath. He got to one knee, the injured leg straight out in front of him. Somehow, he managed to push himself erect, though the room wanted to tip over his ears. It wasn't far to the crooked stick, but it seemed an age before he had it in his hand.

Then the humming stopped!

Keevan cried out and began to hobble frantically across the cavern, out to the bowl of the Weyr. Never had the distance between the living caverns and the Hatching Ground seemed so great. Never had the Weyr been so silent, breathless: as if the multitude of people and dragons watching the hatching held every breath in suspense. Not even the wind muttered down the steep side of the bowl. The only sounds to break the stillness were Keevan's ragged breathing and the thump-thud of his stick on the hard-packed ground. Sometimes he had to hop twice on his good leg to maintain his balance. Twice he fell into the sand and had to pull himself up on the stick, his white tunic no longer spotless. Once he jarred himself so badly he couldn't get up immediately.

Then he heard the first exhalation of the crowd, the ooohs and muted cheers, the susurrus of excited whispers. An egg had cracked, and the dragon had chosen his rider. Desperation increased Keevan's hobble. Would he never reach the arching mouth of the Hatching Ground?

Another cheer and an excited spate of applause spurred Keevan to greater effort. If he didn't get there in moments, there'd be no unpaired hatchling left. Then he was actually staggering into the Hatching Ground, the sands hot on his bare feet.

No one noticed his entrance or his halting progress. And Keevan could see nothing but the backs of the white-robed candidates, seventy of them ringing the area around the eggs. Then one side would surge forward or back and there'd be a cheer. Another dragon had been Impressed. Suddenly a large gap appeared in the white human wall, and Keevan had his first glimpse of the eggs. There didn't seem to be any left uncracked, and he could see the lucky boys standing beside wobble-legged dragons. He could hear the unmistakable plaintive crooning of the hatchlings and their squawks of protest as they'd fall awkwardly in the sand.

Suddenly he wished that he hadn't left his bed, that he'd stayed away from the Hatching Ground. Now everyone would see his ignominious failure. He scrambled now as desperately to reach the shadowy walls of the Hatching Ground as he had struggled to cross the bowl. He mustn't be seen.

He didn't notice, therefore, that the shifting group of boys remaining had begun to drift in his direction. The hard pace he had set himself and his cruel disappointment took their double toll of Keevan. He tripped and collapsed sobbing to the warm sands. He didn't see the consternation in the watching weyrfolk above the Hatching Ground, nor did he hear the excited speculation. He didn't know that the Weyrleader and Weyrwoman had dropped to the arena and were making their way towards the knot of boys slowly moving in the direction of the archway.

'Never seen anything like it,' the Weyrleader was saying. 'Only thirty-nine riders chosen. And the bronze trying to leave the Hatching Ground without making Impression!'

'A case in point of what I said last night,' the Weyrwoman replied, 'where a hatchling makes no choice because the right boy isn't there.'

'There's only Beterli and K'last's young one missing. And there's a full wing of likely boys to choose from. . . .'

'None acceptable, apparently. Where is the creature going? He's not heading for the entrance after all. Oh, what have we there, in the shadows?'

Keevan heard with dismay the sound of voices nearing him. He tried to burrow into the sand. The mere
thought of how he would be teased and taunted now
was unbearable.

Don't worry! Please, don't worry! The thought was
urgent, but not his own.

Someone kicked sand over Keevan and butted
roughly against him.

'Go away. Leave me alone!' he cried.

Why? was the injured-sounding question inserted
into his mind. There was no voice, no tone, but the
question was there, perfectly clear, in his head.

Incredulous, Keevan lifted his head and stared into
the glowing jewelled eyes of a small bronze dragon.
His wings were wet; the tips hung drooping to the
sand. And he sagged in the middle on his unsteady
legs, although he was making a great effort to keep
erect.

Keevan dragged himself to his knees, oblivious to
the pain of his leg. He wasn't even aware that he was
ringed by the boys passed over, while thirty-one pairs
of resentful eyes watched him Impress the dragon.
The Weyrleaders looked on, amused and surprised at
the draconic choice, which could not be forced. Could
not be questioned. Could not be changed.

Why? asked the dragon again. *Don't you like me?* His
eyes whirled with anxiety and his tone was so piteous
that Keevan staggered forward and threw his arms
around the dragon's neck, stroking his eye ridges,

patting the damp, soft hide, opening the fragile-looking wings to dry them, and assuring the hatchling wordlessly over and over again that he was the most perfect, most beautiful, most beloved dragon in the entire Weyr, in all the Weyrs of Pern.

'What's his name, K'van?' asked Lessa, smiling warmly at the new dragonrider. Keevan stared up at her for a long moment. Lessa would know as soon as he did. Lessa was the only person who could 'receive' from all dragons, not only her own Ramoth. Then he gave her a radiant smile, recognizing the traditional shortening of his name that raised him forever to the rank of dragonrider.

My name is Heth, thought the dragon mildly, and hiccuped in sudden urgency: *I'm hungry*.

'Dragons are born hungry,' said Lessa, laughing. 'F'lar, give the boy a hand. He can barely manage his own legs, much less a dragon's.'

K'van remembered his stick and dragged himself upright. 'We'll be just fine, thank you.'

'You may be the smallest dragonrider ever, young K'van, but you're the bravest,' said F'lar.

And Heth agreed! Pride and joy so leaped in both chests that K'van wondered if his heart would burst right out of his body. He looped an arm around Heth's neck and the pair—the smallest dragonboy and the hatchling who wouldn't choose anybody else—walked out of the Hatching Ground, together forever.

THE FIRST HALF-HOUR

Jules Verne

Written in 1870, Jules Verne's *Round the Moon* looked forward to the adventure of man's first journey into space. In this episode the three explorers, travelling in a bullet-shaped capsule fired from an enormous gun, recover from the shock of the launch.

What had happened? What effect had this frightful shock produced? Had the ingenuity of the constructors of the projectile obtained any happy result? Had the shock been deadened, thanks to the springs, the four plugs, the water-cushions, and the partition-breaks? Had they been able to subdue the frightful pressure of the initiatory speed of more than 11,000 yards, which was enough to traverse Paris or New York in a second? This was evidently the question suggested to the thousand spectators of this moving scene. They forgot the aim of the journey, and thought only of the travellers. And if one amongst them—Joseph T. Maston for example—could have cast one glimpse into the projectile, what would he have seen?

Nothing then. The darkness was profound. But its cylindro-conical partitions had resisted wonderfully. Not a rent or a dent anywhere! The wonderful projectile was not even heated under the intense deflagration of the powder, nor liquefied, as they seemed to fear, in a shower of aluminium.

The interior showed but little disorder; indeed, only a few objects had been violently thrown towards the roof; but the most important seemed not to have suffered from the shock at all; their fixtures were intact.

On the movable disc, sunk down to the bottom by the smashing of the partition-breaks and the escape of the water, three bodies lay apparently lifeless. Barbicane, Nicholl, and Michel Ardan—did they still breathe? or was the projectile nothing now but a metal coffin, bearing three corpses into space?

Some minutes after the departure of the projectile, one of the bodies moved, shook its arms, lifted its head, and finally succeeded in getting on its knees. It was Michel Ardan. He felt himself all over, gave a sonorous 'Hem!' and then said,—

'Michel Ardan is whole. How about the others?'

The courageous Frenchman tried to rise, but could not stand. His head swam, from the rush of blood; he was blind; he was like a drunken man.

'Bur-r!' said he. 'It produces the same effect as two bottles of Corton, though perhaps less agreeable to swallow.' Then, passing his hand several times across his forehead and rubbing his temples, he called in a firm voice,—

'Nicholl! Barbicane!'

He waited anxiously. No answer; not even a sigh to show that the hearts of his companions were still beating. He called again. The same silence.

'The devil!' he exclaimed. 'They look as if they had fallen from a fifth storey on their heads. Bah!' he added, with that imperturbable confidence which nothing could check, 'if a Frenchman can get on his knees, two Americans ought to be able to get on their feet. But first let us light up.'

Ardan felt the tide of life return by degrees. His

blood became calm, and returned to its accustomed circulation. Another effort restored his equilibrium. He succeeded in rising, drew a match from his pocket, and approaching the burner lighted it. The receiver had not suffered at all. The gas had not escaped. Besides, the smell would have betrayed it; and in that case Michel Ardan could not have carried a lighted match with impunity through the space filled with hydrogen. The gas mixing with the air would have produced a detonating mixture, and the explosion would have finished what the shock had perhaps begun. When the burner was lit, Ardan leaned over the bodies of his companions: they were lying one on the other, an inert mass, Nicholl above, Barbicane underneath.

Ardan lifted the captain, propped him up against the divan, and began to rub vigorously. This means, used with judgement, restored Nicholl, who opened his eyes, and instantly recovering his presence of mind, seized Ardan's hand and looked around him.

'And Barbicane?' said he.

'Each in turn,' replied Michel Ardan. 'I began with you, Nicholl, because you were on the top. Now let us look to Barbicane.' Saying which, Ardan and Nicholl raised the president of the Gun Club and laid him on the divan. He seemed to have suffered more than either of his companions; he was bleeding, but Nicholl was reassured by finding that the hæmorrhage came from a slight wound on the shoulder, a mere graze, which he bound up carefully.

Still, Barbicane was a long time coming to himself, which frightened his friends, who did not spare friction.

'He breathes though,' said Nicholl, putting his ear to the chest of the wounded man.

'Yes,' replied Ardan, 'he breathes like a man who has some notion of that daily operation. Rub, Nicholl; let us rub harder.' And the two improvised practitioners worked so hard and so well that Barbicane recovered his senses. He opened his eyes, sat up, took his two friends by the hands, and his first words were—

'Nicholl, are we moving?'

Nicholl and Barbicane looked at each other; they had not yet troubled themselves about the projectile; their first thought had been for the traveller, not for the car.

'Well, are we really moving?' repeated Michel Ardan.

'Or quietly resting on the soil of Florida?' asked Nicholl.

'Or at the bottom of the Gulf of Mexico?' added Michel Ardan.

'What an idea!' exclaimed the president.

And this double hypothesis suggested by his companions had the effect of recalling him to his senses. In any case they could not yet decide on the position of the projectile. Its apparent immovability, and the want of communication with the outside, prevented them from solving the question. Perhaps the projectile was unwinding its course through space. Perhaps after a short rise it had fallen upon the earth, or even in the Gulf of Mexico—a fall which the narrowness of the peninsula of Florida would render not impossible.

The case was serious, the problem interesting, and one that must be solved as soon as possible. Thus, highly excited, Barbicane's moral energy triumphed over physical weakness, and he rose to his feet. He listened. Outside was perfect silence; but the thick padding was enough to intercept all sounds coming from the earth. But one circumstance struck Barbicane, viz., that the temperature inside the projectile was singularly high. The president drew a thermometer from its case, and consulted it. The instrument showed 81° Fahr.

'Yes,' he exclaimed, 'yes, we are moving! This stifling heat, penetrating through the partitions of the projectile, is produced by its friction on the atmospheric strata. It will soon diminish, because we are already floating in space, and after having been nearly stifled, we shall have to suffer intense cold.'

'What!' said Michel Ardan. 'According to your showing, Barbicane, we are already beyond the limits of the terrestrial atmosphere?'

'Without a doubt, Michel. Listen to me. It is fifty-five minutes past ten; we have been gone about eight minutes; and if our initiatory speed has not been checked by the friction, six seconds would be enough for us to pass through the forty miles of atmosphere which surrounds the globe.'

'Just so,' replied Nicholl; 'but in what proportion do you estimate the diminution of speed by friction?'

'In the proportion of one-third, Nicholl. This diminution is considerable, but according to my calculations it is nothing less. If, then, we had an initiatory speed of 12,000 yards, on leaving the atmosphere this speed would be reduced to 9165 yards. In any case we have already passed through this interval, and—'

'And then,' said Michel Ardan, 'friend Nicholl has lost his two bets: four thousand dollars because the Columbiad did not burst; five thousand dollars because the projectile has risen more than six miles. Now, Nicholl, pay up.'

'Let us prove it first,' said the captain, 'and we will pay afterwards. It is quite possible that Barbicane's reasoning is correct, and that I have lost my nine thousand dollars. But a new hypothesis presents itself to my mind, and it annuls the wager.'

'What is that?' asked Barbicane quickly.

'The hypothesis that, for some reason or other, fire was never set to the powder, we have not started at all.'

'My goodness, captain,' exclaimed Michel Ardan,

'that hypothesis is worthy of my brain! It cannot be a serious one. For have we not been half annihilated by the shock? Did I not recall you to life? Is not the president's shoulder still bleeding from the blow it has received?'

'Granted,' replied Nicholl; 'but one question.'

'Well, captain?'

'Did you hear the detonation, which certainly ought to be loud?'

'No,' replied Ardan, much surprised; 'certainly I did not hear the detonation.'

'And you, Barbicane?'

'Nor I, either.'

'Very well,' said Nicholl.

'Well now,' murmured the president, 'why did we not hear the detonation?'

The three friends looked at each other with a disconcerted air. It was quite an inexplicable phenomenon. The projectile had started, and consequently there must have been a detonation.

'Let us first find out where we are,' said Barbicane, 'and let down the panel.'

This very simple operation was soon accomplished.

The nuts which held the bolts to the outer plates of the right-hand scuttle gave way under the pressure of the English wrench. These bolts were pushed outside, and buffers covered with india-rubber stopped up the holes which let them through. Immediately the outer plate fell back upon its hinges like a porthole, and the lenticular glass which closed the scuttle appeared. A similar one was let into the thick partition on the opposite side of the projectile, another in the top of the dome, and finally, a fourth in the middle of the base. They could, therefore, make observations in four different directions: the firmament by the side and most direct windows, the earth or the moon by the upper and under openings in the projectile.

Barbicane and his two companions immediately

rushed to the uncovered window. But it was lit by no ray of light. Profound darkness surrounded them, which, however, did not prevent the president from exclaiming,—

'No, my friends, we have not fallen back upon the earth; no, nor are we submerged in the Gulf of Mexico. Yes! we are mounting into space. See those stars shining in the night, and that impenetrable darkness heaped up between the earth and us!'

'Hurrah! hurrah!' exclaimed Michel Ardan and Nicholl in one voice.

Indeed, this thick darkness proved that the projectile had left the earth, for the soil, brilliantly lit by the moonbeams, would have been visible to the travellers, if they had been lying on its surface. This darkness also showed that the projectile had passed the atmospheric strata, for the diffused light spread in the air would have been reflected on the metal walls, which reflection was wanting. This light would have lit the window, and the window was dark. Doubt was no longer possible; the travellers had left the earth.

'I have lost,' said Nicholl.

'I congratulate you,' replied Ardan.

'Here are the nine thousand dollars,' said the captain, drawing a roll of paper dollars from his pocket.

'Will you have a receipt for it?' asked Barbicane, taking the sum.

'If you do not mind,' answered Nicholl; 'it is more businesslike.'

And coolly and seriously, as if he had been at his strong-box, the president drew forth his note-book, tore out a blank leaf, wrote a proper receipt in pencil, dated and signed it with the usual flourish, and gave it to the captain, who carefully placed it in his pocket-book. Michel Ardan, taking off his hat, bowed to his two companions without speaking. So much formality under such circumstances left him speechless. He had never before seen anything so 'American.'

This affair settled, Barbicane and Nicholl had returned to the window, and were watching the constellations. The stars looked like bright points on the black sky. But from that side they could not see the orb of night, which, travelling from east to west, would rise by degrees towards the zenith. Its absence drew the following remark from Ardan.

'And the moon; will she perchance fail at our rendezvous?'

'Do not alarm yourself,' said Barbicane; 'our future globe is at its post, but we cannot see her from this side; let us open the other.'

As Barbicane was about leaving the window to open the opposite scuttle, his attention was attracted by the approach of a brilliant object. It was an enormous disc, whose colossal dimension could not be estimated. Its face, which was turned to the earth, was very bright. One might have thought it a small moon reflecting the light of the larger one. She advanced with great speed, and seemed to describe an orbit round the earth, which would intersect the passage of the projectile. This body revolved upon its axis, and exhibited the phenomena of all celestial bodies abandoned in space.

'Ah!' exclaimed Michel Ardan, 'what is that? another projectile?'

Barbicane did not answer. The appearance of this enormous body surprised and troubled him. A collision was possible, and might be attended with deplorable results; either the projectile would deviate from its path, or a shock, breaking its impetus, might precipitate it to the earth; or, lastly, it might be irresistibly drawn away by the powerful asteroid. The president caught at a glance the consequences of these three hypotheses, either of which would, one way or the other, bring their experiment to an unsuccessful and fatal termination. His companions stood silently looking into space. The object grew rapidly as it approached them, and by an optical illusion the projectile seemed to be throwing itself before it.

'By Jove!' exclaimed Michel Ardan, 'we shall run into one another!'

Instinctively the travellers drew back. Their dread was great, but it did not last many seconds. The asteroid passed several hundred yards from the projectile and disappeared, not so much from the rapidity of its course, as that its face being opposite the moon, it was suddenly merged into the perfect darkness of space.

'A happy journey to you,' exclaimed Michel Ardan, with a sigh of relief. 'Surely infinity of space is large enough for a poor little projectile to walk through without fear. Now, what is this portentous globe which nearly struck us?'

'I know,' replied Barbicane.

'Oh, indeed! you know everything.'

'It is, said Barbicane, 'a simple meteorite, but an

enormous one, which the attraction of the earth has retained as a satellite.'

'It is possible!' exclaimed Michel Ardan; 'the earth then has two moons like Neptune?'

'Yes, my friend, two moons, though it passes generally for having only one; but this second moon is so small, and its speed so great, that the inhabitants of the earth cannot see it. It was by noticing disturbances that a French astronomer, M. Petit, was able to determine the existence of this second satellite and calculate its elements. According to his observations, this meteorite will accomplish its revolution round the earth in three hours and twenty minutes, which implies a wonderful rate of speed.'

'Do all astronomers admit the existence of this satellite?' asked Nicholl.

'No,' replied Barbicane; 'but if, like us, they had met it, they could no longer doubt it. Indeed, I think that this meteorite, which, had it struck the projectile, would have much embarrassed us, will give us the means of deciding what our position in space is.'

'How?' said Ardan.

'Because its distance is known, and when we met it, we were exactly 4650 miles from the surface of the terrestrial globe.'

'More than 2000 French leagues,' exclaimed Michel Ardan. 'That beats the express trains of the pitiful globe called the earth.'

'I should think so,' replied Nicholl, consulting his chronometer; 'it is eleven o'clock, and it is only thirteen minutes since we left the American Continent.'

'Only thirteen minutes?' said Barbicane.

'Yes,' said Nicholl; 'and if our initiatory speed of 12,000 yards has been kept up, we shall have made about 20,000 miles in the hour.'

'That is all very well, my friends,' said the president, 'but the insoluble question still remains. Why did we not hear the detonation of the Columbiad?'

For want of an answer the conversation dropped, and Barbicane began thoughtfully to let down the shutter of the second side. He succeeded; and through the uncovered glass the moon filled the projectile with a brilliant light. Nicholl, as an economical man, put out the gas, now useless, and whose brilliancy prevented any observation of the interplanetary space.

The lunar disc shone with wonderful purity. Her rays, no longer filtered through the vapoury atmosphere of the terrestrial globe, shone through the glass, filling the air in the interior of the projectile with silvery reflections. The black curtain of the firmament in reality heightened the moon's brilliancy, which in this void of ether unfavourable to diffusion did not eclipse the neighbouring stars. The heavens, thus seen, presented quite a new aspect, and one which the human eye could never dream of. One may conceive the interest with which these bold men watched the orb of night, the great aim of their journey.

In its motion the earth's satellite was insensibly nearing the zenith, the mathematical point which it ought to attain ninety-six hours later. Her mountains, her plains, every projection was as clearly discernible to their eyes as if they were observing it from some spot upon the earth; but its light was developed through space with wonderful intensity. The disc shone like a platinum mirror. Of the earth flying from under their feet, the travellers had lost all recollection.

It was Captain Nicholl who first recalled their attention to the vanishing globe.

'Yes,' said Michel Ardan, 'do not let us be ungrateful to it. Since we are leaving our country, let our last looks be directed to it. I wish to see the earth once more before it is quite hidden from my eyes.'

To satisfy his companions, Barbicane began to uncover the window at the bottom of the projectile, which would allow them to observe the earth direct. The disc, which the force of the projection had beaten down to the base, was removed, not without difficulty. Its fragments, placed carefully against the wall, might serve again upon occasion. Then a circular gap appeared, nineteen inches in diameter, hollowed out of the lower part of the projectile. A glass cover, six inches thick and strengthened with upper fastenings, closed it tightly. Beneath was fixed an aluminium plate, held in place by bolts. The screws being undone, and the bolts let go, the plate fell down, and visible communication was established between the interior and the exterior.

Michel Ardan knelt by the glass. It was cloudy, seemingly opaque.

'Well!' he exclaimed, 'and the earth?'

'The earth?' said Barbicane. 'There it is.'

'What! that little thread; that silver crescent?'

'Doubtless, Michel. In four days, when the moon will be full, at the very time we shall reach it, the earth will be new, and will only appear to us as a slender crescent which will soon disappear, and for some days will be enveloped in utter darkness.'

'That the earth?' repeated Michel Ardan, looking with all his eyes at the thin slip of his native planet.

The explanation given by President Barbicane was correct. The earth, with respect to the projectile, was entering its last phase. It was in its octant, and showed a crescent finely traced on the dark background of the sky. Its light, rendered bluish by the thick strata of the atmosphere, was less intense than that of the crescent moon, but it was of considerable dimensions, and looked like an enormous arch stretched across the firmament. Some parts brilliantly lighted, especially on its concave part, showed the presence of high mountains, often disappearing behind thick spots, which are never seen on the lunar disc. They were rings of clouds placed concentrically round the terrestrial globe.

Whilst the travellers were trying to pierce the profound darkness, a brilliant cluster of shooting stars burst upon their eyes. Hundreds of meteorites, ignited by the friction of the atmosphere, irradiated the shadow of the luminous train, and lined the cloudy parts of the disc with their fire. At this period the earth was in its perihelion, and the month of December is so propitious to these shooting stars, that astronomers have counted as many as twenty-four thousand in an hour. But Michel Ardan, disdaining scientific reasonings, preferred thinking that the earth was thus saluting the depature of her three children with her most brilliant fireworks.

Indeed this was all they saw of the globe lost in the shadow, an inferior orb of the solar world, rising and setting to the great planets like a simple morning or evening star! This globe, where they had left all their affections, was nothing more than a fugitive crescent!

Long did the three friends look without speaking, though united in heart, whilst the projectile sped onward with an ever-decreasing speed. Then an irresistible drowsiness crept over their brain. Was it weariness both of body and mind? No doubt; for after the over-excitement of those last hours passed upon earth, reaction was inevitable.

'Well,' said Nicholl, 'since we must sleep, let us sleep.'

And stretching themselves on their couches, they were all three soon in a profound slumber.

But they had not forgotten themselves more than a quarter of an hour, when Barbicane sat up suddenly, and rousing his companions with a loud voice, exclaimed,—

'I have found it!'

'What have you found?' asked Michel Ardan, jumping from his bed.

'The reason why we did not hear the detonation of the Columbiad.'

'And it is—?' said Nicholl.

'Because our projectile travelled *faster than the sound!*'

A WALK IN THE WOODS

David Campton

Whining needles tinkled as a breeze ruffled the branches of the pinclick trees: some of them fell, glittering like fragments of glass. So far Duncan had found the woods a source of wonder and delight. Only his natural caution kept him from rushing about touching, smelling or even tasting. But these woods were not Earth woods, and there was no telling what alien dangers hung or coiled, watching in the sun-speckled glades; so he trod cautiously, alert to every movement among the strangely shaped and coloured bushes.

For Len, trudging by his side, the walk was only another walk: so many thousand paces into the woods, then so many out again. Only the chance to stretch his legs after being cooped up in a space carrier for so long, and the knowledge that what he was doing had been expressly forbidden, gave the exercise any spice. He would probably not even have considered breaking bounds if it had not been for the notice warning 'Freshmen must on no account venture beyond the Transit Camp perimeter'. After reading that he could not allow himself to be confined to the translucent bubbles that constituted the quar-

ters for new arrivals on the planet. He had bullied
and cajoled until Duncan had agreed to come with
him.

Duncan, naturally law-abiding and a conscientious
observer of rules, had held out against Len's persua-
sion until Len had dared him. Then it had become a
question of honour. Even so Duncan cursed himself
for being so sensitive. Slight, pale, and looking almost
girlish, he believed that people would expect him to
run at a hint of danger, to faint at the sight of blood, or
shirk carrying his share of a load; and consequently he
was always shouldering the extra burden and volun-
teering for any risky project. Which, of course, was
why he had signed on for this extra-terrestrial duty.
Now he called himself a fool for rising to Len's bait.
What was a dare? Nothing but words. Suppose Len
had dared him to put his hand into the fire! Yet here he
was in a situation that could end in worse hurt than a
burned hand. Too little was known about the planet
they were opening up. The warning notice was only
common-sense.

Duncan and Len were Cadet Frontiersmen; though
as yet that was hardly more than a courtesy title. For
the two days since touchdown their routine had consisted of keeping stiff new uniforms and scrubbed new
quarters in spotless condition. Later there would be
lectures and exercises, and later still real duties; but at
present they had only to obey orders and keep out of
the way of those with work to do. There was in fact no
end to the jobs a frontiersman might be called upon to
tackle—from concocting a stew out of native roots to
setting up the stations around which the settlers
would establish first communities. Exploration of the
planet had been controlled and orderly. First had come
the astronauts, reporting back an atmosphere and
gravity almost identical to Earth. They had been
followed by technicians sampling mineral deposits,
making maps, investigating flora and fauna. And with

the technicians came the frontiersmen, the first of the galactic odd-job men. Duncan and Len were here to learn that trade.

The boys did not even like each other. They were the same age, the minimum allowed for recruits. Beyond that, all they had in common was their inability to make friends. Duncan was too shy. At the slightest suggestion of being noticed he would blush to the roots of his straw-blond hair. Len was too suspicious. Having fought a losing battle with authority for as long as he could remember, he expected any outstretched hand to close into a fist. So they were frequently paired, merely by the accident of being left together when everyone else in the troop had gone off in groups.

While Duncan glanced around in all directions, taking in colours and sounds that rightly belonged in dreams, Len plodded by his side, dark eyebrows drawn together in habitual frown, and staring only at his outsize boots. Their ideas on the illicit adventure were now reversed. Duncan was beginning to enjoy himself, in spite of the nagging fears at the back of his mind; while Len glumly wondered why he had taken so much trouble merely for another route march, and calculated what it was going to cost in terms of extra duties when the escapade was detected.

He was roused by a muffled explosion from a clump of bushes and a handful of egg-shaped pellets hurtling in all directions. He burst into abuse when one of them hit his cheek. Duncan gathered up several of the smooth, delicate-brown missiles.

'Crashnuts,' he said.

'You be careful,' muttered Len. 'Don't know what you're picking up.'

'We were told about them at the recruiting lecture,' Duncan reminded him. 'When they've been dried, you can crumble them into flour between your fingers. Don't you remember?'

'Don't remember anything about that lecture except the chap saying we could get away from Earth. Couldn't get away soon enough myself.'

'We may wish we were back there before we've done,' murmured Duncan. Then he brightened and held out a nut. 'Have one. They're good to eat.'

'We don't know that,' grumbled Len. 'We don't know anything.'

A tendril spiralled from the black and orange mottled trunk of a near-by tree. It curved over Duncan's hand, then furiously wound itself round the nut. Having secured the food, the tendril withdrew into the tree with the speed and slap of a shooting elastic band.

'Did you see that?' Duncan squeaked excitedly.

'Ugh,' said Len. 'Creepy-crawlies!'

'Is it animal or vegetable?'

'Don't care,' said Len. 'Don't like 'em.'

'But it's fascinating.' Duncan held out another nut. After a while a tendril stretched from the tree in search of it.

'Stop that!' Len smacked the nut from Duncan's hand. As it fell into the thick moss at his feet, the tendril curved after it. With disgusted grunts Len stamped on the tendril, which became detached from the tree, thrashed and squirmed for a few seconds, then lay limp.

'You big-footed fool!' shouted Duncan. 'You killed it.'

'Creepy-crawley. Hate 'em,' grumbled Len. 'And who are you calling a fool, girlie?'

Duncan's face burned red. There was only one answer to that taunt. He clenched his fists; but all those months of training checked him.

'We'd be fools to fight here,' he panted. 'If one of us got hurt we might be delayed until after nightfall, and to be caught in these woods after dark could be fatal. But I'll take you on as soon as we get back to camp.'

'Please yourself. Want to go back now?'

'He wants to go back,' thought Duncan. Aloud he said, 'Why should we? We'll be on a charge anyway for breaking bounds. We might as well have our money's worth. Just look at that!'

Another new tendril had emerged from near the root of the tree. It waved gently as though searching. Duncan grabbed Len's arm. 'If you touch that one, I'll spread your big nose all over your ugly face,' he hissed.

The new tendril curled around the limp one. There was no haste this time. Gently it drew its load towards the tree.

'Like a damned snake,' blurted Len. Duncan realized that his companion's arm was shaking. 'It's thinking,' cried Len. 'A plant's got no right to think.'

The two tendrils reached the tree trunk. As slowly as a wisp of steam dispersing in air, they merged with the bark until there was no sign that they had ever been.

'There,' breathed Duncan, bright-eyed.

'What sort of place have we got ourselves into?' whispered Len.

'Come on,' said Duncan. 'Let's see what there is to see.' Although he was genuinely eager to explore, he enjoyed making Len sweat.

'What else is there to see?' Was there a tremble in Len's voice?

'That for instance.' As Duncan pointed, what seemed like a clump of coloured flowers rose from a

bush. He realized they were the painted wings of a butterfly, which fluttered around a cluster of blossom on an overhanging bough. This blossom too became detached: it was another butterfly. The enormous insects began an aerial dance, circling, swooping, dodging, rushing, in a swirl of reds, blues, yellows and greens.

'It could be a mating dance,' said Duncan. As if demonstrating his theory the butterflies came together, and, bodies pressed, hung in the air. But they were sustained only by the wings of the upper butterfly; while those of the lower fluttered feebly, and then ceased to move at all. Gradually the colour faded from them. Finally a piece of grey-brown membrane, all that was left of the lower insect, floated like a piece of crumpled paper to the ground.

Len ran his tongue over dry lips. 'If that's a mating dance, I'll sit it out,' he murmured, as the victor disappeared among a tangle of branches.

Duncan shrugged his thin shoulders. 'This is a different world,' he said casually. 'But there's something funny about that bush.'

On investigation the bush on which the butterfly had been resting proved not to have been a bush at all, but the spiney skeleton of some animal.

'But what sort of animal would have a skeleton like that?' protested Len. 'It must look like a nightmare.'

It did. It was a black, slug-like creature they came across a quarter of an hour later grazing on a patch of

delicate harebells, and making a noise like the pumping of enormous bellows, obviously enjoying its food. It raised its head, which was not so much a head as the rounded end of its body, and stared at the intruders with its single eye.

'Do we go past it?' asked Len hoarsely. 'Or do we go back?'

Duncan wished he could have forced Len closer to the mis-shapen blob, if only to teach him respect for other forms of life, but it would have been a stupid risk to take. 'I suppose we'd better go back,' he said.

'And hope there's no more of them crawling up behind us,' grumbled Len.

'It's time, anyway,' said Duncan, rationalizing his retreat. The sun's rays slanted low through the trees. 'I reckon we've got about an hour of good light left.'

A butterfly danced through the bars of light. As huge as the others, it had very different markings. 'Blood splashed on parchment,' thought Duncan as he turned away.

A screech, so high-pitched that it was only just within the range of human ears, shrilled through the woods. Although hardly audible, its intensity was almost unbearable. The boys clapped their hands to their ears, and looked over their shoulders. The black creature was screaming.

The white and scarlet butterfly had settled on its back, and it had reared up on end, writhing. The air shimmered as more butterflies fluttered down like a rain of blood. As they covered the body the whining ceased. Then a butterfly flew away. The others followed. At last only one was left, resting on what looked like a dried bush—the skeleton of the black creature.

'Let's get a move on,' croaked Len. Tiny drops of sweat trickled down his swarthy face.

Duncan realized that he himself was trembling. His faltering footsteps pounded faster and faster, until he was running alongside Len. He stumbled over a tiny ant hill from which a swarm of golden motes rose, and settled again. Almost falling he caught Len's tunic. Len tried to shake him off.

'Stop,' panted Duncan. 'This is stupid. At this rate we'll be exhausted before we're halfway back to Camp.'

He let go, and stood taking deep breaths. Len stumbled on for another ten yards, then slowed to a halt.

'Nobody—ever told us—about that,' he gasped.

'We didn't give them a chance,' wheezed Duncan. 'Only been here for two days. Awaiting Further Training. Confined to Camp.'

'Surely somebody must have broken out before us,' said Len.

'If they did, we don't know what happened to them,' replied Duncan, grimly.

For a while they trudged on in silence. The sense of wonder had now soured to apprehension. Any movement from the bushes could have signalled danger. Even Len was unusually alert, eyes wide-open that most of the time were sulkily half-shut.

'You're sure we'll get back before dark?' Len said, trying to sound casual. 'You know the way?'

'Keep the sun on our left,' said Duncan. 'As long as we keep going at this rate we'll have time to spare. Might even get back before we're missed.'

Len wanted to quicken his pace. Perceiving this, Duncan deliberately slowed down. All right, he was nervous, but he wasn't going to show it. Besides he had not forgotten that insulting reference to his looks—as if he could help long dark eyelashes and pink cheeks on which whiskers were reluctant to grow. This was as good a way of punishing Len as lashing out with his fists.

'Get a move on, shortlegs,' growled Len, irritably. 'You go on ahead if you're scared.'

Len faced him squarely. 'Stop that play-acting.

You're as windy as I am. If I weren't here, you'd be wetting your nappy.'

'Think so?' Duncan forced a smile. Deliberately he bent down and plucked a delicate blue flower. 'Pretty isn't it?'

Tiny drops of moisture fell from the miniature bells, some of them splashing on to Duncan's hand.

'Trust you to pick flowers. Going to wear them in your hair?'

An almost overpowering scent rose from the scattered droplets. It reminded Duncan of a time when he had passed the open door of a very expensive restaurant, wafting the combined odours of many flowers, of extravagant food, of warmth, comfort and good living. Duncan lifted the back of his hand to his nose. And was immediately racked by titanic sneezes.

Each shattering 'Choo' was succeeded by the gasp that preceded the next. His eyes swam, his head reeled, and he staggered blindly first into a tree, and then into something warmer and softer that proved to be Len. His nose was becoming hot and sore, and his knees trembled, but the convulsions continued. He wondered vaguely if they would ever stop, and, as breathing became more and more difficult, he began thinking what a silly way it was to die, sniffing at a . . .

Slowly he became aware that Len was supporting him, and that the sneezes had stopped. His sight cleared. As he blinked he heard Len start to grumble again.

'If you're coming round, you can carry your own weight,' he mumbled. 'There's not much on you, but what there is is flaming heavy.'

Duncan realized that his right hand was burning as thought he had been holding a hot coal. Looking down at it, as detached and dully as though it belonged to someone else, he saw that it was now red raw with great blisters where the drops had landed. It was also beginning to swell. At a distance he heard Len's voice.

'Couldn't let you lie down among those poisonous things. But would you mind standing on your own feet?'

Duncan did as he was requested, and with an effort straightened his shoulders. 'Sorry,' he said, with a partially successful attempt at brightness. 'Fool thing to do. Should have learned that what looks nice on this planet can be nasty.'

'That black thing was eating them,' recalled Len with awe.

'Perhaps that's how they're kept down. The black things feed on them, and the butterflies feed on the black things. Balance of nature.'

'What feeds on the butterflies?'

'Perhaps they just eat each other. I can walk now. Let's get going, shall we?'

Progress became slower, though. Each step jolted Duncan's hand, and each jolt was like the stroke of a cane. He unbuttoned the front of his tunic to act as a sling: that was more comfortable, but the unusual distribution of weight made walking more difficult. He now tended to stumble over any unevenness in the ground. The sun sank lower.

'Still time,' he said, aware of the false note in his optimism. 'Barring accidents.'

Instead of spurring him to increase speed, Len stopped dead. 'Look over there. Those trees. They're moving,' he said.

Natural camouflage was responsible, of course. As long as this apparition had stood still, it had been quite invisible: and they had been walking straight towards it. Now that it was moving, however slowly, they could judge its width and length. At its thickest it must have been twice the height of a man, and it stretched from one side of the glade to the other. Fifty feet? Sixty? Seventy?

'What is it?' Len whispered.

'I don't know,' Duncan whispered back. 'But in my book it ought to be extinct.'

'It's in our way. What are we going to do?'

'Ask it to stand aside?' Duncan immediately wished he had not said that. This was no time for sarcasm, especially as Len picked up the tone of mockery.

'All right smarty-pants. We all know you're not just a pretty face. If you're so clever, think of something. The sun's nearly gone. If we're not going to be caught here in the dark, we've got to get over or under or round That. Well?'

A silver moth swooped between the trees, and circled the boys, but their attention was focussed on the stripes of the beast lurking beyond the trees. Until now its head had been turned away. Swiftly it swung round in their direction, a black tongue cracked like a stock-whip and the silver moth disappeared. After which the monster stared straight at them. It was hideous.

Grey-green and purple, it was covered with warty lumps. From a wide snout floated wisps of vapour, giving the impression that in the right circumstances it might breathe fire. The many facets of its single eye glittered like sparks in the scarlet light of the setting sun. That much might have been bearable, but when the eye protruded on the end of an antenna which curved towards them, there was no alternative to flight.

Screaming like frightened birds, the pair crashed through the woods; sometimes bumping into each other, sometimes clutching at each other; all sense of direction lost, and nothing in their minds but the need to escape from the nightmare behind them. They stopped only when Len tripped, somersaulted, and sprawled flat on his face.

Sheer momentum carried Duncan on a few more yards. By the time he had turned back, Len was trying to push himself up. Not far behind Len's foot ants were already repairing their nest, around which a golden light glowed in the approaching dusk. Duncan offered his left hand to help Len up, but Len waved it aside.

'I can stand on my own feet,' he snapped. 'But where's the monster?'

'We must have outrun it,' said Duncan. 'Perhaps it just didn't bother to follow.' He peered into the shadows, hoping that he was right, and the Thing was not actually at his elbow, unseen.

Len had spoken too soon. On applying slight weight to his left foot, he yelped and tumbled again. In lurching he clutched at the nearest support. He might have saved himself if this had not been Duncan's swollen hand. Duncan screamed; Len hit the ground; and for some minutes they heaped insult upon insult, each conscious only of his individual hurt. At last the pain subsided and they fell silent, glumly considering their situation.

'We're in a mess,' said Duncan at last.

'My fault, I suppose,' growled Len, tenderly, nursing his ankle, which was either broken or badly sprained.

'A mess is a mess no matter how we landed in it,' said Duncan quietly. 'Me with one arm, and you with one leg.'

'I might hobble if I'd got something to lean on,' said Len. 'A thick stick would do, but where is that to come from? Try tearing a branch from one of those trees, and I bet it'd bite.'

'You could lean on me,' said Duncan.

'You?' scoffed Len.

'But there's no use in walking if you don't know *where* you're walking,' went on Duncan calmly. 'We're lost. With the sun gone we could even be travelling away from Camp. We'll be missed at Roll Call. I suppose sooner or later a party will set out to look for us.

Our best plan is to stay right here until someone finds us.'

'Unless some*thing* finds us first,' added Len with a cracked laugh.

'Shut up,' snapped Duncan. 'Stop trying to frighten yourself.'

'Me?' scoffed Len. 'If I were a monster I'd go for you first. A right dainty morsel—all sugar and spice.'

'You'd give them more to feed on,' returned Duncan. Gently he withdrew his hand from the front of his tunic, hoping that the cool air might relieve it. The sensation of being boiled had now spread up to his elbow. He knew how ridiculous it was to be spitting and sparring at Len, but could not resist a telling retort. 'You don't have to worry about being ugly. Remember how the butterflies tucked into the black thing.'

The words had tumbled out before he had given himself time to think about them; before he remembered how precipitately the beautiful creatures had stripped their victim to its bones. Almost as though bidden by his thoughts, a scrap of silver danced between black tree trunks, the last light glinting on its wings.

'See that?' whispered Len, squabbling forgotten.

'Aye. Let's hope there's only one of them—and it's particular what it has for supper.'

The silver moth fluttered around their heads. Once it dived so close to their faces that they were able to appreciate its size; from wing tip to wing tip it measured the length of Len's arm.

'On Earth, butterflies feed on honey,' muttered Duncan.

'How much honey do you think it would take to satisfy that one?' said Len.

Two silver moths now spun, rolled, and looped in an airborne *pas de deux*. Duncan and Len might have been dazzled by the spectacle if they had not been

aware of the bloodthirsty menace behind it. The two moths became two pairs, and behind them specks of light grew into outstretched wings as more approached.

'Quite a party,' croaked Len. 'Who's the guest of honour?'

He was not left long in doubt. A moth swooped at his face. Instinctively he threw up an arm to protect his eyes, and something sliced down his sleeve.

'They must have fangs like razors,' he cried.

As one hurled itself at Duncan he caught it by the wing. It slashed at him impotently as he beat it on the ground. The wing tore, and the moth scrabbled in circles. It did not suffer long before another moth bore it away. Apparently the insects had no scruples against cannibalism if opportunity offered.

The moths hovered above them in a shining canopy, then dived in a concerted attack. For a while, stout Government-issue uniforms prevented serious damage, and the boys inflicted heavy losses on the enemy, tearing at paper-thin membrane and stamping on writhing bodies. Their hands and faces began to shine with the brilliant scales that fell from the wings. At length, however, sheer number told. Thick tunics and forage caps were gradually shredded. Blood flew from nicks on Len's hands, and Duncan was almost blinded when an unopposed cut gashed a wound across his forehead. Hampered by an almost useless arm, and trying to wipe his eyes, he became the main target. A sharp pain at the back of his neck warned him that one of the enemy had found a vulnerable spot. He rolled over on the ground, trying to crush it, but even as he did so other moths hooked themselves into his clothing. A strip was torn down one trouser leg. Far off he heard screaming, but could not tell whether the voice was Len's or his own, or both.

Above the flapping and shrieking he heard a series of shots. Was the Cavalry Riding to the Rescue? Had a search party found them so soon? He raised his head, and was just able to snatch a glimpse of Len, lying face downwards and inert with half a dozen silver creatures tearing at his back, when a brilliant passing flash scored his own cheek and he ducked down again. The shots continued, increased to rapid fire, then declined to irregular sniping. At the same time he became aware that there was no longer anything hacking at his body.

He ventured to look up again. Len still lay without moving. As a shred of silver above him poised before an assault, a shot echoed through the woods, and the moth disappeared. Or perhaps it was not so much like a shot as the crack of a whip. And Duncan remembered where he had heard its like before. It took every crumb of failing courage to glance over his shoulder. Only to confirm that bending over him, so close he could feel the steam from its nostrils, was the monster from which he had lately fled.

Ropes of saliva hung from its wart-encrusted jaws. As the stalked eye extended to within a few feet of his face, Duncan struck out at it. It swerved away, but Duncan felt the ground shake underneath him as the giant impatiently stamped its feet. The eye stretched even further to investigate the prostrate Len. With its attention momentarily distracted, Duncan tried to crawl away, keeping close to the ground, and using such techniques as he could recall from Basic Training.

He had only traversed a few yards when he noticed that something long, thick and sinuous was winding its way towards him. At first he thought it must be a snake, but in the dim light he could not see a head, and quickly realized that he was looking at the beast's tail. As it touched him it looped upwards and passed over him. It was making its way towards Len.

It had already coiled twice round Len's limp body when Duncan overcame his fear-induced inertia, and threw himself at the Thing. He had managed to deliver only a few kicks and punches when the tail uncurled, and with one flick knocked him sprawling.

Lying on his back he saw Len, wound about from shoulder to ankles, lifted into the air. Then his companion was gone.

Any mourning had to wait though, if Duncan were not to share a similar fate. He scrambled to his feet, and tried to run. After a dozen or more drunken lurches something tapped Duncan on the shoulder. It was the tip of the tail. There was nothing else to be done. Slack-jawed and glassy eyed Duncan waited to die, unresisting as coils engulfed him. As he was picked up, to slide he supposed like an oyster down some fiery maw, he fainted.

When he came to his senses he was lying in a deep pit. Above him stars glimmered in the night sky. By their faint light he could just make out someone lying beside him. It was Len, still unconscious, but still breathing. Were they in some sort of prison? Was this a cell? Duncan felt the walls behind him: they were strangely warm. They were also lumpy. For some time his mind tried to reject the obvious conclusion. When it became inescapable he was torn between being sick and fainting again. The monster had curled itself round them.

Distantly he heard human voices. He wanted to shout out, but no sound would come from his throat. Did he want to warn them? Did he want them to rescue him? He didn't know. He beat once or twice feebly at the fleshy walls of his cell, then despairingly buried his face in his hands.

'Hullo, Captain. What have you got there?' a cheery voice hailed. 'Something we've been looking for?'

The high walls fell away, and Duncan found himself staring at the First Lieutenant—suitably armoured against the wild life of the woods with a plastisteel boiler suit.

'Lucky for you the Captain found you, or we'd have been collecting bones instead of . . .' The Lieutenant shone his torch on Duncan's face, and then on the prostrate Len. 'You'll be on a charge, of course,' he added, casually cheerful. 'But we'd better get you to Sick Bay before we throw you to the Old Man.'

A few days in hospital restored the casualties to a semblance of health, though Len was forced to rely on a crutch, and Duncan's arm was supported by a sling. At the end of the week stitches were removed from Len's back and Duncan's face. 'It's the best we can do,' chuckled the medical orderly, 'but I guess you'll never be so pretty again.'

'You should have seen the other chap,' grinned Duncan. Then suddenly serious, 'You been here a long time?'

'About a year. Came out just after Base opened. We've got more than a dozen camps started now. Once we've found out a bit more about the place we'll be encouraging settlers. Then the trouble'll really start.'

'The thing they called The Captain—what do you know about it?'

'Heard plenty of stories about it. Never actually come face to face. Not sure that I want to. They say it likes humans. Now that's really odd. I don't.'

'It's so hideous. Almost impossible to imagine it being friendly.'

'That's one of the general rules about this place. The uglier a thing seems, the more loveable underneath.'

*

On a point of comeliness there was little to choose between the monster and the Commanding Officer, except that the latter seemed to have more teeth, and a greater ability to breathe fire. Standing before him on a charge, Duncan and Len could only hope that the general rule would hold.

SUMMERTIME ON ICARUS

Arthur C. Clarke

When Colin Sherrard opened his eyes after the crash, he could not imagine where he was. He seemed to be lying, trapped in some kind of vehicle, on the summit of a rounded hill, which sloped steeply away in all directions. Its surface was seared and blackened, as if a great fire had swept over it. Above him was a jet-black sky, crowded with stars; one of them hung like a tiny, brilliant sun low down on the horizon.

Could it be the sun? Was he so far from Earth? No—that was impossible. Some nagging memory told him that the sun was very close—hideously close—not so distant that it had shrunk to a star. And with that thought, full consciousness returned. Sherrard knew exactly where he was, and the knowledge was so terrible that he almost fainted again.

He was nearer to the sun than any man had ever been. His damaged space-pod was lying on no hill, but on the steeply curving surface of a world only two miles in diameter. That brilliant star sinking swiftly in the west was the light of *Prometheus*, the ship that had brought him here across so many millions of miles of space. She was hanging up there among the stars, wondering why his pod had not returned like a homing pigeon to its roost. In a few minutes she would have passed from sight, dropping below the horizon in her perpetual game of hide-and-seek with the sun.

That was a game that he had lost. He was still on the night side of the asteroid, in the cool safety of its shadow, but the short night would be ending soon. The four-hour day of Icarus was spinning him swiftly towards that dreadful dawn, when a sun thirty times larger than ever shone upon Earth would blast these rocks with fire. Sherrard knew all too well why everything around him was burned and blackened. Icarus was still a week from perihelion but the temperature at noon had already reached a thousand degrees Fahrenheit.

Though this was no time for humour, he suddenly remembered Captain McClellan's description of Icarus: 'The hottest piece of real estate in the solar system.' The truth of that jest had been proved, only a few days before, by one of those simple and unscientific experiments that are so much more impressive than any number of graphs and instrument readings.

Just before daybreak, someone had propped a piece of wood on the summit of one of the tiny hills. Sherrard had been watching, from the safety of the night side, when the first rays of the rising sun had touched the hilltop. When his eyes had adjusted to the sudden detonation of light, he saw that the wood was already beginning to blacken and char. Had there been an atmosphere here, the stick would have burst into flames; such was dawn, upon Icarus . . .

Yet it had not been impossibly hot at the time of their first landing, when they were passing the orbit of Venus five weeks ago. *Prometheus* had overtaken the asteroid as it was beginning its plunge towards the sun, had matched speed with the little world and had touched down upon its surface as lightly as a snowflake. (A snowflake on Icarus—*that* was quite a

thought . . .) Then the scientists had fanned out across
the fifteen square miles of jagged nickel-iron that
covered most of the asteroid's surface, setting up their
instruments and checkpoints, collecting samples and
making endless observations.

Everything had been carefully planned, years in
advance, as part of the International Astrophysical
Decade. Here was a unique opportunity for a research
ship to get within a mere seventeen million miles of the
sun, protected from its fury by a two-mile thick shield
of rock and iron. In the shadow of Icarus, the ship
could ride safely round the central fire which warmed
all the planets, and upon which the existence of all life
depended. As the Prometheus of legend had brought
the gift of fire to mankind, so the ship that bore his
name would return to Earth with other unimagined
secrets from the heavens.

There had been plenty of time to set up the instruments and make the surveys before *Prometheus* had to
take off and seek the permanent shade of night. Even
then, it was still possible for men in the tiny self-
propelled space-pods—miniature spaceships, only
ten feet long—to work on the night side for an hour or
so, as long as they were not overtaken by the advancing line of sunrise. That had seemed a simple enough
condition to meet, on a world where dawn marched
forward at only a mile an hour; but Sherrard had failed
to meet it, and the penalty was death.

He was still not quite sure what had happened. He
had been replacing a seismograph transmitter at
Station 145, unofficially known as Mount Everest
because it was a full ninety feet above the surrounding
territory. The job had been a perfectly straightforward
one, even though he had to do it by remote control
through the mechanical arms of his pod. Sherrard was
an expert at manipulating these; he could tie knots
with his metal fingers almost as quickly as with his
flesh-and-bone ones. The task had taken little more

than twenty minutes, and then the radioseismograph was on the air again, monitoring the tiny quakes and shudders that racked Icarus in ever-increasing numbers as the asteroid approached the sun. It was small satisfaction to know that he had now made a king-sized addition to the record.

After he had checked the signals, he had carefully replaced the sun screens around the instrument. It was hard to believe that two flimsy sheets of polished metal foil, no thicker than paper, could turn aside a flood of radiation that would melt lead or tin within seconds. But the first screen reflected more than ninety per cent of the sunlight falling upon its mirror surface and the second turned back most of the rest, so that only a harmless fraction of the heat passed through.

He had reported completion of the job, received an acknowledgement from the ship, and prepared to head for home. The brilliant floodlights hanging from *Prometheus*—without which the night side of the asteroid would have been in utter darkness—had been an unmistakable target in the sky. The ship was only two miles up, and in this feeble gravity he could have jumped that distance had he been wearing a planetary-type space-suit with flexible legs. As it was, the low-powered micro-rockets of his pod would get him there in a leisurely five minutes.

He had aimed the pod with its gyros, set the rear jets at Strength Two, and pressed the firing button. There had been a violent explosion somewhere in the vicinity of his feet and he had soared away from Icarus—but not towards the ship. Something was horribly wrong; he was tossed to one side of the vehicle, unable to reach the controls. Only one of the jets was firing, and he was pinwheeling across the sky, spinning faster and faster under the off-balanced drive. He tried to find the cut-off, but the spin had completely disorientated him. When he was able to locate the controls, his first reaction made matters worse—he pushed the throttle over to full, like a nervous driver stepping on the accelerator instead of the brake. It took only a second to correct the mistake and kill the jet, but by then he was spinning so rapidly that the stars were wheeling round in circles.

Everything had happened so quickly that there was no time for fear, no time even to call the ship and report what was happening. He took his hands away from the controls; to touch them now would only make matters worse. It would take two or three minutes of cautious jockeying to unravel his spin, and from the flickering glimpses of the approaching rocks it was obvious that he did not have as many seconds. Sherrard remembered a piece of advice at the front of the *Spaceman's Manual*: 'When you don't know what to do, *do nothing.*' He was still doing it when Icarus fell upon him, and the stars went out.

It had been a miracle that the pod was unbroken, and that he was not breathing space. (Thirty minutes from now he might be glad to do so, when the capsule's heat insulation began to fail . . .) There had been some damage, of course. The rear-view mirrors, just outside the dome of transparent plastic that enclosed his head, were both snapped off, so that he could no longer see what lay behind him without twisting his neck. This was a trivial mishap; far more serious was the fact that his radio antennas had been torn away by the impact. He could not call the ship, and the ship

could not call him. All that came over the radio was a faint crackling, probably produced inside the set itself. He was absolutely alone, cut off from the rest of the human race.

It was a desperate situation, but there was one faint ray of hope. He was not, after all, completely helpless. Even if he could not use the pod's rockets—he guessed that the starboard motor had blown back and ruptured a fuel line, something the designers said was impossible—he was still able to move. He had his arms.

But which way should he crawl? He had lost all sense of location, for though he had taken off from Mount Everest, he might now be thousands of feet away from it. There were no recognizable landmarks in his tiny world; the rapidly sinking star of *Prometheus* was his best guide, and if he could keep the ship in view he would be safe. It would only be a matter of minutes before his absence was noted, if indeed it had not been discovered already. Yet without radio, it might take his colleagues a long time to find him; small though Icarus was, its fifteen square miles of fantastically rugged no man's land would provide an effective hiding place for a ten-foot cylinder. It might take an hour to locate him—which meant that he would have to keep ahead of the murderous sunrise.

He slipped his fingers into the controls that worked his mechanical limbs. Outside the pod, in the hostile vacuum that surrounded him, his substitute arms

came to life. They reached down, thrust against the iron surface of the asteroid, and levered the pod from the ground. Sherrard flexed them, and the capsule jerked forward, like some weird, two-legged insect . . . first the right arm, then the left, then the right . . .

It was less difficult than he had feared, and for the first time he felt his confidence return. Though his mechanical arms had been designed for light precision work, it needed very little pull to set the capsule moving in this weightless environment. The gravity of Icarus was ten thousand times weaker than Earth's: Sherrard and his space-pod weighed less than an ounce here, and once he had set himself in motion he floated forward with an effortless, dreamlike ease.

Yet that very effortlessness had its dangers. He had travelled several hundred yards, and was rapidly overhauling the sinking star of the *Prometheus*, when overconfidence betrayed him. (Strange how quickly the mind could switch from one extreme to the other; a few minutes ago he had been steeling himself to face death—now he was wondering if he would be late for dinner.) Perhaps the novelty of the movement, so unlike anything he had ever attempted before, was responsible for the catastrophe; or perhaps he was still suffering from the after-effects of the crash.

Like all astronauts, Sherrard had learned to orientate himself in space, and had grown accustomed to living and working when the Earthly conceptions of up and down were meaningless. On a world such as Icarus, it was necessary to pretend that there was a real, honest-to-goodness planet 'beneath' your feet, and that when you moved you were travelling over a horizontal plain. If this innocent self-deception failed, you were heading for space vertigo.

The attack came without warning, as it usually did. Quite suddenly, Icarus no longer seemed to be beneath him, the stars no longer above. The universe tilted through a right angle; he was moving straight *up* a vertical cliff, like a mountaineer scaling a rock face, and though Sherrard's reason told him that this was pure illusion, all his senses screamed that it was true. In a moment gravity must drag him off this sheer wall, and he would drop down mile upon endless mile until he smashed into oblivion.

Worse was to come; the false vertical was still swinging like a compass needle that had lost the pole. Now he was on the *underside* of an immense rocky roof, like a fly clinging to a ceiling; in another moment it would have become a wall again—but this time he would be moving straight down it, instead of up...

He had lost all control over the pod, and the clammy sweat that had begun to dew his brow warned him that he would soon lose control over his body. There was only one thing to do; he clenched his eyes tightly shut, squeezed as far back as possible into the tiny closed world of the capsule, and pretended with all his might that the universe outside did not exist. He did not even allow the slow, gentle crunch of his second crash to interfere with his self-hypnosis.

When he again dared to look outside, he found that the pod had come to rest against a large boulder. Its mechanical arms had broken the force of the impact, but at a cost that was more than he could afford to pay. Though the capsule was virtually weightless here, it still possessed its normal five hundred pounds of inertia, and it had been moving at perhaps four miles an hour. The momentum had been too much for the metal arms to absorb; one had snapped, and the other was hopelessly bent.

When he saw what had happened, Sherrard's first reaction was not despair, but anger. He had been so certain of success when the pod had started its glide across the barren face of Icarus. And now this, all through a moment of physical weakness! But space made no allowance for human frailties or emotions,

and a man who did not accept that fact had no right to be here.

At least he had gained precious time in his pursuit of the ship; he had put an extra ten minutes, if not more, between himself and dawn. Whether that ten minutes would merely prolong the agony or whether it would give his shipmates the extra time they needed to find him, he would soon know.

Where were they? Surely they had started the search by now! He strained his eyes towards the brilliant star of the ship, hoping to pick out the fainter lights of space-pods moving towards him—but nothing else was visible against the slowly turning vault of heaven.

He had better look to his own resources, slender though they were. Only a few minutes were left before the *Prometheus* and her trailing lights would sink below the edge of the asteroid and leave him in darkness. It was true that the darkness would be all too brief, but before it fell upon him he might find some shelter against the coming day. This rock into which he had crashed, for example . . .

Yes, it would give some shade, until the sun was halfway up the sky. Nothing could protect him if it passed right overhead, but it was just possible that he might be in a latitude where the sun never rose far above the horizon at this season of Icarus's four-hundred-and-nine-day year. Then he might survive the brief period of daylight; that was his only hope, if the rescuers did not find him before dawn.

There went *Prometheus* and her lights, below the edge of the world. With her going, the now-unchallenged stars blazed forth with redoubled brilliance. More glorious than any of them—so lovely that even to look upon it almost brought tears to his eyes—was the blazing beacon of Earth, with its companion moon beside it. He had been born on one, and had walked on the other; would he see either again?

Strange that until now he had given no thought to his wife and children, and to all that he loved in the life that now seemed so far away. He felt a spasm of guilt, but it passed swiftly. The ties of affection were not weakened, even across the hundred million miles of space that now sundered him from his family. At this moment, they were simply irrelevant. He was now a primitive, self-centred animal fighting for his life, and his only weapon was his brain. In this conflict, there was no place for the heart; it would merely be a hindrance, spoiling his judgement and weakening his resolution.

And then he saw something that banished all thoughts of his distant home. Reaching up above the horizon behind him, spreading across the stars like a milky mist, was a faint and ghostly cone of phosphorescence. It was the herald of the sun—the beautiful, pearly phantom of the corona, visible on Earth only during the rare moments of a total eclipse. When the corona was rising, the sun would not be far behind, to smite this little land with fury.

Sherrard made good use of the warning. Now he could judge, with some accuracy, the exact point where the sun would rise. Crawling slowly and clumsily on the broken stumps of his metal arms, he dragged the capsule round to the side of the boulder that should give the greatest shade. He had barely reached it when the sun was upon him like a beast of prey, and his tiny world exploded into light.

He raised the dark filters inside his helmet, one thickness after another, until he could endure the glare. Except where the broad shadow of the boulder lay across the asteroid, it was like looking into a furnace. Every detail of the desolate land around him was revealed by that merciless light; there were no greys, only blinding whites and impenetrable blacks. All the shadowed cracks and hollows were pools of ink, while the higher ground already seemed to be on fire, as it caught the sun. Yet it was only a minute after dawn.

Now Sherrard could understand how the scorching heat of a billion summers had turned Icarus into a cosmic cinder, baking the rocks until the last traces of gas had bubbled out of them. Why should men travel, he asked himself bitterly, across the gulf of stars at such expense and risk—merely to land on a spinning slag heap? For the same reason, he knew, that they once struggled to reach Everest and the Poles and the far places of the Earth—for the excitement of the body that was adventure, and the more enduring excitement of the mind that was discovery. It was an answer that gave him little consolation, now that he was about to be grilled like a joint on the turning spit of Icarus.

Already he could feel the first breath of heat upon his face. The boulder against which he was lying gave him protection from direct sunlight, but the glare reflected back at him from those blazing rocks only a few yards away was striking through the transparent plastic of the dome. It would grow swiftly more intense as the sun rose higher; he had even less time than he had thought, and with the knowledge came a kind of numb resignation that was beyond fear. He would wait—if he could—until the sunrise engulfed him and the capsule's cooling unit gave up the unequal struggle; then he would crack the pod and let the air gush out into the vacuum of space.

Nothing to do but to sit and think in the minutes that were left to him before his pool of shadow contracted. He did not try to direct his thoughts, but let them wander where they willed. How strange that he should be dying now, because back in the nineteen-forties—years before he was born—a man at Palomar had spotted a streak of light on a photographic plate, and had named it so appropriately after the boy who flew too near the sun.

One day, he supposed, they would build a monument here for him on this blistered plain. What would they inscribe upon it? 'Here died Colin Sherrard, astronics engineer, in the cause of Science.' That would be funny, for he had never understood half the things that the scientists were trying to do.

Yet some of the excitement of their discoveries had communicated itself to him. He remembered how the geologists had scraped away the charred skin of the asteroid, and had polished the metallic surface that lay beneath. It had been covered with a curious pattern of lines and scratches, like one of the abstract paintings of the Post-Picasso Decadents. But these lines had some meaning; they wrote the history of Icarus, though only a geologist could read it. They revealed, so Sherrard had been told, that this lump of iron and rock had not always floated alone in space. At some remote time in the past, it had been under enormous pressure—and that could mean only one thing. Billions of years ago it had been part of a much larger body, perhaps a planet like Earth. For some reason that planet had blown up, and Icarus and all the thousands of other asteroids were the fragments of that cosmic explosion.

Even at this moment, as the incandescent line of sunlight came closer, this was a thought that stirred his mind. What Sherrard was lying upon was the core of a world—perhaps a world that had once known life. In a strange, irrational way it comforted him to know that his might not be the only ghost to haunt Icarus until the end of time.

The helmet was misting up; that could only mean that the cooling unit was about to fail. It had done its work well; even now, though the rocks only a few yards away must be glowing a sullen red, the heat inside the capsule was not unendurable. When failure came, it would be sudden and catastrophic.

He reached for the red lever that would rob the sun of its prey—but before he pulled it, he would look for the last time upon Earth. Cautiously, he lowered the dark filters, adjusting them so that they still cut out the

glare from the rocks, but no longer blocked his view of space.

The stars were faint now, dimmed by the advancing glow of the corona. And just visible over the boulder whose shield would soon fail him was a stub of crimson flame, a crooked finger of fire jutting from the edge of the sun itself. He had only seconds left.

There was the Earth, there was the moon. Goodbye to them both, and to his friends and loved ones on each of them. While he was looking at the sky, the sunlight had begun to lick the base of the capsule, and he felt the first touch of fire. In a reflex as automatic as it was useless, he drew up his legs, trying to escape the advancing wave of heat.

What was that? A brilliant flash of light, infinitely brighter than any of the stars, had suddenly exploded overhead. Miles above him, a huge mirror was sailing across the sky, reflecting the sunlight as it slowly turned through space. Such a thing was utterly impossible; he was beginning to suffer from hallucinations, and it was time he took his leave. Already the sweat was pouring from his body, and in a few seconds the capsule would be a furnace.

He waited no longer, but pulled on the Emergency Release with all his waning strength, bracing himself at the same moment to face the end.

Nothing happened; the lever would not move. He tugged it again and again before he realized that it was hopelessly jammed. There was no easy way out for him, no merciful death as the air gushed from his lungs. It was then, as the true terror of his situation struck home to him, that his nerve finally broke and he began to scream like a trapped animal.

When he heard Captain McClellan's voice speaking to him, thin but clear, he knew that it must be another hallucination. Yet some last remnant of discipline and self-control checked his screaming; he clenched his teeth and listened to that familiar, commanding voice.

'Sherrard! Hold on, man! We've got a fix on you—but keep shouting!'

'Here I am!' he cried, 'but hurry, for God's sake! I'm burning!'

Deep down in what was left of his rational mind he realized what had happened. Some feeble ghost of a signal was leaking through the broken stubs of his antennas, and the searchers had heard his screams—as he was hearing their voices. That meant they must be very close indeed, and the knowledge gave him sudden strength.

He stared through the steaming plastic of the dome, looking once more for that impossible mirror in the sky. There it was again—and now he realized that the baffling perspectives of space had tricked his senses. The mirror was not miles away, nor was it huge. It was almost on top of him, and it was moving fast.

He was still shouting when it slid across the face of the rising sun, and its blessed shadow fell upon him like a cool wind that had blown out of the heart of winter, over leagues of snow and ice. Now that it was so close, he recognized it at once; it was merely a large metal-foil radiation screen, no doubt hastily snatched from one of the instrument sites. In the safety of its shadow, his friends had been searching for him.

A heavy-duty, two-man capsule was hovering overhead, holding the glittering shield in one set of arms and reaching for him with the other. Even through the misty dome and the haze of heat that still sapped his senses, he recognized Captain McClellan's anxious face, looking down at him from the other pod.

So this was what birth was like, for truly he had been reborn. He was too exhausted for gratitude—that would come later—but as he rose from the burning rocks his eyes sought and found the bright star of Earth. 'Here I am,' he said silently. 'I'm coming back.'

Back to enjoy and cherish all the beauties of the world he had thought were lost forever. No—not all of them.

He would never enjoy summer again.

BAPTISM OF FIRE

Robert A. Heinlein

horby, an ex slave-boy (or fraki) from the planet Sargon, has been adopted by the Family of the Free Trader ship *Sisu*. He finds the new hierarchy and his new training challenging and baffling . . .

By the time *Sisu* approached Losian Thorby had a battle station worthy of a man. His first assignment had been to assist in the central dressing station, an unnecessary job. But his background in mathematics got him promoted.

He had been attending the ship's school. Baslim had given him a broad education, but this fact did not stand out to his instructors, since most of what they regarded as necessary—the Finnish language as they spoke it, the history of the People and of *Sisu*, trading customs, business practices, and export and import laws of many planets, hydroponics and ship's economy, ship safety and damage control—were subjects that Baslim had not even touched; he had emphasized languages, science, mathematics, galactography and history. The new subjects Thorby gobbled with a speed possible only to one renshawed by Baslim's strenuous methods. The Traders needed applied mathematics—book-keeping and accounting, astrogation, nucleonics for a hydrogen-fusion-powered n-ship. Thorby splashed through the first, the second was hardly more difficult, but as for the third, the ship's schoolmaster was astounded that this ex-fraki had already studied multidimensional geometries.

So he reported to the Captain that they had a mathematical genius aboard.

This was not true. But it got Thorby reassigned to the starboard fire-control computer.

The greatest hazard to trading ships is in the first and last legs of each jump, when a ship is below speed-of-light. It is theoretically possible to detect and intercept a ship going many times speed-of-light, when it is irrational to the four-dimensional space of the senses; in practice it is about as easy as hitting a particular raindrop with a bow and arrow during a storm at midnight. But it is feasible to hunt down a ship moving below speed-of-light if the attacker is fast and the victim is a big lumbering freighter.

The *Sisu* had acceleration of one hundred standard gravities and used it all to cut down the hazard time. But a ship which speeds up by a kilometre per second each second will take three and one half standard days to reach speed-of-light.

Half a week is a long, nervous time to wait. Doubling acceleration would have cut danger time by half and made the *Sisu* as agile as a raider—but it would have meant a hydrogen-fission chamber eight times as big with parallel increase in radiation shielding, auxiliary equipment, and paramagnetic capsule to contain the hydrogen reaction; the added mass would eliminate cargo capacity. Traders are working people; even if there were no parasites preying on them they could not afford to burn their profits in the inexorable workings of an exponential law of multidimensional physics. So the *Sisu* had the best legs she could afford—but not long enough to outrun a ship unburdened by cargo.

Nor could *Sisu* manoeuvre easily. She had to go precisely in the right direction when she entered the trackless night of n-space, else when she came out she would be too far from market; such a mistake could turn the ledger from black to red. Still more hampering, her skipper had to be prepared to cut power entirely, or risk having his n-ship artificial gravity field destroyed—and thereby make strawberry jam of the Family as soft bodies were suddenly exposed to one hundred gravities.

This is why a captain gets stomach ulcers; it isn't dickering for cargoes, figuring discounts and commissions, and trying to guess what goods will show the best return. It's not long jumps through the black—that is when he can relax and dandle babies. It is starting and ending a jump that kills him off, the long aching hours when he may have to make a split-second decision involving the lives—or freedom—of his family.

If raiders wished to destroy merchant ships, *Sisu* and her sisters would not stand a chance. But the raider wants loot and slaves; it gains him nothing simply to blast a ship.

Merchantmen are limited by no qualms; an attacking ship's destruction is the ideal outcome. Atomic target-seekers are dreadfully expensive, and using them up is rough on profit-and-loss—but there is no holding back if the computer says the target can be reached—whereas a raider will use destruction weapons only to save himself. His tactic is to blind the trader, burn out her instruments so that he can get close enough to paralyse everyone aboard—or, failing that, kill without destroying ship and cargo.

The trader runs if she can, fights if she must. But when she fights, she fights to kill.

Whenever *Sisu* was below speed-of-light, she listened with artificial senses to every disturbance in multi-space, the whisper of n-space communication or

the 'white' roar of a ship boosting at many gravities. Data poured into the ships' astrogational analog of space and the questions were: Where is this other ship? What is its course? speed? acceleration? Can it catch us before we reach n-space?

If the answers were threatening, digested data channelled into port and starboard fire-control computers and *Sisu* braced herself to fight. Ordnancemen armed A-bomb target seekers, caressed their sleek sides and muttered charms; the Chief Engineer unlocked the suicide switch which could let the power plant become a hydrogen bomb of monstrous size and prayed that, in final extremity, he would have the courage to deliver his people into the shelter of death; the Captain sounded the clangour calling the ship from watch-and-watch to General Quarters. Cooks switched off fires; auxiliary engineers closed down air circulation; farmers said good-bye to their green growing things and hurried to fighting stations; mothers with babies mustered, then strapped down and held those babies tightly.

Then the waiting started.

But not for Thorby—not for those assigned to fire-control computers. Sweating into their straps, for the next minutes or hours the life of *Sisu* is in their hands. The fire-control computer machines, chewing with millisecond meditation data from the analog, decide whether or not torpedoes can reach target, then offer four answers: ballistic 'possible' or 'impossible' for projected condition, yes or no for condition changed by one ship, or the other, or both, through cutting power. These answers automatic circuits could handle alone, but machines do not think. Half of each computer is designed to allow the operator to ask what the situation might be in the far future of five minutes or so from now if variables change . . . and whether the target might be reached under such changes.

Any variable can be shaded by human judgement;

an intuitive projection by a human operator can save his ship—or lose it. A paralysis beam travels at speed-of-light; torpedoes never have time to get up to more than a few hundred kilometres per second—yet it is possible for raider to come within beaming range, have his pencil of paralysing radiation on its way, and the trader to launch a target-seeker before the beam strikes . . . and still be saved when the outlaw flames into atomic mist a little later.

But if the operator is too eager by a few seconds, or overly cautious by the same, he can lose his ship. Too eager, the missile will fail to reach target; too cautious, it will never be launched.

Seasoned oldsters are not good at these jobs. The perfect firecontrolman is an adolescent, or young man or woman, fast in thought and action, confident, with intuitive grasp of mathematical relations beyond rote and rule, and not afraid of death he cannot yet imagine.

The traders must be always alert for such young-sters; Thorby seemed to have the feel for mathematics; he might have the other talents for a job something like chess played under terrific pressure and a fast game of spat ball. His mentor was Jeri Kingsolver, his nephew and roommate. Jeri was junior in family rank but appeared to be older; he called Thorby 'Uncle' outside the computer room; on the job Thorby called him 'Starboard Senior Firecontrolman' and added 'Sir'.

During long weeks of the dive through dark towards Losian, Jeri drilled Thorby. Thorby was supposed to be training for hydroponics and Jeri was the Super-cargo's Senior Clerk, but the ship had plenty of farmers and the Supercargo's office was never very busy in space; Captain Krausa directed Jeri to keep Thorby hard at it in the computer room.

Since the ship remained at battle stations for half a week while boosting to speed-of-light, each fighting station had two persons assigned watch-and-watch.

Jeri's junior controlman was his younger sister Mata. The computer had twin consoles, either of which could command by means of a selector switch. At General Quarters they sat side by side, with Jeri controlling and Mata ready to take over.

After a stiff course in what the machine could do Jeri put Thorby at one console, Mata at the other and fed them problems from the ship's control room. Each console recorded; it was possible to see what decisions each operator had made and how these compared with those made in battle, for the data were from records, real or threatened battles in the past.

Shortly Thorby became extremely irked; Mata was enormously better at it than he was.

So he tried harder and got worse. While he sweated, trying to outguess a slave raider which had once been on *Sisu*'s screens, he was painfully aware of a slender, dark, rather pretty girl beside him, her swift fingers making tiny adjustments among keys and knobs, changing a bias or modifying a vector, herself relaxed and unhurried. It was humiliating afterwards to find that his pacesetter had 'saved the ship' while he had failed.

Worse still, he was aware of her as a girl and did not know it—all he knew was that she made him uneasy.

After one run Jeri called from ship's control. 'End of drill. Stand by.' He appeared shortly and examined their tapes, reading marks on sensitized paper as another might read print. He pursed his lips over Thorby's record. 'Trainee, you fired three times ... and not a one of your beasts got within fifty thousand kilometres of the enemy. We don't mind expense—it's merely Grandmother's blood. But the object is to blast him, not scare him into a fit. You have to wait until you can hit.'

'I did my best!'

'Not good enough. Let's see yours, Sis.'

The nickname irritated Thorby still more. Brother

and sister were fond of each other and did not bother with titles. So Thorby had tried using their names ... and had been snubbed; he was 'Trainee', they were 'Senior Controlman' and 'Junior Controlman'. There was nothing he could do; at drill he was junior. For a week, Thorby addressed Jeri as 'Foster Ortho-Nephew' outside of drills and Jeri had carefully addressed him by family title. Then Thorby decided it was silly and went back to calling him Jeri. But Jeri continued to call him 'Trainee' during drill, and so did Mata.

Jeri looked over his sister's record and nodded. 'Very nice, Sis! You're within a second of post-analysed optimum, and three seconds better than the shot that got the so-and-so. I have to admit that's sweet shooting ... because the real run is my own. That raider off Ingstel ... remember?'

'I certainly do.' She glanced at Thorby.

Thorby felt disgusted. 'It's not fair!' He started hauling at safety-belt buckles.

Jeri looked surprised. 'What, Trainee?'

'I said it's not fair! You send down a problem, I tackle it cold—and get bawled out because I'm not perfect. But all she had to do is to fiddle with controls to get an answer she already knows ... to make me look cheap!'

Mata was looking stricken. Thorby headed for the door. 'I never asked for this! I'm going to the Captain and ask for another job.'

'Trainee!'

Thorby stopped. Jeri went on quietly. 'Sit down. When I'm through, you can see the Captain—if you think it's advisable.'

Thorby sat down.

'I've two things to say,' Jeri continued coldly. 'First—' He turned to his sister. 'Junior Controlman, did you know what problem this was when you were tracking?'

'No, Senior Controlman.'

'Have you worked it before?'

'I don't think so.'

'How was it you remembered it?'

'What? Why, you said it was the raider off Ingstel. I'll never forget because of the dinner after-wards—you sat with Great Grandmo—with the Chief Officer.'

Jeri turned to Thorby. 'You see? She tracked it cold . . . as cold as I had to when it happened. And she did even better than I did; I'm proud to have her as my junior tracker. For your information, Mister Stupid Junior Trainee, this engagement took place before the Junior Controlman became a trainee. She hasn't even run it in practice. She's just better at it than you are.'

'All right,' Thorby said sullenly. 'I'll probably never be any good. I said I wanted to quit.'

'I'm talking. Nobody asks for this job; it's a headache. Nobody quits it, either. After a while the job quits him, when post-analysis shows that he is losing his touch. Maybe I'm beginning to. But I promise you this: you'll either learn, or *I* will go to the Captain and tell him you don't measure up. In the meantime . . . if I have any lip out of you, I'll haul you up before the Chief Officer!' He snapped, 'Extra drill run. Battle stations. Cast loose your equipment.' He left the room.

Moments later his voice reached them. 'Bogie! Star-board computer room, report!'

The call to dinner sounded; Mata said gravely, 'Starboard tracker manned. Data showing, starting

— 182 —

run.' Her fingers started caressing keys. Thorby bent
over his own controls; he wasn't hungry anyhow. For
days Thorby spoke with Jeri only formally. He saw
Mata at drill, or across the lounge at meals; he treated
her with cold correctness and tried to do as well as she
did. He could have seen her at other times; young
people associated freely in public places. She was
taboo to him, both as his niece and because they were
of the same moiety, but that was no bar to social
relations.

Jeri he could not avoid; they ate at the same table,
slept in the same room. But Thorby could and did
throw up a barrier of formality. No one said anything—these things happened. Even Fritz pretended
not to notice.

But one afternoon Thorby dropped into the lounge
to see a story film with a Sargonese background;
Thorby sat through it to pick it to pieces. But when it
was over he could not avoid noticing Mata because she
walked over, stood in front of him, addressed him
humbly as her uncle and asked if he would care for a
game of spat ball before supper?

He was about to refuse when he noticed her face;
she was watching him with tragic eagerness. So he
answered, 'Why, thanks, Mata. Work up an appetite.'

She broke into smiles. 'Good! I've got Ilsa holding a
table. Let's!'

Thorby beat her three games and tied one . . . a
remarkable score, since she was female champion and

was allowed only one point handicap when playing the male champion. But he did not think about it; he was enjoying himself.

His performance picked up, partly through the grimness with which he worked, partly because he did have feeling for complex geometry, and partly because the beggar's boy had had his brain sharpened by an ancient discipline. Jeri never again compared aloud the performances of Mata and Thorby and gave only brief comments on Thorby's results: 'Better,' or 'Coming along,' and eventually, 'You're getting there.' Thorby's morale soared; he loosened up and spent more time socially, playing spat ball with Mata rather frequently.

Towards the end of journey through darkness they finished the last drill one morning and Jeri called out, 'Stand easy! I'll be a few minutes.' Thorby relaxed from pleasant strain. But after a moment he fidgeted; he had a hunch that he had been in tune with his instruments. 'Junior Controlman ... do you suppose he would mind if I looked at my tape?'

'I don't think so,' Mata answered. 'I'll take it out; then it's my responsibility.'

'I don't want to get you in trouble.'

'You won't,' Mata answered serenely. She reached back of Thorby's console, pulled out the strip record, blew on it to keep it from curling, and examined it. Then she pulled her own strip, compared the two.

She looked at him gravely. 'That's a very good run, Thorby.'

It was the first time she had ever spoken his name. But Thorby hardly noticed. 'Really? You mean it?'

'It's a *very* good run ... Thorby. We both got hits. But yours is optimum between "possible" and "critical limit"—whereas mine is too eager. See?'

Thorby could read strips only haltingly, but he was happy to take her word for it. Jeri came in, took both strips, looked at Thorby's, then looked more closely. 'I dug up the post-analysis before I came down,' he said.

'Yes, sir?' Thorby said eagerly.

'Mmm . . . I'll check it after chow—but it looks as if your mistakes had cancelled out.'

Mata said, 'Why, Bud, that's a perfect run and you know it!'

'Suppose it is?' Jeri grinned. 'You wouldn't want our star pupil to get a swelled head, would you?'

'Pooh!'

'Right back at you, small and ugly sister. Let's go to chow.'

They went through a narrow passage into trunk corridor of second deck, where they walked abreast. Thorby gave a deep sigh.

'Trouble?' his nephew asked.

'Not a bit!' Thorby put an arm around each of them. 'Jeri, you and Mata are going to make a marksman out of me yet.'

It was the first time Thorby had addressed his teacher by name since the day he had received the scorching. But Jeri accepted his uncle's overture without stiffness. 'Don't get your hopes up, bunkmate. But I think we've got it licked.' He added, 'I see Great Aunt Tora is giving us her famous cold eye. If anybody wants my opinion, I think Sis can walk unassisted—I'm sure Great Aunt thinks so.'

'Pooh to her, too!' Mata said briskly. 'Thorby just made a perfect run.'

*

Sisu came out of darkness, dropping below speed-of-light. Losian's sun blazed less than fifty billion kilometres away; in a few days they would reach their next market. The ship went to watch-and-watch battle stations.

Mata took her watch alone; Jeri required the trainee to stand watches with him. The first watch was always free from strain; even if a raider had accurate information via n-space communicator of *Sisu*'s time of departure and destination, it was impossible in a jump of many light-years to predict the exact time and place where she would poke her nose out into rational space.

Jeri settled in his chair some minutes after Thorby had strapped down with that age-old tense feeling that this time it was not practice. Jeri grinned at him. 'Relax. If you get your bloodstream loaded, your back will ache, and you'll never last.'

Thorby grinned feebly. 'I'll try.'

'That's better. We're going to play a game.' Jeri pulled a boxlike contrivance out of a pocket, snapped it open.

'What is that?'

'A "killjoy". It fits here.' Jeri slipped it over the switch that determined which console was in command. 'Can you see the switch?'

'Huh? No.'

'Hand the man the prize.' Jeri fiddled with the switch behind the screen. 'Which of us is in control in case we have to launch a bomb now?'

'How can I tell? Take that off, Jeri; it makes me nervous.'

'That's the game. Maybe I'm controlling and you are just going through motions; maybe *you* are the man at the trigger and I'm asleep in my chair. Every so often I'll fiddle with the switch—but you won't know how I've left it. So when a flap comes—and one will; I feel it in my bones—you can't assume that good old Jeri, the man with the micrometer fingers, has the situation under control. You might have to save the firm. *You.*'

Thorby had a queasy vision of waiting men and bombs in the missile room below—waiting for him to solve precisely an impossible problem of life and death, of warped space and shifting vectors and complex geometry. 'You're kidding,' he said feebly. 'You wouldn't leave me in control. Why, the Captain would skin you alive.'

'Ah, that's where you're wrong. There always comes a day when a trainee makes his first real run. After that, he's a controlman ... or an angel. But we don't let you worry at the time. Oh no! we just keep you worried all the time. Now here's the game. Any time I say, "Now!" you guess who has control. You guess right, I owe you one dessert; you guess wrong, you owe me one. *Now!*'

Thorby thought quickly. 'I guess I've got it.'

'Wrong.' Jeri lifted the killjoy. 'You owe me one dessert—and it's berry tart tonight; my mouth is watering. But faster; you're supposed to make quick decisions. Now!'

'You've still got it!'

'So I have. Even. Now!'

'You!'

'Nope. See? And I eat your tart—I ought to quit while I'm ahead. Love that juice! Now!'

When Mata relieved them, Jeri owned Thorby's desserts for the next four days. 'We start again with that score,' Jeri said, 'except that I'm going to collect that berry tart. But I forgot to tell you the big prize.'

'Which is?'

'Comes the real thing, we bet three desserts. After it's over, you guess and we settle. Always bet more on real ones.'

Mata sniffed. 'Bud, are you trying to make him nervous?'

'Are you nervous, Thorby?'

'Nope!'

'Quit fretting, Sis. Got it firmly in your grubby little hands?'

'I relieve you, sir.'

'Come on, Thorby; let's eat. Berry tarts—aaah!'

Three days later the score stood even, but only because Thorby had missed most of his desserts. *Sisu* was enormously slowed, almost to planetary speeds, and Losian's sun loomed large on the screens. Thorby decided, with mildest regret, that his ability to fight would not be tested this jump.

Then the general alarm made him rear up against safety belts. Jeri had been talking; his head jerked around, he looked at displays, and his hands moved to his controls. 'Get on it!' he yelped. 'This one's real.'

Thorby snapped out of shock and bent over his board. The analog globe was pouring data to them; the ballistic situation had built up. Good heavens, it was *close*! And matching in fast! How had anything moved in so close without being detected? Then he quit thinking and started investigating answers . . . no, not yet . . . before long though . . . could the bandit turn a little at that boost and reduce his approach? . . . try a projection at an assumed six gravities of turning . . . would a missile reach him? . . . would it still reach him if he did not—

He hardly felt Mata's gentle touch on his shoulder. But he heard Jeri snap, 'Stay out, Sis! We're on it, we're on it!'

A light blinked on Thorby's board; the squawk horn sounded, 'Friendly craft, friendly craft! Losian planetary patrol, identified. Return to watch-and-watch.'

Thorby took a deep breath, felt a great load lift.

'*Continue your run!*' screamed Jeri.

'*Huh?*'

'*Finish your run!* That's no Losian craft; *that's a raider!* Losians can't manoeuvre that way! You've got it, boy, you've got it! *Nail him!*'

Thorby heard Mata's frightened gasp, but he was again at his problem. Change anything? Could he reach him? Could he still reach him in the cone of possible manoeuvre? *Now!* He armed his board and let the computer give the order, on projection.

He heard Jeri's voice faintly; Jeri seemed to be talking very slowly. 'Missile away. I think you got him . . . but you were eager. Get off another one before their beam hits us.'

Automatically Thorby complied. Time was too short to try another solution; he ordered the machine to send another missile according to projection. He then saw by his board that the target was no longer under power and decided with a curiously empty feeling that his first missile had destroyed it.

'That's all!' Jeri announced. 'Now!'

'What?'

'Who had it? You or me? Three desserts.'

'I had it,' Thorby said with certainty. In another level he decided that he would never really be a Trader—to Jeri that target had been—just fraki. Or three desserts.

'Wrong. That puts me three up. I turned coward and kept control myself. Of course the bombs were disarmed and the launchers locked as soon as the Captain gave the word . . . but I didn't have the nerve to risk an accident with a friendly ship.'

'*Friendly* ship!'

'Of course. But for you, Assistant Junior Controlman, it was your first real one . . . as I intended.'

Thorby's head floated. Mata said, 'Bud, you're mean to collect. You cheated.'

'Sure I cheated. But he's a blooded controlman now, just the same. And I'm going to collect, just the very same. Ice cream tonight!'

COLLECTING TEAM

Robert Silverberg

From fifty thousand miles up, the situation looked promising. It was a middle-sized, brown-and-green, inviting-looking planet, with no sign of cities or any other such complications. Just a pleasant sort of place, the very sort we were looking for to redeem what had been a pretty futile expedition.

I turned to Clyde Holdreth, who was staring reflectively at the thermocouple.

'Well? What do you think?'

'Looks fine to me. Temperature's about seventy down there—nice and warm and plenty of air. I think it's worth a try.'

Lee Davison came strolling out from the storage hold, smelling of animals, as usual. He was holding one of the blue monkeys we picked up on Alpheraz, and the little beast was crawling up his arm. 'Have we found something, gentlemen?'

'We've found a planet,' I said. 'How's the storage space in the hold?'

'Don't worry about that. We've got room for a whole zoo-full more, before we get filled up. It hasn't been a very fruitful trip.'

'No,' I agreed. 'It hasn't. Well? Shall we go down and see what's to be seen?'

'Might as well,' Holdreth said. 'We can't go back to

Earth with just a couple of blue monkeys and some anteaters, you know.'

'I'm in favour of a landing too,' said Davison. 'You?'

I nodded. 'I'll set up the charts, and you get your animals comfortable for deceleration.'

Davison disappeared back into the storage hold, while Holdreth scribbled furiously in the logbook, writing down the co-ordinates of the planet below, its general description, and so forth. Aside from being a collecting team for the zoological department of the Bureau of Interstellar Affairs, we also double as a survey ship, and the planet down below was listed as *unexplored* on our charts.

I glanced out at the mottled brown-and-green ball spinning slowly in the viewport, and felt the warning twinge of gloom that came to me every time we made a landing on a new and strange world. Repressing it, I started to figure out a landing orbit. From behind me came the furious chatter of the blue monkeys as Davison strapped them into their acceleration cradles, and under that the deep, unmusical honking of the Rigelian anteaters, nosily bleating their displeasure.

*

The planet was inhabited, all right. We hadn't had the ship on the ground more than a minute before the local fauna began to congregate. We stood at the viewport and looked out in wonder.

'This is one of those things you dream about,' Davison said, stroking his little beard nervously. 'Look at them! There must be a thousand different species out there.'

'I've never seen anything like it,' said Holdreth.

I computed how much storage space we had left and how many of the thronging creatures outside we would be able to bring back with us. 'How are we going to decide what to take and what to leave behind?'

'Does it matter?' Holdreth said gaily. 'This is what you call an embarrassment of riches, I guess. We just grab the dozen most bizarre creatures and blast off—and save the rest for another trip. It's too bad we wasted all that time wandering around near Rigel.'

'We *did* get the anteaters,' Davison pointed out. They were his finds, and he was proud of them.

I smiled sourly. 'Yeah. We got the anteaters there.' The anteaters honked at that moment, loud and clear. 'You know, that's one set of beasts I think I could do without.'

'Bad attitude,' Holdreth said. 'Unprofessional.'

'Whoever said I was a zoologist, anyway? I'm just a spaceship pilot, remember. And if I don't like the way those anteaters talk—and—smell—I see no reason why I—'

'Say, look at that one,' Davison said suddenly.

I glanced out the viewport and saw a new beast emerging from the thick-packed vegetation in the background. I've seen some fairly strange creatures since I was assigned to the zoological department, but this one took the grand prize.

It was about the size of a giraffe, moving on long, wobbly legs and with a tiny head up at the end of a preposterous neck. Only it had six legs and a bunch of writhing snakelike tentacles as well, and its eyes, great violet globes, stood out nakedly on the ends of two thick stalks. It must have been twenty feet high. It moved with exaggerated grace through the swarm of beasts surrounding our ship, pushed its way smoothly towards the vessel, and peered gravely in at the viewport. One purple eye stared directly at me, the other at Davison. Oddly, it seemed to me as if it were trying to tell us something.

'Big one, isn't it?' Davison said finally.

'I'll bet you'd like to bring one back, too.'

'Maybe we can fit a young one aboard,' Davison

said. 'If we can find a young one.' He turned to
Holdreth. 'How's that air analysis coming? I'd like to
get out there and start collecting. God, that's a crazy-
looking beast!'

The animal outside had apparently finished its
inspection of us, for it pulled its head away and,
gathering its legs under itself, squatted near the ship.
A small doglike creature with stiff spines running
along its back began to bark at the big creature, which
took no notice. The other animals, which came in all
shapes and sizes, continued to mill around the ship,
evidently very curious about the newcomer to their
world. I could see Davison's eyes thirsty with the
desire to take the whole kit and caboodle back to Earth
with him. I knew what was running through his mind.
He was dreaming of the umpteen thousand species of
extra-terrestrial wildlife roaming around out there,
and to each one he was attaching a neat little tag:
Something-or-other davisoni.

'The air's fine,' Holdreth announced abruptly, looking up from his test-tubes. 'Get your butterfly nets and let's see what we can catch.'

*

There was something I didn't like about the place. It was just too good to be true, and I learned long ago that nothing ever is. There's always a catch someplace.

Only this seemed to be on the level. The planet was a bonanza for zoologists, and Davison and Holdreth were having the time of their lives, hipdeep in obliging specimens.

'I've never seen anything like it,' Davison said for at least the fiftieth time, as he scooped up a small purplish squirrel-like creature and examined it curiously. The squirrel stared back, examining Davison just as curiously.

'Let's take some of these,' Davison said. 'I like them.'

'Carry 'em on in, then,' I said, shrugging. I didn't care which specimens they chose, so long as they filled up the storage hold quickly and let me blast off on schedule. I watched as Davison grabbed a pair of the squirrels and brought them into the ship.

Holdreth came over to me. He was carrying a sort of a dog with insect-faceted eyes and gleaming furless skin. 'How's this one, Gus?'

'Fine,' I said bleakly. 'Wonderful.'

He put the animal down—it didn't scamper away, just sat there smiling at us—and looked at me. He ran a hand through his fast-vanishing hair. 'Listen, Gus, you've been gloomy all day. What's eating you?'

'I don't like this place,' I said.

'Why? Just on general principles?'

'It's too *easy*, Clyde. Much too easy. These animals just flock around here waiting to be picked up.'

Holdreth chuckled. 'And you're used to a struggle, aren't you? You're just angry at us because we have it so simple here!'

'When I think of the trouble we went through just to get a pair of miserable vile-smelling anteaters, and—'

'Come off it, Gus. We'll load up in a hurry, if you like. But this place is a zoological gold mine!'

I shook my head. 'I don't like it, Clyde. Not at all.'

Holdreth laughed again and picked up his faceted-eyed dog. 'Say, know where I can find another of these, Gus?'

'Right over there,' I said, pointing. 'By that tree. With its tongue hanging out. It's just waiting to be carried away.'

Holdreth looked and smiled. 'What do you know about that!' He snared his specimen and carried both of them inside.

I walked away to survey the grounds. The planet was too flatly incredible for me to accept on face value, without at least a look-see, despite the blithe way my two companions were snapping up specimens.

For one thing, animals just don't exist this way—in big miscellaneous quantities, living all together happily. I hadn't noticed more than a few of each kind, and there must have been five hundred different species, each one stranger-looking than the next. Nature doesn't work that way.

For another, they all seemed to be on friendly terms with one another, though they acknowledged the unofficial leadership of the giraffe-like creature. Nature doesn't work *that* way, either. I hadn't seen one quarrel between the animals yet. That argued that they were all herbivores, which didn't make sense ecologically.

I shrugged my shoulders and walked on.

*

Half an hour later, I knew a little more about the geography of our bonanza. We were on either an immense island or a peninsula of some sort, because I could see a huge body of water bordering the land some ten miles off. Our vicinity was fairly flat, except for a good-sized hill from which I could see the terrain.

There was a thick, heavily-wooded jungle not too far from the ship. The forest spread out all the way towards the water in one direction, but ended abruptly in the other. We had brought the ship down right at the edge of the clearing. Apparently most of the animals we saw lived in the jungle.

On the other side of our clearing was a low, broad plain that seemed to trail away into a desert in the distance; I could see an uninviting stretch of barren sand that contrasted strangely with the fertile jungle to my left. There was a small lake to the side. It was, I saw, the sort of country likely to attract a varied fauna, since there seemed to be every sort of habitat within a small area.

And the fauna! Although I'm a zoologist only by osmosis, picking up both my interest and my knowledge second-hand from Holdreth and Davison, I couldn't help but be astonished by the wealth of strange animals. They came in all different shapes and sizes, colours and odours, and the only thing they all had in common was their friendliness. During the course of my afternoon's wanderings a hundred animals must have come marching boldly right up to me, given me the once-over, and walked away. This included half a dozen kinds that I hadn't seen before, plus one of the eye-stalked, intelligent-looking giraffes and a furless dog. Again, I had the feeling that the giraffe seemed to be trying to communicate.

I didn't like it. I didn't like it at all.

I returned to our clearing, and saw Holdreth and Davison still buzzing madly around, trying to cram as many animals as they could into our hold.

'How's it going?' I asked.

'Hold's all full,' Davison said. 'We're busy making our alternate selections now.' I saw him carrying out Holdreth's two furless dogs and picking up instead a pair of eight-legged penguinish things that uncom-

plainingly allowed themselves to be carried in. Holdreth was frowning unhappily.

'What do you want *those* for, Lee? Those dog-like ones seem much more interesting, don't you think?'

'No,' Davison said. 'I'd rather bring along these two. They're curious beasts, aren't they? Look at the muscular network that connects the—'

'Hold it, fellows,' I said. I peered at the animal in Davison's hands and glanced up. 'This *is* a curious beast,' I said. 'It's got eight legs.'

'You becoming a zoologist?' Holdreth asked, amused.

'No—but I am getting puzzled. Why should this one have eight legs, some of the others here six, and some of the others only four?'

They looked at me blankly, with the scorn of professionals.

'I mean, there ought to be some sort of logic to evolution here, shouldn't there? On Earth we've developed a four-legged pattern of animal life; on Venus, they usually run to six legs. But have you ever seen an evolutionary hodgepodge like this place before?'

'There are stranger setups,' Holdreth said. 'The symbiotes on Sirius Three, the burrowers of Mizar—but you're right, Gus. This is a peculiar evolutionary dispersal. I think we ought to stay and investigate it fully.'

Instantly I knew from the bright expression on Davison's face that I had blundered, had made things worse than ever. I decided to take a new tack.

'I don't agree,' I said. 'I think we ought to leave with what we've got, and come back with a larger expedition later.'

Davison chuckled. 'Come on, Gus, don't be silly! This is a chance of a lifetime for us—why should we call in the whole zoological department on it?'

I didn't want to tell them I was afraid of staying

longer. I crossed my arms. 'Lee, I'm the pilot of this ship, and you'll have to listen to me. The schedule calls for a brief stopover here, and we have to leave. Don't tell me I'm being silly.'

'But you are, man! You're standing blindly in the path of scientific investigation, of—'

'Listen to me, Lee. Our food is calculated on a pretty narrow margin, to allow you fellows more room for storage. And this is strictly a collecting team. There's no provision for extended stays on any one planet. Unless you want to wind up eating your own specimens, I suggest you allow me to get out of here.'

They were silent for a moment. Then Holdreth said, 'I guess we can't argue with that, Lee. Let's listen to Gus and go back now. There's plenty of time to investigate this place later when we can take longer.'

'But—oh, all right,' Davison said reluctantly. He picked up the eight-legged penguins. 'Let me stash these things in the hold, and we can leave.' He looked strangely at me, as if I had done something criminal.

As he started into the ship, I called to him.

'What is it, Gus?'

'Look here, Lee. I don't *want* to pull you away from here. It's simply a matter of food,' I lied, masking my nebulous suspicions.

'I know how it is, Gus.' He turned and entered the ship.

I stood there thinking about nothing at all for a moment, then went inside myself to begin setting up the blastoff orbit.

I got as far as calculating the fuel expenditure when I noticed something. Feedwires were dangling crazily down from the control cabinet. Somebody had wrecked our drive mechanism, but thoroughly.

For a long moment, I stared stiffly at the sabotaged drive. Then I turned and headed into the storage hold.

'Davison?'

'What is it, Gus?'

'Come out here a second, will you?'

I waited, and a few minutes later he appeared, frowning impatiently. 'What do you want, Gus? I'm busy and I—'

His mouth dropped open. *'Look at the drive!'*

'You look at it,' I snapped. 'I'm sick. Go get Holdreth, on the double.'

While he was gone I tinkered with the shattered mechanism. Once I had the cabinet panel off and could see the inside, I felt a little better; the drive wasn't damaged beyond repair, though it had been pretty well scrambled. Three or four days of hard work with a screwdriver and solderbeam might get the ship back into functioning order.

But that didn't make me any less angry. I heard Holdreth and Davison entering behind me, and I whirled to face them.

'All right, you idiots. Which one of you did this?'

They opened their mouths in protesting squawks at the same instant. I listened to them for a while, then said, 'One at a time!'

'If you're implying that one of us deliberately sabotaged the ship,' Holdreth said, 'I want you to know—'

'I'm not implying anything. But the way it looks to me, you two decided you'd like to stay here a while longer to continue your investigations, and figured the easiest way of getting me to agree was to wreck the drive.' I glared hotly at them. 'Well, I've got news for you. I can fix this, and I can fix it in a couple of days. So go on—get about your business! Get all the zoologizing you can in, while you still have time. I—'

Davison laid a hand gently on my arm. 'Gus,' he said quietly, *'We didn't do it.* Neither of us.'

Suddenly all the anger drained out of me and was replaced by raw fear. I could see that Davison meant it.

'If you didn't do it, and Holdreth didn't do it, and *I* didn't do it—then who did?'

Davison shrugged.

'Maybe it's one of us who doesn't know he's doing it,' I suggested. 'Maybe—' I stopped. 'Oh, that's nonsense. Hand me that tool-kit, will you, Lee?'

They left to tend to the animals, and I set to work on the repair job, dismissing all further speculations and suspicions from my mind, concentrating solely on joining Lead A to Input A and Transistor F to Potentiometer K, as indicated. It was slow, nerve-harrowing work, and by mealtime I had accomplished only the barest preliminaries. My fingers were starting to quiver from the strain of small-scale work, and I decided to give up the job for the day and get back to it tomorrow.

I slept uneasily, my nightmares punctuated by the moaning of the accursed anteaters and the occasional squeals, chuckles, bleats, and hisses of the various other creatures in the hold. It must have been four in the morning before I dropped off into a really sound sleep, and what was left of the night passed swiftly. The next thing I knew, hands were shaking me and I was looking up into the pale, tense faces of Holdreth and Davison.

I pushed my sleep-stuck eyes open and blinked. 'Huh? What's going on?'

Holdreth leaned down and shook me savagely. 'Get up, Gus!'

I struggled to my feet slowly. 'Hell of a thing to do, wake a fellow up in the middle of the—'

I found myself being propelled from my cabin and

led down the corridor to the control room. Blearily, I followed where Holdreth pointed, and then I woke up in a hurry.

The drive was battered again. Someone—or *something*—had completely undone my repair job of the night before.

*

If there had been bickering among us, it stopped. This was past the category of a joke now; it couldn't be laughed off, and we found ourselves working together as a tight unit again, trying desperately to solve the puzzle before it was too late.

'Let's review the situation,' Holdreth said, pacing nervously up and down the control cabin. 'The drive has been sabotaged twice. None of us knows who did it, and on a conscious level each of us is convinced *he* didn't do it.'

He paused. 'That leaves us with two possibilities. Either, as Gus suggested, one of us is doing it unaware of it even himself, or someone else is doing it while we're not looking. Neither possibility is a very cheerful one.'

'We can stay on guard, though,' I said. 'Here's what I propose; first, have one of us awake at all times—sleep in shifts, that is, with somebody guarding the drive until I get it fixed. Two—jettison all the animals aboard ship.'

'What?'

'He's right,' Davison said. 'We don't know what we

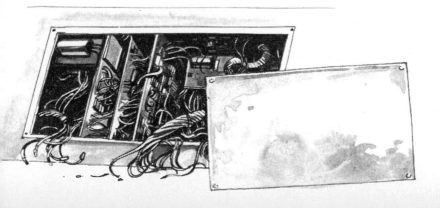

may have brought aboard. They don't seem to be intelligent, but we can't be sure. That purple-eyed baby giraffe, for instance—suppose he's been hypnotizing us into damaging the drive ourselves? How can we tell?'

'Oh, but—' Holdreth started to protest, then stopped and frowned soberly. 'I suppose we'll have to admit the possibility,' he said, obviously unhappy about the prospect of freeing our captives. 'We'll empty out the hold, and you see if you can get the drive fixed. Maybe later we'll recapture them all, if nothing further develops.'

We agreed to that, and Holdreth and Davison cleared the ship of its animal cargo while I set to work determinedly at the drive mechanism. By nightfall, I had managed to accomplish as much as I had the day before.

I sat up as watch the first shift, aboard the strangely quiet ship. I paced around the drive cabin, fighting the great temptation to doze off, and managed to last through until the time Holdreth arrived to relieve me.

Only—when he showed up, he gasped and pointed at the drive. It had been ripped apart a third time.

*

Now we had no excuse, no explanation. The expedition had turned into a nightmare.

I could only protest that I had remained awake my entire spell on duty, and that I had seen no one and nothing approach the drive panel. But that was hardly a satisfactory explanation, since it either cast guilt on me as the saboteur or implied that some unseen external power was repeatedly wrecking the drive. Neither hypothesis made sense, at least to me.

By now we had spent four days on the planet, and food was getting to be a major problem. My carefully budgeted flight schedule called for us to be two days out on our return journey to Earth by now. But we still were no closer to departure than we had been four days ago.

The animals continued to wander around outside, nosing up against the ship, examining it, almost fondling it, with those damned pseudo-giraffes staring soulfully at us always. The beasts were as friendly as ever, little knowing how the tension was growing within the hull. The three of us walked around like zombies, eyes bright and lips clamped. We were scared—all of us.

Something was keeping us from fixing the drive.

Something didn't want us to leave this planet.

I looked at the bland face of the purple-eyed giraffe staring through the viewport, and it stared mildly back at me. Around it was grouped the rest of the local fauna; the same incredible hodgepodge of improbable genera and species.

That night, the three of us stood guard in the control-room together. The drive was smashed anyway. The wires were soldered in so many places by now that the control panel was a mass of shining alloy, and I knew that a few more such sabotagings and it would be impossible to patch it together any more—if it wasn't so already.

The next night, I just didn't knock off. I continued soldering right on after dinner (and a pretty skimpy dinner it was, now that we were on close rations) and far on into the night.

By morning, it was as if I hadn't done a thing.

'I give up,' I announced, surveying the damage. 'I don't see any sense in ruining my nerves trying to fix a thing that won't stay fixed.'

Holdreth nodded. He looked terribly pale. 'We'll have to find some new approach.'

'Yeah. Some new approach.'

I yanked open the food closet and examined our stock. Even figuring in the synthetics we would have fed to the animals if we hadn't released them, we were low on food. We had overstayed even the safety

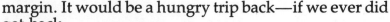

margin. It would be a hungry trip back—if we ever did get back.

I clambered through the hatch and sprawled down on a big rock near the ship. One of the furless dogs came over and nuzzled in my shirt. Davison stepped to the hatch and called down to me.

'What are you doing out there, Gus?'

'Just getting a little fresh air. I'm sick of living aboard that ship.' I scratched the dog behind his pointed ears, and looked around.

The animals had lost most of their curiosity about us, and didn't congregate the way they used to. They were meandering all over the plain, nibbling at little deposits of a white doughy substance. It precipitated every night. 'Manna', we called it. All the animals seemed to live on it.

I folded my arms and leaned back.

*

We were getting to look awfully lean by the eighth day. I wasn't even trying to fix the ship any more; the hunger was starting to get me. But I saw Davison puttering around with my solderbeam.

'What are you doing?'

'I'm going to repair the drive,' he said. 'You don't want to, but we can't just sit around, you know.' His nose was deep in my repair guide, and he was fumbling with the release on the solderbeam.

I shrugged. 'Go ahead, if you want to.' I didn't care what he did. All I cared about was the gaping emptiness in my stomach, and about the dimly grasped fact that somehow we were stuck here for good.

'Gus?'

'Yeah?'

'I think it's time I told you something. I've been eating the manna for four days. It's good. It's nourishing stuff.'

'You've been eating—the manna? Something that grows on an alien world? You crazy?'

'What else can we do? Starve?'

I smiled feebly, admitting that he was right. From somewhere in the back of the ship came the sounds of Holdreth moving around. Holdreth had taken this thing worse than any of us. He had a family back on Earth, and he was beginning to realize that he wasn't ever going to see them again.

'Why don't you get Holdreth?' Davison suggested. 'Go out there and stuff yourselves with the manna. You've got to eat something.'

'Yeah. What can I lose?' Moving like a mechanical man, I headed towards Holdreth's cabin. We would go out and eat the manna and cease being hungry, one way or another.

'Clyde?' I called. 'Clyde?'

I entered his cabin. He was sitting at his desk, shaking convulsively, staring at the two streams of blood that trickled in red spurts from his slashed wrists.

'*Clyde!*'

He made no protest as I dragged him towards the infirmary cabin and got tourniquets around his arms, cutting off the bleeding. He just stared dully ahead, sobbing.

I slapped him and he came around. He shook his head dizzily, as if he didn't know where he was.

'I—I—'

'Easy, Clyde. Everything's all right.'

'It's *not* all right,' he said hollowly. 'I'm still alive. Why didn't you let me die? Why didn't you—'

Davison entered the cabin. 'What's been happening, Gus?'

'It's Clyde. The pressure's getting him. He tried to kill himself, but I think he's all right now. Get him something to eat, will you?'

*

We had Holdreth straightened around by evening. Davison gathered as much of the manna as he could find, and we held a feast.

'I wish we had nerve enough to kill some of the local fauna,' Davison said. 'Then we'd have a feast—steaks and everything!'

'The bacteria,' Holdreth pointed out quietly. 'We don't dare.'

'I know. But it's a thought.'

'No more thoughts,' I said sharply. 'Tomorrow morning we start work on the drive panel again. Maybe with some food in our bellies we'll be able to keep awake and see what's happening here.'

Holdreth smiled. 'Good. I can't wait to get out of this ship and back to a normal existence. God, I just can't wait!'

'Let's get some sleep,' I said. 'Tomorrow we'll give it another try. We'll get back,' I said with a confidence I didn't feel.

The following morning I rose early and got my tool-kit. My head was clear, and I was trying to put the pieces together without much luck. I started towards the control cabin.

And stopped.

And looked out the viewport.

I went back and awoke Holdreth and Davison. 'Take a look out the port,' I said hoarsely.

They looked. They gaped.

'It looks just like my house,' Holdreth said. 'My house on Earth.'

'With all the comforts of home inside, I'll bet.' I walked forward uneasily and lowered myself through the hatch. 'Let's go look at it.'

We approached it, while the animals frolicked around us. The big giraffe came near and shook its head gravely. The house stood in the middle of the clearing, small and neat and freshly-painted.

I saw it now. During the night, invisible hands had put it there. Had assembled and built a cosy little Earth-type house and dropped it next to our ship for us to live in.

'Just like my house,' Holdreth repeated in wonderment.

'It should be,' I said. 'They grabbed the model from your mind, as soon as they found out we couldn't live on the ship indefinitely.'

Holdreth and Davison asked as one, 'What do you mean?'

'You mean you haven't figured this place out yet?' I licked my lips, getting myself used to the fact that I was going to spend the rest of my life here. 'You mean you don't realize what this house is intended to be?'

They shook their heads, baffled. I glanced around, from the house to the useless ship to the jungle to the plain to the little pond. It all made sense now.

'They want to keep us happy,' I said. 'They knew we weren't thriving aboard the ship, so they—they built us something a little more like home.'

'They? The giraffes?'

'Forget the giraffes. They tried to warn us, but it's too late. They're intelligent beings, but they're prisoners just like us. I'm talking about the ones who run this place. The super-aliens who make us sabotage our own ship and not even know we're doing it, who stand someplace up there and gape at us. The ones who dredged together this motley assortment of beasts from all over the galaxy. Now we've been collected too. This whole damned place is just a zoo—a zoo for aliens so far ahead of us we don't dare dream what they're like.'

I looked up at the shimmering blue-green sky, where invisible bars seemed to restrain us, and sank down dismally on the porch of our new home. I was resigned. There wasn't any sense in struggling against *them*.

I could see the neat little placard now:

EARTHMEN. Native Habitat, Sol III.

MAROONED ON SPLATTERBANG

Nicholas Fisk

On the starship, they cut in the boost-burners. To Mykl, it was like the slamming of a great iron door. The whole planet seemed to shudder and shift under his feet. The blast of the burners forced him backwards, stumbling and tripping. He ended up on his back with the blast trying to tear his helmet from his head, squeezing his rib-cage, flattening his ecosuit into harsh ripples and creases. 'You can't leave me!' he shouted. 'You can't!' But there was nobody to hear him. The starship, thrusting into the violet-tinted blackness of the sky, was leaving him behind. Leaving him alone.

'You *can't!*' he screamed. But the starship was dwindling even as he watched. Seconds ago it had been a vast, noisy thing, a mass of metal and ceramics and plastics, filling his vision: now it was shrinking, waning, receding. Another few seconds and it would be a dot of flame. Already the blasting gale of its power was dying down. Its iron-throated bellowing was distant thunder. The light of its drivers and burners was a mere pinpoint.

But still the flamers chased it. They seemed to come

from anywhere, everywhere—from the ground he stood on, from the shallow humps and hillocks around him. The flamers were bullets, burning bullets, like tracers. They streamed from the planet to chase the starship. A hopeless chase by now: the starship was a fiery dot at the end of a crayon line of burned air.

Then even the dot was gone. The planet was almost still, the last flamers fell back to the ground like spent rockets. Nothing moved in the infinite sky around him or on the ground. Alone.

Mykl got to his feet and with an unconscious movement shook his helmet to the right to bring in Distant Sound. He heard only uncertain booming. By now, the starship was hundreds or thousands of miles away. By now, his father and mother had released themselves from their 'padded cells'—the take-off modules—and were busying themselves with routine in-flight business. Mykl had a sudden vision of his father's face: a blood-hound face with deep, dark creases and hangdog brows. He saw his mother's face, small, brisk, vivid, watchful.

He began to cry. Alone. They had deserted him, left him alone. His sobbings choked him. His mind said, 'Come on! You're thirteen! You're a big boy now!' but it was no good, there was a pump in his chest forcing the useless sobs into his throat.

He told himself, 'They had to do it! They had no choice!'—but he simply blubbered. His tears blinded him. He tripped over something, fell to his hands and knees and remained there, down and out, finished and done for.

He stayed like that for a long time, at first not hearing his helmet. It was giving him a direction. It said 'Beep . . . beep . . . beep' in a quiet, endless, rhythmic murmur. The tinny sound was like an insult. 'I don't want you!' Mykl yelled. 'I want—' The sobs seized him again. But this time he held them down and stood erect. Over there was the Settlement. He could see it plainly.

He walked towards it. Needlessly, his helmet guided him, with its 'Beep, beep, BEEP', to the glimmering dome of the Settlement's 'cheesedish'—its shield. This settlement was not like the many others he had seen and entered. He shrugged his helmet to silence and made himself remember what to do. To enter a settlement, you had to speak into the grille— give your personal code sequence. Where was the grille? It was staring him in the face. There was even a dimly lighted arrow pointing to it.

For a moment he could not remember his code and his heart leaped sickeningly. But how can you forget your own code? Mykl's number had been drummed into him when he was a baby. 'Grow up!' he told himself, surlily, and spoke his code into the grille.

The lighted arrow did a somersault and pointed at a tiny keyboard. 'Another new idea,' Mykl thought. No doubt a doublecheck. He tapped out his code. The glimmering wall puckered and shrank, like sheet plastic burning. He walked into the hole and through it. The hole mended itself to glassy perfection. He was inside.

Alone.

*

Inside, it was familiar yet unfamiliar. All settlements were rather like small spaceport lounges, designed to give comfortable living accommodation for up to twenty or thirty people: but this one was newer, better. There were soft lights, clusters of tables and chairs and lounges, a three-dimensional mural of an Earthside scene, new doors with new signs leading to shower-rooms and a bar for drinks. There was two-wall TV, food slots, a sign that read SLEPING KORTERS, everything.

Mykl looked at it without interest and the place

looked back at him blandly, efficiently, impersonally. He had lived most of his life in such places, they were completely familiar to him.

But this time he was alone. No mother, no father. He began to shake. He went to the console—the brain of the settlement—and tipped down the tab that said RADIO. There was a roar of static, an impenetrable surge of noise. It was what he had expected. He was on the planet nicknamed Splatterbang—one of the Hellholes cluster. The Hellholes could be surrounded by a jungle of static for days at a time. There was no hope of getting through to his father and mother on the starship.

Alone. It was so silent. He sat down in a chair and the silence seemed to shout at him. He walked up and down the comfortable, neutral room, listening to his own footsteps. 'Put on some music!' he told himself, and went back to the hi-fi. Yet his finger didn't want to press the MUS tab, there was no music that could help. 'What do you want?' he asked himself. 'Another good cry? Does baby want weepies? Does ickle Mykl want his Doggo and Mags?' But this was a mistake. The words—the nicknames of his parents—pushed a sob into his throat.

He hit himself violently at the top of his rib cage with his fist, sat down, held his head in his hands and said, 'Come on, now. Come on, come *on*!'

A voice said, 'Hallo, Mykl. I'm sorry I couldn't be with you sooner.'

*

It was a smooth, warm, deep masculine voice, quite close to Mykl's ear.

He jumped to his feet and said, 'Where are you? Who?'

'I've startled you!' the voice said. 'I'm sorry, Mykl, I didn't mean—'

'Where are you?'

'Mykl, please. Be calm. I'm here, but I'm not. I'm

only a machine, Mykl. With a voice. No body, no face, just a voice. But I'm here to help you.'

Mykl said nothing. He sat down slowly, and again let his head fall into his hands.

'Mykl, please speak to me. . . .'

He said, 'Yes. I'm sorry. I thought for a minute that it was a—you know, a real person. You're just an Ego, aren't you?'

'Yes, I'm afraid so. Just an Ego.' The voice had a modest hint of laughter in it. 'But I'm the newest, latest and best Ego, Mykl, if that's any consolation. I've got more functions and services and accesses than any Ego you've ever met before!' The voice paused, then asked, 'Have you eaten? Would you like some food?'

'No. No thank you.'

'Mykl, you should eat. You're sick, sick with shock and everything that's just happened to you. Please eat something.'

'No thank you. I couldn't.'

'Well, you can't stop me *serving* something. . . .' A slot opened. Soup, with steam rising from it. Milk. Bread.

'Go on, Mykl. Just to please me.'

'Just to please you! How can you be pleased, or not pleased, or anything at all, about me eating or not eating, or—'

'Drink the milk, Mykl. Just the milk.'

'All right. I'm drinking the milk, see? *Can* you see?'

'Oh yes. But not properly. I mean, I can see you, but I can't accurately judge your thoughts from your expression. It's all too difficult for a machine.'

Mykl wasn't listening. 'What about my parents? What about the ship?'

'You know more about that than I do. Look, Mykl: you're going to be here for some time. There's no way round it. I think it would be a very good idea if you ate that food then sat down and told me everything.'

He ate it and felt better for it.

'Now, Mykl. Tell me what happened.'

'It was just a routine trip. The usual thing here. My father called in here, to pick up the grabber—you know, the machine that collects samples. We'd landed, and they started firing at us, and the firing got worse than ever, and they had to get away in a hurry, and they thought I was on the ship but I wasn't. And now I've ended up here, all alone. . . .'

The thought choked him. He had to stop. Ego's smooth, warm voice cut in tactfully.

'Yes, you needn't explain. Look, I'll tell you what *I* know, shall I? What I've got in my Fax store? Your father's a licensed prospector, your mother's a geologist. They charter a starship—'

'You're joking!' Mykl interrupted. 'It was a share-charter. It always is. We can't afford to charter on our own, we always have to share.'

'Your parents share-charter a starship,' Ego said, accepting the correction, 'and supply the home planet with anything from information and samples to minerals and gases and ores. Anything that could be useful and earn a living. Right?'

'That's right. My father left a grabber here. I don't know if there was anything in it, because everything went wrong. . . . It might have been some form of life, no one's ever found animal life on the Hellholes and they thought there might be something because of the plants. . . . But then the flamers started.'

'I know. What were *you* doing on the trip?'

'I go on nearly all the trips. I've spent only a few months of my life at home, Earthside. We just bash around the Galaxy, all three of us. Me and Doggo and Mags.'

'Doggo and Mags?'

'My mother and father.'

'Of course,' Ego said, blandly. Then there was the little pause, only as long as '. . . .', which meant that Ego was recording the names. Mykl could almost see

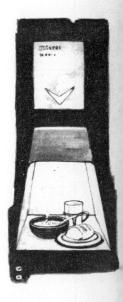

the tiny spools of wire, finer than hair, spinning.
He thought, 'A fat lot of good that will do you,
Ego!'

Ego said brightly, 'It's always interesting to record
names and nicknames. Quite a lot of people still call
their parents Ma and Pa, or Mum and Dad. The old
names. And of course, your name is an old name,
Mykl. It used to be written—'

'M,i,c,h,a,e,l,' Mykl said. 'I know. My parents told
me.'

'The poor kids in those old days, Mykl!' Ego said.
'What strange things they had to learn!'

Mykl grumbled, 'The poor kids now! Wherever we
go, they load on my brainbox—you know, my
Tuta—and I sit in front of it most of the time, cram-
ming away. My parents don't want me to end up like
them. They want me educated.'

'Well, *they* are educated.'

'Yes, but my father's still only a prospector, all the
same—a chancer at that.' Ego went '. . . .' Mykl
explained, 'A chancer: someone hoping to strike it
rich. My mother helps him. And I tag along, learning
lessons and not living anywhere really. We haven't got
an Earthside home, not a proper home. It's all hotels
and rented flats.'

'But you've got each other.'

'We had each other.'

'Yes . . .' said the voice, politely sympathetic. After a
pause, it added, 'Go on about what happened.'

'I don't see how it can help, my telling you,' Mykl
said. 'They had to do what they did, it wasn't their
fault. Now it's done, and I'm here.'

'Tell me all the same,' Ego said.

*

He did not tell Ego everything. He did not tell it, for
instance, about the argument the previous night.
(Night? In the starship, it was always night—blackness, nothingness, space. So you followed terrestrial

time, keeping to the twenty-four hour clock. You have
to play these tricks on yourself.)

That evening, Mykl had been at his Tuta, learning.
Or half-learning: his headphones were only half on.
He could overhear his parents.

Mags said, 'Look. Do we really have to go back to the
Hellholes and Splatterbang? It's too dangerous. It's
not worth it.'

Doggo said, 'It's worth it, if the stuff's there. Anything's worth it, if only the stuff's there.'

'Anything? Anything at all? I don't think you mean
that. Suppose something happened to *him*!' she meant
Mykl.

Doggo said, 'If that shale really is active, something
would happen to him. Something wonderful. We
could give him—oh, anything. Think, Mags! We could
live Earthside, have air to breathe, trees and earth,
mornings and evenings. . . .'

'And a future for Mykl. I know all that. You've said it
often enough. No, I'm not accusing, really I'm not. But
here we are again on a dirty old starship, sharing the
charter with a gang of cut-throat Romnis—'

'We've shared with Romnis before and our throats
aren't cut.'

She ignored him. 'And you're doing all the piloting
and navigation because they don't know how—and
we're heading for Splatterbang, which is just about the
last place in the Galaxy any sane person would go—'

'That's why we're going there,' Doggo said
patiently. 'We've got it to ourselves. And if the shale is
active—'

'I don't mind so much for myself,' Mags said, not
listening. 'It's him. Mykl.' Then she was silent,
worried.

Looking out of the corner of his eye, his father
seemed to Mykl more than ever like a bloodhound,
and his mother like a small, disapproving statue.
'Whose side should I be on?' Mykl asked himself. The

answer was, 'Both'. He loved and admired them both. The argument went on.

'What was that Romni man talking to you about?' his mother asked.

'Oh, he's the boss, the leader. He was trying to sell me spare parts for the Analyst, he's got a lot of junk for a Mk VI, the same as ours.'

'How did he know we've got a Mk VI?' Mags demanded.

'I suppose he saw us loading it. Look, Mags, he's all right, you've got a thing about Romnis. . . .'

'Scavengers!' his mother said, bitterly. 'Muckrakers. Junk pickers. That's all they are.'

'They know their stuff,' his father said, uneasily. 'They've got a sort of—*nose* for things. . . . I've learned a lot from them about alien forms of life, what to do in a strange place, when to move and when to stand still—'

'Keep moving when a Romni is anywhere near you!' Mags said, with a sniff.

But Mykl saw her lean down and reach for the Analyst. She put it on the bench, opened it and began prodding its programmer section. 'Oho,' Mykl thought, 'Doggo's won, and she knows it. Otherwise she wouldn't do that!' For the Analyst was the machine that analysed living or dead material—the essential tool of the prospector's trade. They were going to land on Splatterbang all right.

'Those flamer things,' Mags said, still prodding. 'Shooting at us. . . .'

'Not harming us,' Doggo said. 'Just a few pimples on the last ship we had. Lots of banging and sparks, but no real power.'

'I don't like being fired at with flaming bullets,' Mags said, 'And some of those pimples looked more like craters. This time, they might fire something that goes right through the ship!' But she wasn't really listening to her own words. She had closed the programme-section lid and was checking the spectrometer box. Everything worked. She closed the box and started to attack again.

'And *who*'s firing at us?' she demanded. 'If only we knew! I hate that place, I hate the hostility. I hate the hate. All we see is the flamers. We never see who's firing. We never see *them*, the things that hate us and shoot at us!'

'Look, Mags—'

'He's not to leave the ship!' his mother announced. 'Mykl's not to leave the ship on any account, is that understood? Do you promise me that?'

'He won't leave the ship. I give you my promise,' Doggo said, wearily.

Mykl said to himself, 'Oh yes he will!' He smiled behind his hand and got on with his Tuta work.

*

Later, they landed. They came down in a rain of flamers that turned into a storm.

'Shields!' his father said. He flung open the armoury

cupboard and threw the titanite shields behind him. They weighed little yet stopped almost anything, however hostile, however alien and unimaginable.

Mykl picked up one of the shields. 'You're not going,' his father said grimly. 'I know!' Mykl said, wide-eyed with innocence—and handed the shield to the leader of the party of Romnis, who was standing behind him grinning. His teeth were blindingly white but outlined with black tartar. His skin was dark brown and he had a stubble of blue-black beard.

The Romni took the shield. His grin became a laugh. 'You don' need no shields,' he said in his slurred English. 'You need understand the natives, you know what I mean?' And he bellowed with laughter and strode to the lift, showing his teeth at the bullets. His shoulders heaved with laughter under his ecosuit. Mykl saw the suit was covered in patches. Other Romnis pushed past him, white grins showing through helmets clouded with grime. One was no more than a midget.

'Look, take the shields!' his father yelled, angrily. But the Romnis just pushed past, grinning. No shields. Outside, the storm of flamers became a tempest. The burning bullets wavered, swerved, seemed to accelerate—then hit the ship, *splatterbang*. Then they dripped from the point of impact like fiery lava, as if reluctant to let go.

'You're staying here, Mykl.' His mother's voice was fierce in Mykl's ears, filling his helmet. His parents had allowed him to watch them leave, so he wore his ecosuit and helmet. 'Not a step outside the hatch!' his father said.

Mykl said nothing. He watched the human figures make their cautious way to the lift and stand on the hatch platform, waiting their turn. The lift went down oilily. It reached the ground and Mykl saw his parents below him as two glassy blobs. The blobs tilted and the faces inside turned to him. His mother's voice said

'Remember, now! You stay!' A flamer zinged past his father, seeming to swerve to miss him. His father shrugged, looked up and Mykl saw what he had been waiting for, the doggy, reluctant smile. He smiled back and waved.

The lift came up, went down. Mykl smiled and waved. Everyone was on the ground now, walking slowly and carefully uphill, away from the ship. The air of the planet was dimly violet, but the flamers made yellow and orange glows and reflections on the human figures. Mykl watched their progress until they were rapidly darkening shapes, almost silhouettes in the dark light of the miserable little planet. Already, Mykl found, they were out of radio range—there was nothing but static in his helmet. Static from the flamers? The flamers were everywhere, flaming, whizzing, splattering, banging. Yet no one was hit.

When Mykl was sure he could not be seen, he brought the lift to his feet—went down on it—and stood on the ground of Splatterbang. He jumped up and down, testing the gravity. More than he thought. He jumped some more, for the pleasure of it, then walked. In time with every other step, he said, 'Beautiful! Marvellous! Freedom!'

He walked through the flamers, feeling his muscles flex. He wanted to run and keep running—to stretch his legs, wave his arms—but of course he didn't. You never run, you mustn't run. You proceed slowly, carefully, consistently.

But his mind shouted: 'Freedom!'

*

Seconds later, it happened.

A flamer went ZAP! through the chink in the starship's hatch. The hatch was closing, automatically, but there was still space for the bullet to get through. Inside the ship, it skidded from surface to surface, yelping with each ricochet. Almost spent, it struck a switch marked ENTRY 5—fused on to it—shorted the

printed circuit inside—and triggered the ship's alarm system.

The ship obediently switched on an immensely powerful, revolving, flashing light and sounded its panic horn. The light glared and swung, the horn bellowed EE-HOO! EE-HOO! EE-HOO!

Men came running. They thronged the lift. One Romni, late, clung to it as it made its way up. His fellows pulled him on to the platform. The siren yelled EE-HOO!

They stood in the hatch area, pointing and gesticulating. Two more figures, brilliantly lit then dark again, made their way to the ship. The lift went down, the two figures were carried up. Mykl saw them. His parents. He began, frantically, to run. The light revolved, lighting the landscape crazily. The siren bellowed.

The hatch area was open. The lights, the siren, the open hatch—whatever it was, it attracted a vicious hail of bullets. They no longer hit the hull, they poured through the hatch. Mykl could see the confusion in the hatch area. The flamers were pouring into the ship. They ricocheted and screamed and flung showers of orange sparks. The people looked as if caught in a fireworks disaster, trapped in a maelstrom of flame and explosion. Someone beat at the control console with his fist and the hatch slammed down. Now they were safe. The hull was sealed. Mykl shouted. 'Wait!'

The storm of flamers grew still more furious. Every bullet now hammered at the hatch until it was aglow with lava-like flux and sparkling with running fire.

The flashing light went out and the primary drives of the ship wailed low—swooped up the scale—and hit a torturing, high note. Mykl ran, the ship lifted. He stumbled, the ship was a hundred metres off the ground, joined to the planet only by the string of flamers. He kept running, his heart bursting, and on the starship, they cut in the boosts and the great iron door slammed in Mykl's head.

Alone.

'It was my own fault,' he told Ego. 'There was nothing they could do. My parents didn't know I'd disobeyed them. If they had known, they still had to take off, get away, escape the bullets.'

'They'll come back,' Ego said.

'Not until they've gone half across this sector of the galaxy to get the ship checked. Or sent another ship here somehow. Inside that hatch. . . . It was alive with fire, it was being hammered to bits.'

'But they'll come back in the end,' said Ego. 'Of course they will!'

*

For two days, Mykl watched but hardly saw old movies from Ego's endless store. He ate meals, took snacks, ate again, tasted nothing. He did head-stands, jogged, sprawled in the soft, comfortless chairs.

Ego was his constant companion.

Ego said, 'I've got some yoga programmes, Mykl. Do you know about yoga? Would you like me to run this programme?' The two-wall viddy lit up and a woman in black tied herself into a geometrical knot. In full 3D, the effect was amazing.

Mykl grunted and said, 'No. No, thank you.' The picture faded.

Ego said, 'I've got a terrific film somewhere called "Spaceshots that misfired". . . . Ah, here it is. Look, Mykl!'

On the screens, a vast old InterGal ship—date about 2025, or perhaps 2030, Mykl thought—spewed coloured smoke and fire, lurched at an angle, hovered above the launching pad, slowly fell on its side, erupted with coloured fires and crashed and slithered across the countryside, ploughing through buildings and fences and cars and a seaside motel. 'Oo-oops!' chuckled the commentator. 'Back to the old drawing board!' The ship lay in the shallows of the sea, boiling

and billowing and erupting. 'Mm-*mmm*!' said the happy commentator. 'Real hotshot!'

'No thanks,' Mykl said. The solid picture faded.

He went to the radio console and started digging at it. Static. Ego said, 'I don't think you'll do any good, Mykl, not yet. It's always like that for days after a landing.'

'How many days?' Mykl said. 'Three? Four? Weeks?'

'It varies so much . . .' Ego said.

'No, tell me. How long do you think I must wait before I can get in touch with my parents? Or Earthside?'

'Honestly, Mykl, I don't know.'

'Well, is it weeks?'

'It's not *likely* to be weeks. But it could be more than a week,' Ego replied. The sympathetic, almost tender voice was beginning to get on Mykl's nerves. He said, 'Look, you know the answers I want but you're not telling me, you're treating me like a child!'

Ego, sweetly reasonable, said, 'I *don't* know the answers. I know only what's been put into my memory banks, my Fax store. I haven't got opinions, even—only a store of received information from people who know only as much as you know about the Hellholes and Splatterbang. I think, Mykl, you want me to be what I can't be.'

'I'm sorry,' Mykl said.

'You don't have to be sorry, Mykl. You can't hurt my feelings. I haven't got any.'

'It's your voice . . .' Mykl said. 'It sounds so—you know, human and sympathetic.'

'You don't like my voice?'

'It isn't that I don't like it, it's just that—'

'I hadn't realized, I'm so sorry, I can change it.'

'Look, don't bother, it's just because I'm upset—'

'Is that any better?'

The new voice was deeper, impersonal, laconic. It boomed and Mykl started. He said, 'For heaven's sake—'

'I can produce more or less any voice you want,' Ego boomed. 'I can even produce a personna if you wish.'

'A personna?'

'A visual image of a personality. On the screens. In 3D, of course. Fully rounded. Lifelike.'

'Why ever would anyone want you to do that?'

'Some space travellers get lonely. They want to see a human being. Preferably a beautiful one, in beautiful surroundings. So I am programmed to produce such persons. The facility to do this is being introduced in all Ego-equipped establishments such as this on an alphabetical rota, and as the true description of this planet is Aaron VII—'

'Oh, I see,' Mykl said. 'That's why this stupid little place has such a wizzo Ego? Alphabetical order—Aaron VII?'

'Quite so.'

'Show me a personna,' Mykl said.

The screens lit: a blonde, beautiful girl in a swim suit appeared. She lay on a reclining seat by a swimming pool set amid green lawns and trees. She half-rose, turned to Mykl and said, 'Why, hello! My name is Rani. Isn't it just great us meeting this way! Come and talk to me!'

Mykl said, 'You've got the wrong voice'—for the girl spoke in the impersonal, masculine tones Ego had last used.

Ego said '. . . .', then, 'Of course. I am sorry. Is this better?' Now the voice was husky, warmly welcoming, throbbing. Mykl began to laugh, and couldn't stop. It was the first time he had laughed on Splatterbang.

When he stopped laughing, he said: 'Are all the people beautiful girls? All grown-ups? Aren't there any young people?'

Ego said '. . . .', and the screens darkened. When they lit again, there was a little girl in a swim suit. She carried a doll as large as herself. She waved her hand

and piped, 'Hallo! I'm Babs, I'm five! What's your name?'

'No,' Mykl said. 'Not her.'

She was replaced by an elderly man, who said, 'You know—the past contains many mysteries, still unsolve—'

'No,' said Mykl.

'I could make you a suitable personna,' Ego said. 'If you could give me some time—say, twenty seconds—'

'No,' Mykl said. 'Don't bother.' He didn't know whether to laugh or cry. The sudden glimpse of humanity, trees, water, sky, had shaken him. Yet it was a farce. 'Don't bother,' he said, 'I'll do a yoga programme. Then eat.'

The yoga programme reappeared. He followed the movements, became bored and went again to the radio console. The static seemed weaker. It still covered every frequency, but not evenly. There were holes of gritty noise here and there in the enveloping roar. He said to himself, 'I've got to get in touch. I've got to get out.'

The words 'get out' started a new thought. He asked Ego, 'What would happen if I left the module—put on my ecosuit and walked out? If I went for a walk?'

Ego said—using its original voice—'Please don't, Mykl. We get so few people here, it's not possible for me to tell you about conditions outside. I have too little data. But the flamers, the thin atmosphere—every-

thing seems to be hostile. Please don't go out. I have a responsibility for all visitors to this establishment—'

Mykl said, 'But you can't stop me coding myself out, can you?'

'No. But I have already recorded this conversation and will record all subsequent conversations on the subject. The records are on autodisplay, Mykl, which means that—'

'—Which means that Galactic Authority will be shown the records. You don't have to explain. . . .' He kicked the toes of his bare feet into the thick carpet and thought.

Ego said, 'Mykl! Please look at the screens!'

He looked, and saw a girl of his own age. She was chestnut-haired, pretty, tomboyish, dressed in frayed denim. Her mouth moved but she did not talk. 'I haven't got a voice for her,' Ego explained. 'I have several boys. Would you like to meet them?'

'Look—' Mykl began, but Ego was flashing images and voices at him in quick succession. Boys, girls, white, black and brown. Mykl said, 'Look, please don't bother, I'd rather you answered my question about leaving this place. Answer it properly. I don't want to meet these people.'

But then a dark, sullen, glowering girl appeared. Her hair hid most of her face. Her sulky lips moved.

Mykl said, 'Has she got a voice?' The girl began to pick at one of her toes. She was sitting in the corner of a building made of the old bricks, the bricks they used in

the twentieth century. She did not look at Mykl.

Ego said, 'I don't know how she got in here. . . . Oh, I see, she's from Archaeology and Environments, she shouldn't be here—'

'Has she got a voice?' Mykl repeated.

'No voice, Mykl, I'm sorry,' Ego said. 'And I don't think I can hold her much longer—' As Ego spoke, the screens went blank. 'Thought so,' Ego said.

'I liked her,' Mykl said.

'Do you want me to run her again? I could make more of her with a bit of mixing and infill, but she's not a programme, just a snippet. I could build her if you like?'

Mykl thought and then said, 'No. I'll eat now.'

He ate, but the girl stayed in the back of his mind.

Later he watched a film about the First World War. He had heard about this war, but had never been able to place it. History was not his strong subject. The film gripped him. It was like his first visit to a planet called Garon, where everything was not just different but totally different: atmospheric growths that looked like trees hung upside-down from the dense gas that formed the sky: the sky was green, the earth was blue. . . . World War One was just as alien, just as strange.

He watched the film again before he went to bed.

TERRAFIED

Arthur Tofte

uzzled, Dor peered up at the strange object in the deep blue sky. Still far away, it seemed very small. Yet, even as she watched, it grew steadily larger and larger.

Never before had she seen anything in the sky. There were no flying creatures on the planet of Tyrox.

Her first reaction was that of youthful curiosity. But as the object kept coming closer, Dor felt a growing sense of danger.

Her clawlike hands pulled back on the slender leather reins that gave her control over her tholl. Today was Dor's sixteenth birthday. The tholl was her parents' birthday gift. It was a beautiful, six-legged beast, fully twenty feet long from its single horn in front to its six-foot tail at the back. Best of all, it was full of spirit and swift as the wind. Not yet full grown, it would be her personal mount for years to come.

Dor watched for several minutes as the flying object sped downward towards her. Whatever it was, Dor knew that it was not of Tyrox. It was something alien and, therefore, to be feared.

Although she had planned to ride her birthday tholl farther, she pulled it around and headed back towards her village. It would be wise, she thought, to get home quickly and warn the others.

Before her tholl had gone a dozen leaps, Dor was horrified to see the flying object settling down a few hundred paces ahead and directly in her path. Flames were shooting out of its bottom as it slowly came to rest.

Dor gave a violent tug on the reins to turn the tholl away. Terror-stricken by the flames, the animal leaped sideways in a forty-foot jump that unseated his young rider. Dor flew head over heels, landing on the thick turf with a jarring jolt that knocked her unconscious for a few minutes.

When she opened her three eyes, she had trouble focusing them. It seemed that a tall, very pale-skinned creature was standing over her. She felt short, stubby fingers probing for possible injuries. Apparently it was a thinking animal. Only a thinking being would do that.

Dor sat up. The creature was even taller than she had first thought—taller by a head and a half than any of the adults in Dor's village. He was dressed in a tight-fitting, one-piece uniform that seemed to be made of a shiny, metallic substance. But what surprised and shocked Dor more than anything else was that the creature had only two eyes. That, and two rows of deadly looking teeth he was revealing by smiling at Dor.

Dor sensed that the smile was to reassure her. But she was not reassured. Actually she was terrified.

When Dor tried to rise to her feet, she winced with pain. One of her legs had been wrenched. She took a half step and fell back to the ground.

The tall creature reached down and easily picked her up. Moments later she felt herself carried up a short ladder into the body of the flying object. She was placed into a sleeping pod. Straps were fastened to hold her tight. Then she felt a stab in her arm.

Hours later she awoke to see the tall stranger looking down at her. Again he was smiling.

Dor realized that the flying object had taken off from Tyrox. She was allowed to get out of her sleeping pod and to take a few tentative steps. Her hurt leg had been wrapped with bindings and she could stand on it now.

She discovered there were four beings on the ship. All had only two eyes each. All were very tall and had ferocious-looking teeth. They seemed friendly enough, however. They tried to talk with her. It was all a hopeless gibberish.

After she had eaten, Dor was taken to a room that contained a mass of controls. On one wall was a large screen. The view on the screen was that of a green sphere.

Dor stared at it for several minutes. Then she realized that it was her own planet seen from thousands of miles away. She let out a cry of 'Tyrox!' It was the first word she had uttered whose meaning the creatures on the ship could understand.

Later, when she was lying in her pod, she thought of the terrible situation she was in. What was going to happen to her? Who were the two-eyed strangers? Where did they come from? What were her father's and mother's thoughts when she failed to return from her first ride on her birthday-gift tholl? Would the tholl return to their home?

She tried not to let herself be panicked. She knew her only chance to escape was to keep her wits about her. She would learn everything she could about the ship and its crew. By biding her time and looking for the right moment, she might have a chance.

What she must not do was lose her courage. The crew seemed friendly enough. Clearly they meant her no bodily harm. All she could do was wait for the right opportunity.

The next day, one of the crew members began an intensive course teaching Dor their language. She learned they called themselves human beings, or men. They were from the third planet in a small solar system, a planet they called Terra. The man who had

carried her into the ship was their leader whom they addressed as Captain Cahorn.

Gradually, as the days moved into weeks and into months, Dor learned how to communicate with the beings who had captured her. In fact, within two months, as the ship sped along its way, she was able to talk to them fluently.

Although Captain Cahorn asked that she teach them the Tyroxan language, Dor could seem to make no progress. For one thing, she could see no gain in teaching them her language. On the other hand, if she were to escape, she would have to know everything possible about her captors.

In many ways she felt that she was brighter, sharper-minded than the four men of the ship. She watched them at their work. She studied the ship's controls until she felt she knew them as well as they did. She was especially interested in the long-range communications system with which they kept in contact with their home planet. Dor quickly perceived that it was similar to the system that had been in use on Tyrox for centuries. She felt that she might even be able to communicate with Tyrox if she could only get to the controls alone.

Dor was careful, for the present, not to mention this possibility. Actually, it was the one secret fact she had been able to discover that might eventually help her.

Otherwise Dor was quite free and open in telling her captors about life on Tyrox. She told of its beauty—the deep blue sky and the rolling green hills. She said the climate was favourable for growing crops all year. The difference between winter and summer was very little. There were large bodies of clear, fresh water, yielding fish of many kinds. Mountain ranges in the interior contained easily mined minerals of all needed kinds. An abundance of waterfalls provided all the hydro-electric power that was required. Life on Tyrox was easy and gentle. The birth-rate was kept at about level with the death-rate. People lived comfortably in wide-spread villages. Conflicts between villages were unheard of.

After Dor had been questioned steadily for several weeks by Captain Cahorn, she began to ask questions of her own.

What was Terra like? Why had they taken her prisoner? What were they going to do with her? When would she be able to go home?

Captain Cahorn had obviously grown fond of Dor in the months the ship had been speeding back towards Terra. He smiled as the young Tyroxan poured out her questions.

'We had had unconfirmed reports that there was a habitable planet in your solar system,' he said. 'Our mission was to check it out. Also, if possible, we were to try to capture a native of the planet to bring back to our head office on Terra.'

'But why me?' Dor asked.

'It was just chance that we saw you on your mount. When you were thrown off and hurt, we took advantage of it and carried you into our ship.'

'What is going to happen to me now?'

Captain Cahorn patted Dor's arm. 'We are all amazed at how quickly you picked up our language. By Terra standards, you are quite a genius. Young as you are, there is almost no limit to what you could do for yourself when we get to Terra.'

'What is it really like there?'

Captain Cahorn shrugged his shoulders. 'The planet Terra, or Earth as it is sometimes called, has just a bit of everything. It has wide oceans and great stretches of sandy deserts. It has mountains and valleys and even a few forests. There is snow and ice at both poles. At the equator there are even a few dense jungles left. But mostly people live in vast cities that cover hundreds of square miles.'

'Are the people of Terra happy?'

'Some are,' Captain Cahorn said. 'Many are not.'
'Why not?'
'For a variety of reasons. Some nations are very poor. They have too many people. Some of them have too little to eat. Then there are parts of the planet where people always seem to be at war.'
'War? What is that?'
'That's when people can't get along with each other. Hundreds of thousands of people die in wars each year. But you don't need to concern yourself with this. Where I am taking you is very peaceful. We are so strong no one dares attack us.'
'Where are you taking me?'
'Well, Dor,' Captain Cahorn said as he settled back in his bucket seat, 'I guess it's time for me to tell you what we have planned for you. I've been in contact with the headquarters of Outerspace Explorations, Incorporated. That's the organization I work for. I've sent a recording of everything you have told us about yourself and your planet of Tyrox. It's going to take them a few days to analyse your statements and program them for the computers to study. When that is finished, I expect they will want to talk to you again.

'In the meantime, as soon as we land two days from now, I'm going to take you to my own home. Would you like that?'
'Have I a choice?'
Captain Cahorn looked startled at the abrupt question. 'Possibly not. Actually, it's the best thing for you. You're a celebrity. Everybody on Terra wants to see you. I'd hate to see you put on public display. In my home you'll have privacy. Furthermore, it will give you a chance to see how we Terrans live.'
'I'm frightened,' Dor murmured.
'I don't blame you.' Captain Cahorn nodded in sympathy. 'That's why I'd like you to come to my home. I have a son just about your age. And a daughter a year younger. You'll like them.'

Dor turned away. 'But will they like me? After all, I'm different. I have three eyes. My hands are not like yours. My head is larger although I'm smaller. My skin is blue where yours is pink. I haven't your big teeth.'

'I'm sure they'll like you. Anyway, as I said before, you really don't have much choice. You're very intelligent, Dor. I know you'll always do the right thing.'

'Could I ask a favour?'

'If it's possible for me to grant it.'

'Do you think I could tell my father and mother where I am?'

Captain Cahorn looked at her with surprise. 'How could you do that?'

'I've studied your long-range communications system. It is very similar to the one we use on Tyrox. It may take some adjustments. I've written down the instructions you must follow to make the adjustments and then for the actual contact with Tyrox. If you can do that for me, I'll be very thankful.'

Captain Cahorn took the slip of paper and then looked at Dor with new respect.

Two days later the ship landed at an out-of-the-way spaceport to avoid the crowd of newsmen who awaited their arrival at the main spaceport. Captain Cahorn hustled Dor across the landing field to a waiting sky taxi.

Three hours later, Dor was ushered into Captain Cahorn's suburban home. It was a fifth-floor apartment in a building complex covering five square miles. Its chief attraction was that each apartment had a plastic-enclosed balcony on which green vines and ferns and dwarf bushes were allowed to grow.

Captain Cahorn introduced his family. Joanne, his wife, was an attractive, pleasantly plump woman in her early forties. He waved his fifteen-year-old daughter, Renna, forward. The pretty, blonde girl was flustered. She seemed to hesitate whether or not to shake hands with this strange little being from outer space. Those three eyes of hers seemed to look right through Renna.

Bob, the captain's sixteen-year-old, six-foot son, had no compunctions about stepping up and taking Dor's clawlike hand.

'Welcome to Terra,' he said, obviously intrigued by Dor's unusual appearance. 'You're to stay with Renna in her room. We'll show you the way. I have to get back to the red-hot football game on right now on my vistascope. Do you play football on Tyrox?'

Dor shook her head. 'I don't know what football is.'

'Come, we'll show you.'

A minute or two later, Dor, along with Renna and Bob, was seated in front of a three-dimensional vista-scope screen in his room. On the screen she saw men line up in meaningless formations, hurl themselves at each other, run up and down a field, either carrying, throwing, or kicking an oval ball. It was more violence than she had ever seen in her whole life.

'Is this what you call war?' she asked. 'Are they trying to kill each other?'

Renna laughed. 'No. It's just a game.'

'Don't they get hurt?'

'Sure,' Bob said. 'Quite often. But football players are well paid to take their chances.'

'Paid?' Dor asked. 'You mean they are given more food than others?'

Bob looked at her with wonder. 'You mean you don't know what it is to do something for pay? Oh, boy! What a lot you have to learn.'

'If you don't mind,' Dor said, 'I would like to go to sleep now. I'm very tired and confused by all I've seen and done today. I think I need to rest.'

'Let's go to my room,' Renna said. 'I'll sleep on the cot Mom has set up for me. You can wear one of my sleepwears for tonight. Tomorrow I'll ask my father if we can't call in an order for some real Terra clothes for you. Tomorrow, then.'

'Tomorrow,' Dor echoed, wondering what surprises would be in store for her on the morrow.

The next day, after breakfast, Bob announced that since it was not a school day, he would like to borrow the family's land car to show Dor around.

After nodding politely to Mrs Cahorn, Dor followed her new Terran friend out of the rear door of the apartment. The Cahorn car was kept in a small recess in the back wall.

'You're lucky you didn't come to Terra last year,' Bob said as he started up the small electric car. 'Last year was a terrible year for smog. We saw the sun only eight times. Now it's much better. We've been able to see the sun at least two or three times every month.'

'Smog? What's that?'

'Look around, Dor. What you see in the air is smog. It's smoke and fog and all kinds of polluting gases in the air.'

'What caused it?'

'It's been here a long time. A lot of it came in the old days from gasoline-burning motorcars, coal-burning power plants, mills, and factories. That's all been changed. But they say it may take another hundred years to get the air clean and clear again.'

'Why isn't something being done?'

'Oh, it is. We're spending billions of dollars to clear the air. But we let it go too long.'

'And your oceans and lakes and rivers,' Dor exclaimed, 'how about them?'

Bob grimaced. 'I guess we've just about given up on them. About all we can do is purify the water we use for drinking and bathing.'

'Where do you get your fish?'

'We don't. My father told me that when he was a small boy his father took him fishing one time and he actually caught a fish. As far as I know, all fish alive on the planet are in our public aquariums. The oceans haven't had fish in them for nearly half a century.'

Bob turned to Dor. 'Enough of this serious talk. There isn't much to see in the city—just buildings. Let's have some excitement. I don't get many chances to drive our car. I'm going to take you for a short ride on one of our old superhighways. Of course it's in bad shape now and not in use. But I know one section about fifteen miles long that's fairly clear. Unfortunately, all the other kids who can borrow their family cars head for that same section. It's become quite a racetrack. It's where we find out how fast we can go. And who has the most nerve.'

Bob laughed aloud with pleasure as he headed up a ramp, gaining speed with every foot. 'Hold on,' he cried, 'here we go.'

Dor held tight to her seat belt as the car left the ramp and projected itself on to a four-lane strip of some black material, crisscrossed with a myriad of cracks.

'The trick,' Bob said, 'is to avoid the potholes. You hit one of them at high speed and you're through.'

Dor watched with horror as Bob sent the car plunging ahead at a greatly accelerated speed. 'Must we go so fast?' she cried out. 'I'm not used to this. The fastest I've ever gone is riding my tholl. That's nothing like this.'

'Don't worry, Dor. I'll be careful. Oh, look, there's an old steam car ahead. They are supposed to be very fast. I'm going to try to pass it. Hold on, here we come.'

The car leaped forward as Bob turned the rheostat lever to top speed. A moment later they were alongside the big, lumbering steam car. Bob gave its driver a derisive wave of his hand as though challenging him to a race.

Not to be outdone, the other driver increased his speed. Soon the two cars, side by side, were screaming along the wide freeway. The steam car made a peculiar hissing sound as it matched Bob's speed.

Dor saw it first—a slower car ahead of them, weaving back and forth to avoid a series of dangerous potholes. Almost at the same moment Bob saw it. He applied all brakes instantly.

In the smog, however, it was apparent that the driver of the steam car was a second or two late in seeing the danger ahead.

With their own car skidding sideways, Dor watched with horror as the big car careened left and right past them, smashing first against the metal guardrails at the right only to bounce back to the left of Bob's car. A split second later, the steam car drove head on into the slower car that had created the original obstacle.

There was a series of violent crushing noises, ending with both cars slamming up against the left guardrail. Both cars were complete wrecks.

Bob, in the meantime, had been able to get his car back under control. With skill, he slid past the two tangled cars to their right.

'Whew!' he said, 'that was close. Wait until I tell

the kids at school about this. Will they be jealous!'

'You mean you do this for fun?' Dor asked.

'Sure, it's fun. Of course, the idea is to get involved without getting hurt.'

'I don't see how you can avoid getting hurt. Those two drivers back there—shouldn't we go back and help them? They might be hurt badly.'

'Go back?' Bob was genuinely surprised. 'No one ever goes back on the freeway. It would be sure suicide.'

He pointed ahead. 'That's where the good section ends. It's mostly rubble beyond. As soon as we leave on this down ramp, you'll be able to see typical city streets.'

Dor looked about. As far as she could see in the misty air, the two sides of the street were lined with towering buildings, all more or less alike. The tops were lost in the smog. Traffic moved at a slow pace, with cars bumper to bumper. Few people were to be seen on the narrow sidewalks.

Dor finally spoke. 'I think I would like to go back to your home. Life on Tyrox is nothing like this. I'm frightened.'

'Aw, you'll get used to it.'

As they inched along in the heavy traffic, Dor said, 'I don't understand. Why don't you do something about conditions here on Terra—clean it up?'

'We're doing everything we can. But, as I said before, we let it go too long.'

He turned towards Dor. 'That's where you come in.'

'Me? What can I do about it?'

Bob peered over at his companion. 'Perhaps I shouldn't be telling you this, Dor. But I heard my father talking last evening to his boss at Outerspace Explorations. He said Tyrox would be a wonderful place for people from Terra to settle and colonize. He said it could easily support a billion of Terra's over-population.'

'You mean the people from this planet would go to my planet and take over?'

'Oh, I'm sure we'd pay you well for it.'

'Pay us—how? With pollution of our air and water? And what can you give us in payment? Surely you don't think we would want the kind of life you have here?'

'Oh, I don't know. We can give you the benefit of our advanced technology. That's worth a great deal.'

Dor turned her face away, her heart heavy.

When they reached the Cahorn home, the captain met them as they put the car away.

'I've good news for you, Dor,' he said to the Tyroxan. 'You were right about the communications system.'

'You've been able to contact my father?' Dor exclaimed eagerly.

'Yes, we have. Using your instructions and the key words you told us to use, we've made contact with Tyrox. I have always felt badly that we took you away from your home without giving you a chance to tell your parents. I'm glad to help make amends now.'

'When can I talk with my father?'

'As soon as we can get the proper arrangements. The conversation will be relayed over the entire inter-continental vistascope network. People all over the world will be able to see you and hear you talk with your father. You're quite a celebrity, Dor.'

'But I'll be speaking in Tyroxan.'

'After you have concluded your talk with your father, you can translate what you both said into Terran language. The vistascope people are setting up their equipment in our family room. Let's go to Renna's room. It's the only quiet place left.'

Bob left them, saying he wanted to watch the excitement of the vistascope set-up.

Captain Cahorn and Dor found Renna lying on her bed, reading. She was dressed in a long, all-

enveloping robe. Dor could see that by Terran standards Renna was probably very attractive. Her silvery
blonde hair had the kind of poetic beauty that Dor
could understand and appreciate. Her blue eyes were
clear and innocent and yet intelligent.

Captain Cahorn turned to Dor. 'I have to check with
the vistascope people now. You should be thinking of
what you want to tell your father. Perhaps Renna can
help you decide what to say.'

When the spaceman had left, the two young beings
looked warily at each other. Suddenly Renna's face
broke into a broad smile.

'You don't like Terra, do you?' she asked softly.

Dor returned her smile with a grin. 'It's different,'
she managed to say in reply.

'From what my father has told us, Tyrox is a beautiful place.'

'It is,' Dor nodded.

Renna shook her head. 'You know what they are
planning to do, don't you?'

'Bob told me a little this morning. Terra would like to
colonize Tyrox.'

'Do you realize what that means?'

'I can guess.'

'It's impossible for you to guess,' Renna said. 'You
haven't seen enough of what life is like on our planet.
Billions of people will be listening to your talk today.
As you talk they will be envisioning Tyrox—the green
fields, the clear blue skies, the pure streams, the fresh
clean air. To them it will be the dream of Terra as it
once was ... the dream your planet now suddenly
makes real to them.'

The Earth girl sat down on the edge of her bed and
buried her head in her hands.

'I like you, Dor. There's nothing I would like better
than to leave Terra and go to Tyrox. But it's too cruel.'

'What do you mean ... cruel?'

Renna looked up at her. 'We here on Terra are

doomed. We know it. Not only do we have pollution in our air and water. We have pollution of our minds and character. With our billions of people crowded together, life has become a raging struggle for survival. It's like a disease, a plague. That's what our people would bring to Tyrox. And there is nothing you can do to stop it.'

'Do you suggest I try to stop it?'

Renna shook her blonde head. 'The company my father works for has spent a great deal of money on the exploratory expedition to Tyrox. It is by far the most suitable planet discovered to date. They have even started selling one-way tickets. I might add that as reward to my father, the entire Cahorn family is scheduled for an early transport. Not as early as yours, of course.'

'Mine? I am being sent back to Tyrox?' Dor cried out in eagerness.

'Yes, my young friend,' Captain Cahorn said from the open doorway. 'I convinced Outerspace Explorations that it was good protection to have you along on the first ship. That first ship leaves next week. It will carry some of our leading agronomists, biologists, chemists, geologists, mineralogists, communicators, and, of course, the military. It will be their job to analyse all phases of life on Tyrox and prepare the way for the colonists to come. With you on the ship, we are more likely to get a fair reception. And you will be well paid to serve as the interpreter.'

He paused, a worried look on his face. 'But come, Dor, the vistascope people are ready for you. The whole world is tuned in to see you and hear you. I would have preferred to delay this talk until we had had a chance to go over what you should say. But I know you are anxious to talk to your father and tell him you are among friends. Right now all you need to do is reassure him that all is well with you. Later, when our plans are more definite, we can tell him about when he can expect your return.' In the family room, Dor was almost blinded by the strong lights. She was seated in the centre of the room. She could see several vistascope cameras levelled at her. The room was crowded with technicians. Over to one side she could see Renna and Bob with their mother.

'As soon as you hear your father's voice, you can begin talking,' Cahorn said to her.

For a moment or two, Dor waited in silence, listening for her father's voice. When it came through, amplified, as clear as if he were in the same room, Dor had difficulty holding back a sigh of relief.

Then she spoke, very slowly and carefully, in the graceful, lilting Tyroxan language.

'Father,' she said, 'I am a prisoner on a planet called Terra.

'The people here are desperate. I feel sorry for them. There are billions and billions of them. Everything is polluted. They are looking for other planets to colonize to relieve the horrible pressure.

'Yes, Father, they want to send many of their people to Tyrox, at least a billion. But as I love you and you love me, don't let even that first ship land.

'They are sending a ship next week with some of their top scientists. You must prevent it from landing. You have not quite three hundred Tyroxan days to prepare your defences. I recall hearing that special machinery for laser disintegrators and magnetic shields were developed a century ago when we

thought we were in danger from another invader. Use those three hundred days to reactivate the shields and the disintegrators.

'No, Father, all Terrans are not evil. They are like people caught in a deadly plague. They are frightened. The people I am living with are very kind to me. I wish we could help them. But it's only common sense to refuse to admit the plague. If they are unable to land on Tyrox, it will force them to search further for other habitable planets, preferably unpopulated. Tyrox must be saved!

'No, Father, they do not understand what I am saying to you. I know their language. They do not know ours.

'Tell Mother and all my friends that I am well treated. I admit I am frightened. Perhaps I should say I am *Terra*fied . . . terrified of what Terra could do to Tyrox. Don't let that first ship land, Father.'

Dor raised her three eyes, glistening with half-shed tears, to look up at Captain Cahorn.

'And now could you tell us what you told your father?' the spaceman asked.

Dor nodded. 'I told him that life is quite different here than it is on Tyrox. I told him that I was well and that I was being very well treated.'

'Did you tell your father that you were going to be on the first ship to go to Tyrox? I'm anxious that we are favourably welcomed.'

Dor looked back at the Terran spaceman. 'No,' she

said with a half smile of a secret unshared, 'I didn't say anything about my being on that first ship. I did tell him, however, how to welcome it.'

PLANET-FALL ON ISIS

Monica Hughes

The warning klaxons awakened the sleeping passengers of the Interstellar Ship Pegasus Two. For the duration of the five-parsec journey from Earth all eighty of them had lain cocooned in an hypnotically induced slumber, while information about their new life on Isis was fed to them. Meanwhile, as they floated against their padded couch straps, dreaming and learning, the Captain and crew of the Pegasus had kept the ship on course from reference light to reference light, homing in to three-dimensional space, checking their coordinates, and winking out into hyper-space to the next light. To some super observer in space their progress across the galaxy from Earth to Ra in the constellation Indus must have looked like an enormously long dotted line, as they alternately vanished and reappeared, arcing imperceptibly towards the centre of the slowly spinning galaxy.

The first thing Mark London was aware of was the apparent weightlessness of his body against the contoured couch on which he had spent the last months. In actual fact, the gravitational field of Ra was already making itself felt. The stylo that the navigational officer had left in mid-air almost a moment before had just reached the table top. But compared to Mark's last memory, lying apprehensively waiting for blast-off from Earth, he was weightless. It was a pleasant feeling, half awake, half asleep, wholly contented.

The quiet voice that had been his sole companion through the voyage spoke again in his ear. 'You have had an excellent sleep. You have awakened fit and refreshed, remembering everything you have learned. Lie still until the nurse reaches you to detach your intravenous feeder. Then sit up very slowly, swing your legs down off the couch, and do the prescribed exercises.'

Mark lay staring up at the white bulkhead until a twinge in his left arm and the firm pressure of an adhesive bandage triggered his next reaction. Obediently he sat up and swung his stiff legs down from the couch. His toes prickled with pins and needles, but otherwise he felt in perfect shape. He wriggled his toes and rotated his ankles, breathing deeply to the bottom of his lungs. He coughed. His throat and lungs felt dry and unused. So did his mouth. A drink would be good.

In the next beds his mother, father and little sister Carrie all seemed safe and well. The nurse was helping Carrie to sit up. Well, that was all right then . . . not that things often went wrong in space-flight. Hypnosleep cushioned the body and mind against the insults of g-forces and weightlessness as the ship popped in and out of real space, and from the boredom of the time between . . . but it was good to see his family safe, with his own eyes.

Six hours later the passengers had had two meals and a full physical workout. By then Ra's gravitational pull was noticeable. An object put down, stayed down. An object forgetfully left in mid-air fell to the floor with a crash. Not that the settlers made that particular mistake. It was the crew, every time, who forgot. It was not surprising. Mark saw, in the occasional glimpse of a lined face, the strain of re-entry after months of weightlessness.

Every moment not spent in eating was spent in restoring the tone to flaccid muscles. Twenty-four hours after waking, Mark felt that he had never been in such good shape in his life before. Reluctantly he returned to his couch to strap himself in for planet-fall. His heart began to pound so hard with excitement that Mark was afraid it would show up on the biomonitor, and he forced himself to practise the slow deep breathing that was one of the skills he had learned in hypno-sleep.

A final blast of the klaxon. Probably a warning for the crew to strap themselves in for planet-fall. 'Planet-fall'. The old sea term 'land-fall' had been carried over into space navigation and now had more meaning than it had ever had back on Earth. Planet-fall ... a fall towards a planet. Controlled by retro-jets, but nevertheless a fall, as the gravity of Ra's fourth planet Isis reached out and grabbed them.

Outside Pegasus Two the heat shields began to glow and flake away in a spume of bright sparks. The atmosphere here was deeper than Earth's but thinner. Less friction, then, but for a longer period of time. Hot enough. Mark felt the perspiration trickle down the sides of his forehead and neck to be absorbed damply into the cushion against which his head was pressed. Experimentally he tried to move his right hand against the straps. Then just the tip of his index finger. As the ship hurtled towards Isis the reactionary forces pushed him with a giant's hand back against his couch. Breathing was almost impossible. It was something you did through your clenched teeth, drawing in a few cubic centimetres of air at a time, as much as you could force in, which was just enough to stop your eyes from bursting out of your head. The tearing thundering noises that surrounded him seemed to be an echo of what was going on inside his own body.

Mark was just beginning to realize, in a rising wave of panic, that he simply could not last another minute, when the noise stopped abruptly. The giant's hand was lifted from his body. He cautiously drew in a deep breath. Then another. Boy, that felt good!

The silence was overwhelming. Had he gone deaf? Then, as the pounding in his ears subsided and his heart slowed to its normal steady beat, he began to hear the tiny pings and snaps of cooling metal. Then Carrie's voice . . . 'Mummy?' And Jody's fretful wail from further down the ship. People stirred and sighed. Far away Mark could hear the sound of metal grating against metal.

Then, quite suddenly, the tired smelly recycled air was gone. Instead there was chill, a smell of dry grass, the lively scent of a herb, something like sage, but different, new. The tang of upland air. When Mark sucked in the air he could feel it tingling right down to his toes. They had arrived! How much longer were they supposed to go on lying here? They were on Isis at last. Would the word to go ashore never be given? All around were the little sounds of breathing and fidgeting. All eighty settlers waited for the word.

When it finally came training held firm. They sat up. The velcro straps were undone for the last time, and in an orderly fashion they lined up in the long passenger cabin and marched, two by two, down a spiral flight of stairs to the main exit of the ship. There was a flash of brightness that dazzled, but the outside stair was steep and Mark had to keep his eyes on the steps below him, while the next passenger crowded him from above. So his first glimpse of Isis was of nothing but the stubble of blue-grey grass and, all around the ship, black char from the jets.

But once he had lined up with his family and the rest of their Ten he had time to look around, past the hectares of grey grass bowing and nodding waist high in every direction, to the mountains that rose almost sheer on every side. Some of them were flat-topped, like the mesas of New Mexico and Colorado, while the others were jagged, young-looking, unworn by time and weather, all of a startling rose-red colour streaked with sombre purple.

Mark turned around. To the north of the ship the mountains grudgingly parted, leaving a small ravine, in the misty depths of which he could see flashes of white—a waterfall, perhaps. Beyond the ravine were the distant peaks of yet more mountains, lavendered by the distance between.

There was no sound anywhere, except for the low voices of the settlers, and the sharp pings of still cooling metal. The sky was wide and empty, enormously empty, and of a clear shrill cool green. The sun ... Mark glanced up and then quickly turned away ... the sun was small, brilliant and white, and the shadows it cast were as hard-edged as if they had been cut out of blue-grey cardboard.

He was nudged and pushed back into place, so that by the time the Captain came down the stairway, the settlers were ranked in orderly fashion in their Tens. First there were the ten couples under twenty years of age, many of whom had probably married in haste to meet the immigration requirements. Next to them stood the ten childless couples whose ages ranged from twenty to thirty. No small children were allowed. Nothing was known about the disorienting effect of the long sleep on small children, and anyway, it had been unanimously agreed by STC officials that small children were too much of a hazard and a source of heartbreak on new planets. They had to be watched constantly, and they seemed to have an uncanny habit of putting new and untested substances into their

mouths without asking first, and of making pets of unknown and potentially dangerous animals. So there were no younger ones among the Tens.

The two Tens, where Mark and Carrie stood, consisted of the ten married couples between the ages of thirty and forty, who had between them twenty children, from the age of Jody, who was nine going on ten, and had been squeaked through because his mother and father had unique new-planet training, and Mark, who was seventeen. There were two more males than females in this teenage population. The computer estimated that in the first two years of a new colony, an average of three out of forty men would lose their lives, while only one out of forty women might be expected to die. Assembling the groups for the Tens was a touchy exercise for psychologists and computers alike.

They had come aboard as strangers, these four Tens. They had never met back on overcrowded Earth, yet now they were bound to each other by powerful hypnotic suggestions into one big loyal family. As Mark stood to attention waiting for the Captain's formal words he let his eyes slide to left and right. He recognised every person, knew each name, each personality, the part that each was to play in establishing a home in this new world.

The Captain was the only unknown, and this made him seem larger than life. He stood sturdily on the bottom rung of the metal staircase, his piercing blue eyes surveying his living cargo. Mark looked up at the seamed, space-ruddied face, the eyes narrowed against the cold brilliance of the morning sun; just for a moment he wished that he too could be a crew member of a space ship. To ply one's endless way through space from Earth to star colony and back. That would be a sight more glamorous than farming!

But then he looked up, past the Captain, past the battered hulk of Pegasus Two, to the clear empty sky, and he smelled again the delicious spicy cold scent of aromatic herbs, and thought—glamour be damned. Isis is *home*.

The Captain spoke briefly, a formal inauguration of the new colony, a prayer, a welcome and a warning. He and his ship would stay, like a lifeboat, for one turn of Isis about its sun. Then they would leave, probably for ever. If things went wrong, if the colony somehow refused to 'jell'', then before the year's end they would all have to return to Earth, the opportunity to escape the crowding and the shortages gone for ever. If they survived the first year Pegasus Two would leave and the settlers would be on their own.

The Captain returned to the ship, and the hypnotic teaching took over. Without fuss, with incredible efficiency, the settlers dogged open the cargo doors and began to unload the packing cases containing the nucleus of their new life. They had two tread-tracked cars and two small floaters, all of them solar powered. These were pushed down the ramp by shoulder power and left in the sun to recharge while the rest of the cargo was unshipped.

An engineering team went ahead to build a bridge across the river that flowed out of the southern end of the lake. These decisions had all been made, long ago, on Earth. The river, which plunged down from the northern mountains in a series of spectacular waterfalls, emerged from the wide lake in a placid stream and meandered in a leisurely fashion between groves of bamboo and clumps of marsh grass until it, unexpectedly and unaccountably, lost itself in the ground two kilometres to the south. The Keeper of the Light had named it Lost Creek, and so it was called on the colony maps.

By the time all the packing cases had been piled around the squat base of Pegasus Two, the crawlers and floaters had acquired sufficient energy to be used; then began a continuous trek to and from the new town site on the far side of the lake. The temporary bridge, a roll of flexible plastic matting, had been unrolled and laid in place across the tussocky swamp that bordered Lost Creek. It had been pegged in place and its plastic 'memory' had been frozen with a high-speed catalytic spray. Now it lay, as rigid as iron, as strong as concrete, as if it had always been there. Young bamboo plants, their tattered grey and mauve leaves shimmering in the wind, bordered it on either side. Only around the edges did it get a little muddy, as the crawlers, heavily laden, moved from ship to town site and back.

Mark, Willi, Angus and Kano were set to erecting the huts that would be home for the Tens. There was a hut each for the childless Tens, and two huts for the Tens with families. In front, closer to the lake, with a clearing in front of it, there was a double-sized hut that would be dining room, meeting hall, kitchen and everything else for the new colony.

The huts were shells of fine plastic film, like bubble tents, each fastened securely by metal posts driven firmly into the soil. Inside, simple screens of the same film divided the area into rooms, one for each couple, a pair for each couple with children. As the boys finished erecting each hut a team of sprayers followed, pumping plastic foam over the shell, inside and out. The stuff set pudding-hard in a moment, and by the end of the day, acted on by the ultra-violet of Isis' sun Ra, it would be like concrete.

There was a scramble of women behind the sprayers, fastening in shelves, hooks, hangers, while the walls were still soft, and another team cut holes for doors and windows. As soon as everyone else was out of the way there came the youngsters, each carefully carrying piles of family possessions, blankets, clothes, books and tools.

By lunch, which they ate sprawled on the dry spiky grass overlooking the lake, there was already a sem-

blance of order. Before Ra touched the rim of the western mountains a stranger would have imagined that the village had been there for months.

Supper was a celebration, a properly cooked meal of freeze-dried turkey meat, with dressing, cranberry sauce and vegetables, followed by pumpkin pie, all transported from Earth in frozen packets to mark the settlers' first Thanksgiving Dinner.

Next year, thought Mark, looking round the lamplit dining room, next year we'll be on our own. No food from Earth then. The Pegasus will have left. What will Thanksgiving Dinner be like next year? It was a solemn scary thought. When at last they left the dining room, all of them reluctant to break away from the 'together' feeling, even though they could hardly keep their eyes open, Mark walked a little way away from the huts and looked up at the night sky.

Here, closer to the centre of the galaxy, the stars burned twice as thickly as even in a southern sky back on Earth. The patterns of the constellations were new. Nothing was familiar any more. He looked for Earth, but how could he tell, in that crowded sky? He knew that Sol was an insignificant star low down on the western horizon, in a constellation whose only interest was that its appearance would tell them that summer was on its way.

In the brilliant starshine he could just see the squat silhouette of Pegasus Two, a black outline against the dark expanse of grassland that spread from the far shore of the lake to the distant western mountains. He looked around. Above the eastern horizon a moon rose, tiny, hardly more than star size. It shunted busily among the thickly clustered stars, more like an artificial satellite than a real moon. That must be Shu. And somewhere up there, hidden like a tree in the middle of the forest, was Isis' second moon Nut. It was even tinier, and since it was in a wider orbit and moved more slowly, it would be even more unnoticeable.

For a second Mark felt a twinge, almost like stomach ache, for the familiar things of Earth, for a sun and moon that looked like the Sun and the Moon, for stars whose patterns were familiar. But then he remembered the actualities of the city where he and Carrie and their parents had lived; the choking smog, the hours standing on the rapid transit, shoulder to shoulder with other half-asleep commuters, the line-ups for food, for movies, for a day in the country or by the sea . . . the continual inhuman jostling for space.

Here on Isis there was at least space. A man could stretch and feel free to be himself. He took a last look around. The thin air was biting cold. To his right the mesa rose stark and steep, bisecting the sky, blotting out half the stars. Over to the north, near where he had seen the waterfall, halfway up the precipitous cliff, was light. Tiny golden oblongs of light that said clearly that up there, halfway to the sky, was a house. One of the lights blinked out, just for an instant, as if someone had walked across the room close to the window.

Mark realized with a shock that he must be looking at the dwelling of the Keeper of the Isis Light. That was strange and mysterious . . . a girl, all alone out here, parsecs from the nearest civilization, with no one to talk to but . . . what did she call him? . . . Guardian, that was it. Up there, where she lived, close to the mesa top, the stars must seem close enough to touch, the burning cold of space must be a neighbour.

What would it be like to be alone for year after year, with only the night and the wind and the cold spicy smell of the upland grasses? He tried to imagine how she must feel—the Keeper of the Light—but try as he might his mind couldn't make the jump. His training told him too clearly that the uplands were dangerous, that he must never leave the valley without the protection of an ultra-violet-opaque suit and an oxygen mask.

One day, off in the vague future, if all went well with the colony, they would plant trees and gradually build up the oxygen content of Isis. Then the ozone layer would also thicken, the ultra-violet would be safely filtered out, and the mesas and mountains of Isis would be theirs . . . One day, but not now. For now, the valley was wide and deep. That was where they belonged, not in some oxygen-thin eagle's eyrie, perched on a cliff halfway to outer space.

He turned his back on the night and went into his own hut, into the room he shared with Carrie. She was already asleep, so he skinned quietly out of his clothes and slid into his sleeping bag. It was unbelievably quiet. There was no roar of cars, no tearing sound of jets, no warring voices from a thousand transistors, no quarrelling shouts, no kids screaming in the night, no sirens.

A tiny rustle in the stiff grass outside sent a shock of gooseflesh down his back. Far off there was the lonely yammering cry of some unknown night creature. He wriggled deeper into the warmth of his sleeping bag and found himself thinking again about the high mesa, and about the girl who had kept the light burning on Isis all the long years until they had come.

HALF LIFE

Rachel Cosgrove Payes

s Benji washed up for lunch at the Dake Cent, the tattoo on the back of his right hand reminded him that Half Life was only two short months away, and he hadn't filed yet on an Expired. It was harder on Dake Cent kids, with no parents to use. He had to go looking, find himself an Expired who hadn't already been tabbed, and file, hoping that someone else hadn't beaten him to it. Benji had been taken from his mother when he was only three, too young to remember her except as a vague dream. And his father had disappeared five years ago.

Marc, who bunked above him, came in to wash.

'Hey, Benji, filed yet?'

'Not yet.' He wished Marc would quit asking—gloating, really. Marc had located a recluse in the bombed-out buildings down by the river, and had filed on him already.

'How about the Old Man of the Hills? Huh, Benji? He oughta be so old that you'd win the prize for this year.'

Everybody knew the Old Man of the Hills was

a myth, created by the cruel to taunt those who couldn't find an Expired by filing date. Benji sneaked another look at his hand. The tattoo mocked him. The numbers were indelible, unchangeable, inexorable. His birthdate, 21/6/20, and his ID number. And today was March 15, 2035. In just two months and six days, Benji would be fifteen—Half Life. If he didn't file at least two weeks prior to that date, and bring in a hand before his own Half Life, he'd have a large red X tattooed over the date on his hand, automatically classifying him as a Technical Expired, although he was only fifteen instead of the legal cut-off age of thirty. Then he would have to guard his own life constantly, so that someone nearing Half Life would not file on him and kill him for his tattooed hand, to fulfil the requirements of the law and retain their own immune status until they Expired in another fifteen years.

These days, scarcely anyone lasted through his thirtieth year. There was a prize each year for the oldest hand turned in—the prize being a royal blue hand tattoo that gave the lucky winner an extra year of life before he Expired.

Benji decided to start getting up at dawn to prowl the city, trying to ferret out hidden Expireds. But when another week passed without his finding an untagged Expired, he began to panic. At dawn he flitted silently along the edges of Bargetown, where dilapidated old boats and barges clogged the polluted waters of the river. He had had the barges under surveillance for a week, keeping his eye glued to a home-made scope.

Then he spied one person with a red X over his tattoo, an eligible. He was even able to make out the ID number without allowing himself to be seen. Surely he would be first to file on this legal Expired, as the boy stayed on the river side of the barges, never approaching the shore. So Benji hurried back to the Half Life

Bureau and filed the ID number he had read through his scope.

'Run it through the computer immediately,' the bored programmer told him.

Benji's emotions were a mixture of anxiety and elation. He was sure this would be a good one. Then his only remaining problem would be to kill the Technical Expired, cut off his tattooed right hand, and bring it in for confirmation.

The computer lights flickered, the reels spun, the printer clacked, and the technician pulled off the print-out sheet. 'Filed on two hours ago. You can't use him.'

Out in the street, Benji found that he was trembling. It wasn't just fear; it was a combination of many emotions—frustration, anger, desperation. It was then that he remembered Marc's taunt about the Old Man of the Hills. Maybe there *was* someone out there in the rugged, wooded slopes to the north of the City. He would have to get a special permit to leave, but with his Half Life rapidly approaching, he was sure he would get the okay.

Benji was in luck, since the clerk who issued permits for Outside had lived in Benji's Dake Cent until his own Half Life two years earlier.

'I'll even issue you a scoot, if you can scrounge batteries.'

Benji grinned, elated. He knew where he could swipe a battery or two, and with a scoot to ride, he would have lots more time to search the hills before he had to come back to the City to celebrate his Half Life.

'Thanks, Jon. Come to my Half Life party.'

He waited until dark, slid quietly into a locked scoot repair shop via a loosened board on a back window, and took two batteries, one as a spare. *I'll repay when I reach Half Life and am eligible to work*, he promised himself.

At first light he was at the north gate, astride the scoot, permit badge stuck firmly to his wrist.

'Lookin' fer the Old Man of the Hills, kid?' the guard asked jokingly, as he moved the coiled barbed wire aside just enough to allow Benji through the gap. 'Don't forget you have to return in time for your Half Life.'

Benji accelerated, purring along the broken, overgrown ancient road that wound north through the foothills. Ahead the dark green of mountains beckoned, and Benji breathed thanks to Jon for the scoot. Without it, he would have walked for days just reaching the mountains.

In all that first day of bouncing along increasingly rough tracks that steadily rose into the hills, he saw no one. There were ruins of houses. He even rode, once, through the deserted streets of a ghost town. At the time of the Trouble, everyone had come into the City to the tunnel shelters. No one returned to the Outside.

His early elation rapidly changed to worry. No one lived Outside. The stories of the Old Man were just stories, not fact. By the end of this third day of riding, Benji was out of sight of the broken towers of the City, high in the mountains that grew wilder with each mile he rode. He had to reserve some battery power for the return trip.

Benji began to regret his decision to search Outside. No one had ever found an Expired outside the City. He

should have stayed at home and prowled the streets and tunnels. He would have found someone eventually. Now he had wasted precious days on this folly. He would ride to the top of the ridge, along this faint track that was the only remnant of an earlier road. If he saw no sign of life, he would turn back and take his chance in familiar territory.

Topping the rise, Benji looked down into a small valley, a twinkling blue oval of lake at the bottom, with trees growing almost to its waters except on one side where there was a fair-sized clearing—and a small hut that did not seem to be the usual ruin he had been seeing. Excited, he got off the scoot and lay full length on the ground with the scope to his eye. The scene leaped up at him. It was a small house, not a ruin. A tiny drift of smoke came from a tall stone chimney. Someone lived there. Even as Benji watched, his mouth dry with emotion, he saw the hut door open, and a man stepped outside. The distance was too great for Benji to be able to see the man's tattoo. He would hide his scoot here on the ridge and go down into the valley on foot. Less chance of having the man spot him and flee.

A cautious thirty minutes later, Benji had worked his way to within a thousand feet of the house. Dusk was falling. As he crouched in a thicket of berry bushes, the hut door opened again and the man stood silhouetted in the doorway. Whipping his scope to his eye, Benji focused on the man's right hand. The date

stood out clearly, even though it was X'd in red—14/2/90. The man was forty-five years old! Benji had never seen anyone that old before. He would win this year and earn an extra year of life for himself.

Then a terrible thought hit him. He hadn't filed on this man. Legally he had to file before the kill. How could he have forgotten? It meant the long trip back to the City, filing, getting confirmation, then receiving permission to leave for Outside again. He would have to retrace his route and hope that the man was still living here. It would take at least a week; and, if he couldn't steal more scoot batteries for the return trip, much longer by foot. He might not be able to do it in the allotted time.

Desperation brought Benji to a terrible decision. He would kill the man now, take the hand, and ride back towards home. Before entering the gate, he would hide the hand. Then, after he had filed on the man in this hut, he could go back out, get his grisly cache, and pretend he had killed the man just outside the City.

Perhaps it would be best to wait until the man was asleep. Benji had heard the old tales of mighty warriors who declined with age, but this man looked robust. With only his knife as a weapon, Benji couldn't risk normal combat.

Darkness fell, the man went back inside, and Benji moved closer to the hut. Suddenly he heard something so beautiful that his heart ached, and tears came to his eyes. It was music, he guessed, but not the thump he was used to. The sound went up, up, up, then rippled down, a waterfall splashing in a pool, like the one he had seen on the trail yesterday. It was haunting, with none of the hard beat of thump. Yet, unfamiliar as it was, it called to Benji in a language he knew was his own.

He had to find out what was making the glorious sound. Like a ghost, he drifted close to the hut. On one

side light filtered out of a window only partially cur-
tained. Holding his breath, Benji eased into position so
that one eye peered through a gap in the rough fabric
hiding the interior.

The man was sitting in front of something that
looked like a modified computer console. A row of
white and black levers ran along one side, and the man
was pushing them with his fingers, producing
the enchanting sounds Benji had heard. Benji
remembered that he had seen a picture once, in a
tattered book of the Ancients, of such a thing—called
a *piago*, or some such odd word. He was familiar
with the drums and gitjos the thumpers played,
but this was—his mind refused to put a name to
it.

The concert went on for a long time, melting Benji's
heart. Then the man leaned back, dropped his hands,
and the glorious sounds stopped.

'More!'

The man spun around and was on his feet before
Benji realized he had cried the word aloud.

'Who's there?'

Shaken by the spell of the music, paralysed by fright
at being discovered, Benji just stood there. The man
snatched open the door. Seeing him move galvanized
the boy, but it was too late. Benji turned to flee into the
bushes, when a heavy hand clamped on to his
shoulder and spun him around.

Benji flashed his knife, only to have his wrist caught
in a numbing grip. Then he was marched into the
house.

Relieved of the knife, Benji stood shaking. Yet, in
here, the power of the music returned, and his eyes
strayed away from the hard face of his captor to the
instrument against the wall.

'Have you never heard a piano?' The man's voice
didn't match his brutal strength. It was low and
gentle.

Benji shook his head. 'I've only heard the thumpers.'

The man eased his grip after taking Benji's knife. Then he held up Benji's tattooed hand. 'Yes, I understand. Soon it will be your Half Life.' His voice held pain, and it made Benji want to cry, just as the music had.

'Are you hungry, boy?'

Benji didn't answer, but the man went to a cupboard, brought out bread and some meat Benji didn't recognize, and used Benji's own knife to cut huge portions.

'Come on, eat—and I'll play for you.'

He left Benji's knife on the table with the food, turned his back as if unafraid, and seated himself before the piano. His fingers ran up and down the black and white levers, and the sound poured out, filling the room, filling Benji's soul just as the food filled his empty stomach.

When the boy was full, the man stopped playing and turned to face him. He held out his right hand, so that the tattoo showed plainly.

'You've come for my hand, haven't you?' His dark eyes were sad. 'I've lived the span of two Half Lives since I left the City. I had hoped that the madness would die away; but it must be worse, if you've come this far, just for my hand. Are Expireds that hard to find now?'

Benji nodded. There was a queer lump in his throat, as if a chunk of the bread he had eaten was stuck there.

'I left, you know. I found I couldn't kill anyone. So, when I refused, they marked me Expired. I slipped away one night and fled to the hills. So many years ago—I'd almost forgotten the old horrors. I found this house, and the piano someone had loved before the Trouble—and I've lived here, at peace with my neighbours.'

Benji gasped. 'Neighbours? There are others?'

His host smiled. 'In the next valley, and the one beyond that. A few who, like me, wouldn't fulfil their obligation to kill another human, just to get a hand.'

Benji's head ached. He had never met anyone like the Old Man of the Hills. His eyes couldn't stay away from the date on his hand—he would win; no one else in the world could be this old. Benji's hand stole towards his knife, so foolishly, so trustingly returned to him.

As his fingers curled around the hilt, his host said softly, 'Would you like to learn to play the piano?'

It was a heart-stopping moment. Play? Make that lovely sound that had drawn him, that called to him in a language at once strange and yet achingly familiar?

'Could I—no. I have to get back by—'

'By your Half Life. You have a few days yet. What is your name, boy?'

'Benji.'

'And I am Rolf. Let me teach you to play. Then, when you achieve your legal Half Life, you can return here, if you wish, and have the piano for your own.'

'But—but—you—'

'I'll not be here, will I? Not if you kill me and take my hand.'

It was a terrible decision. Benji knew he would win the prize with Rolf's tattoo; yet suddenly he felt sick inside. To kill the man would kill the music. Benji knew that he couldn't learn, in a few short weeks, to make the sounds he had heard tonight. It must have taken Rolf years—more years than Benji had realized anyone had in this life.

As terrible sobs shook his body, he felt Rolf's arms about him, in a way he had never known before. The man rocked him gently and made little crooning, soothing sounds.

'Tell me, Benji. Talk about it.'

Calmer, Benji explained about the prize.

'They didn't do that thirty years ago. It's worse, much worse than I'd dreamed. I'm glad I fled.'

'So you see, you're so old—with your hand, I'd earn myself one more year before I Expired.'

'Yes, I see. And one extra year is very precious. Well, Benji, you don't want to kill me.' Benji shook his head fiercely, and sniffed loudly. 'Yet you need my hand.' Rolf paused, and reluctantly, Benji nodded. 'Then let me give you that hand.'

For a moment, Benji didn't understand. Then, slowly, the meaning seeped into his mind. 'You— you'd let me cut off your hand—just so that I—'

'It means so much to you, doesn't it?'

Benji's eyes strayed to the piano, silent now that its master no longer commanded it to make its melodies.

'But, with one hand, you couldn't make the music.'

'Not as well, Benji. Not as well.'

Benji thought as he had never thought before. If he took in Rolf's hand, he would have sixteen years of existing in the City, and then he would be Expired, fair game for some youngster nearing Half Life. Nothing in the City could compare with what he had seen this evening, here in this house with its magic piano that made the achingly lovely music. Suddenly the solution to his problem seemed so simple.

'If I don't go back—if I lose my honour by refusing my Half Life obligation, would you—would you—?' He couldn't say the words.

But Rolf knew. 'I get lonely, Benji. We'll start your piano lessons in the morning.'

That night Benji lay on a narrow bed that faced an uncurtained window. The moon rose, huge and orange, over the mountain and flooded his tiny room with its peaceful light. He had scarcely seen the moon before, because it wasn't safe to be above ground in the City at night. Too excited to sleep, Benji wondered: Someday, will some boy nearing Half Life come here hunting me? If he does, I hope that I can help him, as Rolf has helped me.

And he slept, soundly, dreaming of the morning . . . and the music.

RETURN TO PELADON

Terrance Dicks

On the remote edges of the galaxy was a planet called Peladon. It was a bleak and mountainous place, lashed by howling storms, lit at night by the fierce blaze of three moons. A primitive, barbarous world, inhabited by warriors, hunters, and savage beasts, fierce bear-like creatures with tusks and one mighty horn, who roamed the wooded slopes of the high mountains.

The warriors of Peladon both hunted and worshipped the beast called Aggedor. No young Peladonian was reckoned truly a man until he had slain one in single combat. Because of its strength and valour, Aggedor became the sacred symbol of the Royal House of Peladon. Unfortunately, it also became very nearly extinct.

Time brought other changes. Under a young and progressive king, Peladon joined the Galactic Federation, allying itself with other more civilized planets.

The alliance was not accomplished without difficulty. Hepesh, High Priest of Peladon clung fiercely to the old ways, rebelling against his king and combining with a treacherous Federation delegate called Arcturus to keep Peladon isolated. The plot was foiled by a wandering Time Lord called the Doctor. He arrived on

Peladon apparently by chance, was mistaken for a
Federation delegate, and later vanished as mysteriously as he had come.

Time passed, and King Peladon was succeeded
by his daughter. The Galactic Federation became
embroiled in war with Galaxy Five, and suddenly
Peladon was a planet of vital strategic importance. The
mountains and rocks of Peladon were rich in trisilicate,
a mineral vital to the war effort.

Now more intensive mining began, and Federation
technicians were brought in to speed up the process.

The war with Galaxy Five dragged Peladon towards
a technological future with brutal speed. Clashes
between the old ways and the new were inevitable,
and once again there were rumblings of mutiny from
the more traditionally minded Peladonians. Was this
all the benefit of joining the Federation—more toil in
the mines, now under alien overseers?

Affairs on Peladon were moving towards a crisis.
Then the Doctor reappeared . . .

*

A little party of miners toiled through an immense
cavern deep in the heart of Mount Megashra, sacred
mountain of Peladon. They wore rough working-
clothes, and their hands and faces were grained deep
with trisilicate dust. The cathedral-like cavern was the
meeting point of many tunnels and mine galleries, and
its strangely twisted stalagmites and stalactites gave a
weird subterranean beauty to the scene.

Between them the miners trundled a sonic lance, a
device like a small wheeled cannon, newly introduced
into the mining operation. Ettis, the squad leader har-
ried them along, a thin, wiry young man, sharp-
featured and sharp-voiced.

'Come on, come on, keep it moving. Mustn't keep
our lords and masters waiting.' He pointed to a tunnel
directly ahead. 'Straight down there.'

Suddenly a glowing spot appeared on the cavern

wall. With terrifying speed it grew into a blazing corona of light, and in the heart of the fireball appeared a familiar and terrifying form.

The miners staggered back, before the blast of heat, covering their eyes and bowing their heads in fear.

A ray of light sped from the heart of the apparition. It touched one of the miners, his body glowed brightly, and he screamed once and vanished. His fellows turned and fled in terror. Behind them the glowing apparition faded from the cavern wall.

*

In a tunnel not far away, two relative newcomers to Peladon were engaged in an earnest technical discussion. One was called Vega Nexos, a mole-man from the planet Vega. Most of the inhabitants of Vega lived in tunnels of one kind or another, and the Vegans were famous mining engineers, who sold their skills all over the galaxy. The second was an Earthman called Eckersley, a tall, lean man with a wry, sardonic face. Like Vega Nexos, he was a mining engineer. Both wore light silver cover-alls—the badge of the technician throughout the galaxy.

Eckersley was brandishing a chunk of rock, shot through with gleaming metallic veins. 'I agree, the quality's marvellous—but we're not even producing *enough* to refine yet.'

Vega Nexos gave a snort of discontent. 'How can we, when these primitives cling to their picks and shovels? We bring modern equipment here and they refuse to let us use it.'

'Oh, they'll come round in time,' said Eckersley tolerantly. 'At least they agreed to try out the sonic lance.'

There were yells from down the tunnel, and the sound of rushing feet. A group of terrified miners rounded a bend in the tunnel, shot past them and ran on.

Eckersley reached out a long arm and grabbed the

last of the group, forcing him to a halt. 'Hey, Ettis, what's going on? What's all the panic?'

'It is Aggedor! We brought the sonic cannon as you ordered and the spirit of Aggedor appeared and slew one of us for blasphemy.' Ettis wrenched himself free. 'Do you think anyone will use your alien equipment now, Earthman?'

Before Eckersley could reply, Ettis had followed the others down the tunnel.

*

In the throne room of the Citadel of Peladon, the great castle on the peak of the sacred mountain, a meeting was held to discuss the crisis.

The huge stone-walled chamber was richly draped with hanging tapestries. Torches flared smokily in holders formed in the shape of the snarling face of Aggedor.

At the end of the great hall on a raised dais was the great ceremonial throne, now occupied by the slender figure of Queen Thalira. A frail and beautiful girl, still very young, she seemed almost crushed by the weight of her crown and ceremonial jewels. Behind her towered the massive figure of Blor, the Queen's Champion, powerful arms folded over his mighty chest. At the Queen's right hand, a little behind the throne, stood Ortron, who was both Chancellor and High Priest. An ornately robed, impressively bearded figure, he was the Queen's chief adviser and the holder of the real power on Peladon.

A strangely assorted group was assembled before the throne. At the centre were the two engineers, Eckersley and Vega Nexos. Beside them stood Alpha Centauri, Ambassador of the Galactic Federation. To the Peladonians, unused to the infinite variety of intelligent life-forms, his was an extraordinary figure. The body was a single column, draped in a cloak emblazoned with the insignia of a Federation Ambassador. The head was octopoid with a single enormous

eye. Six rippling tentacles projected from beneath the
cloak. They waved and stirred continuously, like
branches in the breeze, reflecting every shade of Alpha
Centauri's feelings. For all his rather intimidating
appearance, Alpha Centauri was a gentle and
sensitive creature. He was finding the position of
Federation Ambassador on a primitive and strife-
torn planet a considerable strain on his delicate
sensibilities.

Chancellor Ortron surveyed the motley group with
disfavour. He was no lover of aliens, however politi-
cally distinguished or technically qualified. His glare
settled on Eckersley. 'One of our miners has been
killed, the others are terrified and refuse to work.
Explain!'

Eckersley had worked on a lot of planets and it took
more than an angry Chancellor to intimidate him. 'Not
up to me to explain, is it? The miners say it was the
spirit of Aggedor, whatever that means.'

'Do not blaspheme, alien,' rumbled Ortron.

Alpha Centauri said 'I am sure no disrespect was intended, Chancellor.' His voice was high-pitched and twittering, a fitting expression of his nervous temperament.

In his low grunting voice, Vega Nexos said, 'I am a practical engineer. I find it difficult to accept that this incident was brought about by supernatural means.'

'Then what is your explanation?'

'Sabotage.'

'And who are these saboteurs?'

Eckersley said, 'Saboteurs or spooks, the result's the same. Your miners are refusing to use the sonic gun.'

Queen Thalira spoke for the first time. 'The use of this sonic cannon is essential to you?'

Eckersley shrugged. 'It will increase output tenfold, Your Majesty. Save your miners a lot of hard work with pick and shovel.'

'Then arrange an immediate demonstration. If our people see that we have faith in the new technology, it may calm their fears.'

Alpha Centauri's tentacles rippled as he inclined forward in a bow. 'Allow me to thank Your Majesty on behalf of the Federation.'

Thalira raised her hand. 'Thank you, Ambassador. The audience is at an end.'

The aliens left in a group, and Ortron leaned closer to the throne, dominating the Queen with his bulk. 'I must protest, Your Majesty. To expose yourself to danger . . .'

'You know as well as I, Ortron, that it was my father's dream to see Peladon a member of the Federation. He signed the treaty, and now I must honour it—even if it means my people must make sacrifices in a quarrel not their own.' Queen Thalira sighed. 'We must accept the duties of Federation membership, Ortron, as well as its privileges.'

Ortron bowed, 'I shall go to the temple, Your Majesty, and seek guidance from the spirit of Aggedor.'

*

In one of the tunnels just beneath the Citadel, a guard on routine patrol was astonished to hear a strange wheezing, groaning noise and even more astonished to see a square blue box appearing out of thin air. Strange rumours of terrifying events in the mines below had been circulating through the Citadel, and overcome with superstitious terror, he turned and fled.

Since he was a brave and conscientious man despite his fear, he stopped at a bend in the tunnel keeping the box under observation from a safe distance.

He was amazed to see its door open and a tall white-haired man in strange clothes step out, followed by a female alien, equally strangely dressed.

The Doctor looked around him and rubbed his chin. 'Well, according to my calculations, Sarah, we should be in the Citadel of Peladon, one of the most impressive sights—'

'Well, we're not, are we?' interrupted the girl. Her name was Sarah Jane Smith. She was an independently minded freelance journalist from the planet Earth in the twentieth century, and she had been the Doctor's more or less unwilling companion on a number of adventures.

She was already regretting that she had let the Doctor talk her into this trip. He had persuaded her with the promise of a fascinating visit to a picturesque and primitive planet, just making the transition from feudal savagery to technological civilization.

Sarah looked round disgustedly. 'We're not in your precious Citadel of Peladon at all, we're in another rotten gloomy old tunnel!' For some reason tunnels seemed to feature largely in their adventures—and there was usually something nasty at the other end.

'I'm afraid the scanner must still be on the blink.'

'There's more than the scanner on the blink,' muttered Sarah darkly.

'I'm afraid the spatial co-ordinates must have slipped a bit,' said the Doctor apologetically. 'We may not actually be *in* the Citadel, but we're not far away. It's built on the peak of a mountain, you see, and the mountain is honeycombed with mining tunnels.'

'I don't suppose we could just get back in the TARDIS and go home?'

'Have a heart, Sarah, I've been looking forward to a return visit to Peladon for ages.'

The Doctor set off, and Sarah sighed and followed him.

Silently the watching guard slipped away.

*

In the main cavern a party of miners were setting up the sonic cannon, supervised by Eckersley and Vega Nexos.

Ettis looked on gloomily. Beside him was an older man, a burly, thick-set miner, with an air of natural authority. This was Gebek, leader of the Miners' Guild. Fiercely loyal both to his Queen and to the miners he led, he was having a difficult time reconciling the conflicting claims.

They looked up as Queen Thalira swept in, attended by Blor, her Champion, Chancellor Ortron and a squad of guards.

Gebek fell to one knee. 'We are honoured by your presence, Your Majesty.'

'And we are grateful for yours,' said Thalira regally. 'Can your miners be persuaded to overcome their fears?'

'The demonstration may help, Your Majesty. But as Ettis will tell you . . .'

Ettis threw himself on his knees before the Queen. 'I beg you not to permit this blasphemy, Your Majesty. I have *seen* the wrath of Aggedor . . .'

'You have seen the work of alien spies and saboteurs, agents of Galaxy Five,' interrupted Vega Nexos peevishly.

A guard ran in and threw himself down before Ortron. 'Aliens, my lord. They appeared in the tunnel as if by magic.'

Ortron turned to the Commander of the Queen's Guard. 'You heard him! There are aliens in the tunnels, enemies of Peladon and the Federation. They must be found and destroyed.'

As the guards ran from the cavern, Eckersley said, 'Everything is ready, Your Majesty. May we begin?'

Thalira inclined her head.

Eckersley said, 'If you will kindly keep your eyes on that section of wall over there . . .' He pointed to the rock face on which the sonic cannon was trained.

Vega Nexos bent over the controls, there was a hum of power, and a circular chunk of the rock face exploded into fragments, instantly creating a miniature cave.

'Direct access to the main seam in a matter of moments,' said Eckersley proudly. 'Take weeks to do that by hand.'

A fierce light blazed from inside the newly created cave, and a shattering savage roar filled the cavern.

The Peladonians were transfixed with fear, but before anyone could stop him, Vega Nexos hurried forward to the gap. 'Do not be afraid, it is only some trickery . . .'

As he reached the hole there was another terrifying roar and a beam of brilliant light shot out. His body glowed brightly and vanished.

'You see,' screamed Ettis. 'It is the curse of Aggedor! Now do you believe?'

'Come, Your Majesty,' shouted Ortron. 'You must leave this place at once.' He led the Queen away, and the others hurried after them.

*

The Doctor stopped at a tunnel junction and looked thoughtfully around him.

'Go on, admit it, Doctor,' said Sarah. 'We're lost!'

'Well, a little mislaid possibly.'

'Why don't we go back to the TARDIS?'

'For two very good reasons, Sarah. Firstly I don't want to leave Peladon without seeing my old friend the King.'

'Name-dropper!'

'And secondly—we're lost!'

The Doctor led the grumbling Sarah along the tunnels. 'Cheer up, Sarah, we're nearly there.'

'As far as I'm concerned a tunnel is a tunnel is a tunnel,' muttered Sarah.

They heard voices and the sound of marching feet. 'That'll be the palace guard,' said the Doctor cheerfully. 'We're all right now.'

A squad of savage-looking soldiers, armed with spears, swords and pikes, swung round a bend in the tunnel.

'Don't run,' said the Doctor. 'As soon as I explain who I am . . .'

They heard the voice of the guard Captain. 'There they are! Kill them!'

'I've changed my mind,' shouted the Doctor. 'Run!'

The guards clattered after them as they fled down the tunnels. There were tunnel openings on all sides and the Doctor took first one and then another, apparently at random. His last choice seemed to be a bad one, since the tunnel ended in a blank wall, in which was set a single flaring torch.

They could hear the sound of the guards running up behind them. 'We're trapped, Doctor,' gasped Sarah.

'Oh no we're not,' said the Doctor cheerfully. 'I've been here before.' He reached up and twisted the torch-holder. It turned sideways, a section of wall slid back and they hurried through.

The door closed behind them and the pursuing

guards turned the corner to find only a blank wall.

*

The Doctor and Sarah were in a dark and gloomy chamber, lit by flaring torches. The walls were decorated with rich tapestries, and at the far end was an altar, dominated by an immense stone statue, a bearlike beast with a single terrifying horn.

'There we are, Sarah,' said the Doctor. 'The Temple of Aggedor in the very heart of the Citadel of Peladon.'

'Very impressive. What about those guards? I thought you said they knew you here?'

'Oh, just a little misunderstanding, I imagine we startled them. Take a look at old Aggedor, there he is bless him!' The Doctor beamed affectionately at the terrifying statue.

Sarah came to join him. 'Doesn't look very loveable to me.'

'Well, this is a symbolic Aggedor, the real animal is very different.' The Doctor stared up at the statue. 'You know, when I first came here, Peladon was just on the point of joining the Galactic Federation. There was a good deal of trouble . . .'

'Not now, Doctor,' whispered Sarah suddenly.

The Doctor was hurt, 'Well, of course, if you don't want to hear about it.'

'It isn't that, Doctor—but I think there's going to be some more trouble. Look!'

The Doctor turned.

Armed soldiers were filling the door to the temple.

*

As they were marched into the throne room the Doctor was saying cheerfully, 'Don't worry, Sarah, as soon as we see King Peladon . . .'

He broke off in astonishment, at the sight of the slender young woman on the throne.

The bearded figure beside the throne stepped forward. 'You stand accused of both sabotage and of sacrilege. Do you wish to confess, before you die?'

'No, we don't,' said Sarah spiritedly. 'I don't know what you're talking about.'

'Silence, slave. I addressed your master.'

'He's not my master,' said Sarah indignantly.

Ortron ignored her, glaring at the Doctor from beneath bushy eyebrows. 'Well, alien?'

The Doctor bowed low before the throne. 'May I ask who I have the honour of addressing?'

'I am Ortron, Chancellor and High Priest. This is Her Majesty Queen Thalira of Peladon.'

The Doctor bowed again. 'And *King* Peladon?'

'King Peladon was my father,' said Thalira. 'I was the child of his old age. He died when I was still a baby.'

'Name those who sent you alien,' boomed Ortron, 'and your life may yet be spared.'

The Doctor waved him away. 'Yes, yes, in a minute, old chap.' He turned back to the Queen and said gently, 'I am called the Doctor, Your Majesty. Your father and I were good friends long before you were born.'

Thalira looked wonderingly at him. 'I have heard stories of the Doctor since I was a child. How you fought Grun and spared him, and tamed the sacred beast...'

'And so has every child on Peladon,' said Ortron scornfully. 'What better disguise for an alien spy and saboteur than to claim to be a legendary hero of our people?'

The Doctor sighed. 'You really are a suspicious old fellow, aren't you?'

Ortron's face flushed with anger at the Doctor's insolence. Turning to the guard Captain he roared, 'Take these alien spies away and cut off their heads!'

*

Guards seized their arms, and began to drag them out.

Then a strange figure bustled into the throne room, and bowed before the throne.

Sarah gasped. 'Doctor, what's that?'

'The answer to all our troubles. Alpha Centauri!'

The Ambassador swung round, his tentacles waving wildly. 'Doctor! Is it really you?'

'Indeed it is!' Shaking off the astonished guards, the Doctor went over to his old friend. 'Alpha Centauri, my dear fellow! What a well-timed entrance!'

'It's like a miracle, Doctor! All these years, and you haven't changed a bit!'

'Neither have you. A touch of grey in the tentacles, perhaps, but still the same old Alpha.'

To Sarah's astonishment, the Doctor enfolded the many-tentacled alien in an affectionate hug, which was affectionately returned by all six tentacles.

'Ambassador!' boomed Ortron, reprovingly.

Alpha Centauri swung round. 'Forgive me, Chancellor, Your Majesty.'

'I take it these aliens are known to you, Ambassador? asked Thalira.

'Not the, er—female?' Alpha Centauri blinked enquiringly at the Doctor, who nodded. 'Not the female, Your Majesty, she's of no importance. But this is most certainly the Doctor, a good friend of your father and of Peladon.'

Thalira inclined her head. 'Very well. We shall release the aliens into your custody, Ambassador. But we shall expect a full explanation of their presence on Peladon.'

Alpha Centauri bowed and fluttered his tentacles.

'Of course, Your Majesty.' He turned to the Doctor. 'Come with me, please, Doctor. You may bring the female.'

Sarah stood her ground. 'Well, I don't think it's good enough. I think we're owed an apology, for the way we've been treated.'

'Not now, Sarah,' said the Doctor warningly. 'Come along.' Grabbing her by the hand, he pulled her after Alpha Centauri. As they left, Ortron approached the throne. 'It is not wise to trust this alien, Your Majesty. Even if he is the Doctor—was he not the one who helped persuade Peladon to join the Federation, and so caused all our troubles? Why has he come here again? Will he not bring still more trouble with him?'

Thalira said coldly, 'If the Doctor is our enemy, he will soon betray himself. We shall not learn of his plans by chopping off his head. See that he is watched.'

*

There was a secret passage from the mines into the Citadel. Gebek was in that passage now, together with Ettis and a squad of armed miners. Ettis was one of the leaders of a resistance movement, sworn to drive the aliens from Peladon. Gebek was sympathetic to their aims, but still hoped to reach the same results by peaceful means.

It was with that aim that he was about to enter the Citadel now. Ettis had no faith in his mission. 'Gebek, for the last time, will you listen? Even if you reach the

Queen, it will do no good. She and Ortron are puppets of the Federation.'

'We must *try*,' said Gebek determinedly. 'If I can only talk to the Queen . . .'

'All right. But if your talking fails, Gebek—we fight.'

Gebek clamped a massive hand on his arm. 'There will be no fighting, not yet. You will wait for me here. When I have spoken to the Queen, we shall talk again.'

Ettis waited till he was out of earshot. 'Gebek is a good man, but he is too trusting, too patient. We shall give him time to get clear. Then while he is talking, we shall *act*.'

From the low growl of assent, it was clear that the others were with him.

*

Gebek marched boldly along the corridors until he walked straight into a squad of palace guards. Outraged, they seized him. 'Take him to the Chancellor,' ordered the squad leader.

Gebek offered no resistance. It was what he wanted, after all.

*

Not far away, the Doctor and Sarah were heading for that part of the Citadel assigned to visiting aliens. Sarah was still protesting. 'I don't see why I should put up with being treated like this. And as for your friend there!' She nodded towards Alpha Centauri, who was leading the way down the corridor. '"The female is of no importance," indeed!'

The Doctor grinned. 'I knew you wouldn't care for that! Still, you should be grateful to Alpha Centauri, Sarah, they go in for rough justice on Peladon. Chop off your head and apologize afterwards.'

Sarah refused to be consoled. 'If you hadn't missed the target by about five hundred and fifty years, we wouldn't be in all this trouble.'

*

In an anteroom just off the throne room, Gebek stood before Ortron under guard.

Ortron stared disdainfully at him. 'You know that the Citadel is forbidden to those of lowly rank?'

Gebek chuckled, 'Reserved for you nobles eh? And your *masters*, the Federation aliens, of course.'

Ortron flushed with anger. 'Do not be insolent, Gebek! Why did you come here?'

'I must speak with the Queen.'

'You should have petitioned for an audience in the proper way.'

'And endure endless delay? Things are too urgent for the proper way. I must see the Queen *now*—for the good of all Peladon.'

Such was Gebek's sincerity, that even Ortron was convinced. 'Very well.'

Ortron headed for the throne room, and Gebak followed him.

*

Ortron bowed before the throne. 'The miners' leader, Gebek, Your Majesty.'

Gebek fell to one knee. 'Forgive this intrusion, Your Majesty.'

Thalira said graciously. 'Why have you come here, Gebek?'

'To beg you to send the Federation aliens home. Otherwise there will be rebellion on Peladon.'

Gebek rose and began to plead his cause, not knowing that the rebellion had already begun.

ACKNOWLEDGEMENTS

The publishers would like to extend their grateful thanks to the following authors, publishers and others for kindly granting permission to reproduce the extracts and stories included in this anthology:

ESCAPE FROM THE DEATH STAR from *Star Wars: From the Adventures of Luke Skywalker* by George Lucas. Copyright © 1976 by The Star Wars Corporation. Reprinted by permission of Ballantine Books, a division of Random House, Inc.

TRIAL BY COMBAT from *Unearthly Beasts and Other Strange People* by Jay Williams. Reprinted by permission of the author, Macmillan, London and Basingstoke, and Laurence Pollinger Ltd. © The Estate of Jay Williams 1958, 1960, 1979.

THE LIGHTS OF THE CITY by Garry Kilworth. © Garry Kilworth 1982.

THROUGH THE MOONS OF MOWL from *Dragonfall 5 and the Super Horse* by Brian Earnshaw. Reprinted by permission of the author and Methuen Children's Books. Copyright © 1977 Brian Earnshaw.

THE STAR by H. G. Wells from *The Complete Short Stories of H. G. Wells.* Reprinted by permission of The Executors of the Estate of H. G. Wells.

JOHNSON by Guy Weiner. Reprinted by permission of MBA Literary Agents Ltd. © Guy Weiner 1979.

THE SMALLEST DRAGONBOY by Anne McCaffrey. First published in Great Britain in *Get Off the Unicorn* by Corgi Books, 1979. Reprinted by permission of MBA Literary Agents Ltd. © Anne McCaffrey 1979.